Triple Crown Publications
presents

Hoodwinked

By Quentin Carter

Compilation and Introduction copyright © 2004 by
Triple Crown Publications
2959 Stelzer Rd., Suite C
Columbus, Ohio 43219
www.TripleCrownPublications.com

Library of Congress Control Number: 2005930552
ISBN# 0-9762349-6-3
Cover Design/Graphics: www.MarionDesigns.com
Editor: www.PhoenixBlue.com
Junior Editor: Sheniqua Sharp
Editor-In-Chief: Mia McPherson
Consulting: Vickie M. Stringer

First Trade Paperback Edition Printing
10 9 8 7 6 5 4 3 2

Printed in the United States of America

Acknowledgements

First and foremost I would like to thank my mother and father, Charles & Lois Williams. Whether I'm right or wrong ya'll always have my back. My brothers, Christopher "Fuzz" Carter, Dewayne "Black" Jones and Brad Reeder, you three support my bankroll so I can keep my fronts up, 'cause y'all know I be up in here poppin' off at the mouth.

A special thanks to all my children, biological and step, who always show me much love. Quentez, Mi'Kelle, Brianna, Breanna, Brandis, Michael, CC, Tashay, Ebony and Kendal. Damn, that's a lot of kids! My nephews, Treshawn * lil Chris, Brad Jr. and Dewayne Jr.

The women in my life, though some of you are long gone, I still appreciate your efforts. This time ain't easy for me to do either. My babies' mommas: Danika, Keosha, Lady and Shawna. My friends, Mauri, Kelly, Shirmesse, Ladel and Kiria, who even today have yet to fail me.

R.I.P. my niggaz who didn't make it to see this book get released. Lamar Reece, Vonzale, Willis Johnson, Reggie Finch, Uncle Ricky, Uncle Odie, Sammy and Kay Williams, y'all are gone but definitely not forgotten. My grandmother Mary Carter, God bless her soul.

A very special thanks to Vickie Stringer for putting me on. Words alone can't describe how truly grateful my family and I are to you. The T.C.P Family, Tammy, Mia and the others whom I don't know by name, thank y'all as well.

Gotta holla at my hoodfellas, Skatterman (keep that music pumpin' playboy), Boo Dewey, Jawan, Benny, Mike Fluker, Chris, Jay, Roland, Reggie, Red, Dagwood, Bucky, Lil Jay, Veto, Rich, Gary, Pork, Cortez, Rico, Big Perry, Tyrone Miller, Lamont, Big Ant, Shelby, Tony, Marcus, Bobby Joe, Monte, D.G., Monster, Joe Burkes, Talib, Greg Preston, Jeff Baker, Renzo, 40-Cal, Wayne Bush, Derrick, Bertha, Tracy, Mika, Dave Hanes, Torey and Mac (keep ya head buried deep in those law books nigga!), By best friend Denisha and her crew, Nikki, Tish, Natalie, Kamisha, Debbie, Tay and Author.

Can't forget the people who read the manuscript in the raw three years ago, and encouraged me to send it in, ED & Christine Dryden. My toughest critics who sat up all night reading it, Duley, Clay Powell, Kevin King, Keese from the Lou, Big Geno and Ray Duck, y'all don't know how many times your comments have wounded my feelings.

My family, Benard Carter, Ricky, Steve, Barbara, Aunt Mary, Uncles Willie & Ronnie, Dalvin Carter, Joey Jackson, T.T., Michael, Vickie, Ashley, Tashay, Tony, D-Loc, Shante, Kosha, Lisa, Grandma Williams, Peanut, Connie, Bunchie, David Jones, Larry* Kathy, Ebony, Casy, Triecy, Willis, Shawn, Raslynn, Spanky, Sweet Pea and anybody else that I forgot, it's because I probably haven't heard from you.

My Jail house partners, My son* friend Wonyell, Keith Haliburton, Chris, Al, Sweatt, Hawk, Big Willie, Kenny, Freak, Juice, Tico, T-Nutt, Rafiel, Adam, Steve Wright, Sirron, Mike Simmons, Twain, Myrel, Honeycutt, B.D., Tee, Jamar, Hollis, Anthony Hodges, Ray Ray, Kesan, T-Rip, D.K., Fat Pat, Jeff, Chris Anderson, Clay, T.C., Cavy, Taz, K-9, Mustafa, Mick, Melvin, T.A., and Shakur and Lil Derrick and P.B., who are currently hard at work on two novels, White Rich, Big Hamp and Big Woods, Ali and Tank.

From the Lou, Bryan Warren, Jimmie, Nu-Nu, Big Lee Ill

Will, Osama, Norman Sheppard, EightBall, Spade, PJ, Cat, Adale, Beno, Will, Stuffy, Easley-Bey, Capone, E, Danyell, Mums, U.T., Herb, Temple, Twin, Cole, and Turtle, even though you ain't from the ST.L.

From Illi; Smooth, Short Reed, Jesse James, K.B., Travis, Chris, Drizzle, Alf, T.C., Wolf, Raboni, Chop, Coop, Wayne Bond, Big Ron and Q.

Last but not least, the Acklin family, Granny, Tony, Lonnie, Greg, Marlon, Eli, Duke, Cynthia, Jamie, Jawanna, Montez, Tamika, Nikki, Angel, T.C., Joe, Lil Bit, Gaylon, Michelle, Kim, Rodrick and Charles Ann.

Every story has been told - it's the way I tell it that keeps the reader turning pages.

Q. Carter

Chapter 1

It was a warm summer night in June. Keith Banks and his younger brother, Kevin, were cruising the streets in Keith's silver Lexus coupe. They slowly sipped Hennessy and Coke while listening to Too Short pumping out of the fifteen-inch subwoofers.

Keith loved the attention that he received, from both men and women, when he flossed through his city on twenty-inch chrome rims. Nothing excited him like attention. It was like his drug, and one of the main reasons that he got into the dope game.

Years back when he was just a shorty, Keith used to envy the attention that dope boys got from men and women of all ages. To most it didn't matter if they were selling poison to their own people. What mattered was what the dope boys could put into their empty palms.

In Keith's mind not even basketball, football or baseball players got attention like a dope boy. When he was faced with a choice between the four professions, he chose the easy one: dope boy. The money was faster and most of all, it was guaranteed. No one could promise him that he'd be scouted by the NBA, NFL or Major League Baseball scouts in college, and drafted. Nope, million-dollar contracts only came to those he saw on TV.

Keith winced when he saw flashing lights in his rearview mirror. The cognac had his eyes out of focus. He couldn't tell if it was the police or a regular car.

"Who in the hell is that, flashing their lights behind us?" Keith asked.

Kevin flipped the visor down to gaze into the mirror.

"It looks like a bitch. A light-skinned bitch," Kevin replied.

"Yeah?" Keith hit his signal light. He turned into a car wash parking lot and stopped under a tall light pole. He wanted the light to reflect off his spotless rims.

Keith relaxed in his leather seat as a green two-door Neon pulled alongside him. The woman got out of the car slinging her long hair over her shoulders. Keith's nature rose at the sight of her skirt that was short enough to reveal a half-inch of green underwear. Her camel toe was cussing him out.

She was short with a perfect tan and perky titties. The muscles in her legs let him know that she worked out or was some kind of athlete.

She stopped halfway and crooked her finger for Keith to come to her. Keith checked his spiral waves in the mirror before he got out and approached her.

"Ummm," she said under her breath as she watched Keith step his tall, lean and well-toned frame out of the car. He had on a pair of Jordans, heavily starched jean shorts and a fresh, white Stafford t-shirt. No jewelry, but she didn't know that Keith only wore jewelry when he went to clubs.

"Whassup?" Keith asked in his smooth tone. He flashed his gold and diamond grill at her.

She put her hand over her mouth and said, in a surprised voice, "I am sorry. I thought you were someone else. I am so sorry."

"You thought I was someone else?" Keith asked, curious.

She nodded. "Umm-hmm. You're not gonna believe this," she said with a Hispanic accent, "but I met this dude earlier today, driving this same kinda car. He told me to meet him here tonight."

Keith knew right then that she was spitting game at him. He liked her style.

He said, "Well, don't look like your boy's gonna show up. But since you obviously have a thing for men in big cars...why don't I pick up his slack?"

"I don't know if I dig you; not like I did him, anyway."

Keith smiled that player smile of his. The one that made you focus on the solid half-carat diamond on his side tooth. "Listen, baby, I'm a bad muthafucka, I know this. And I can see it in yo' eyes that you digging me."

She smiled at his confidence. Apparently arrogance impressed her. "You are kinda sexy," she said, stroking Keith's ego. Subconsciously, she put her small, freshly manicured hand on his stomach. Her expression was seductive.

"Feel anything you like?" Keith smirked.

She looked up at him. "I love a man who takes care of his body," she said softly.

Her accent was getting the best of Keith. "The feeling's mutual." Once again he gave her that smile.

"Your teeth are so cute," she said in a high-pitched voice. "How much did they cost?"

"Ain't important," Keith answered. "What's important is me getting your name, number and when I can come by."

Everything about this woman impressed Keith. Her walk, look, smell, even the pretty little toe ring that he noticed on her second toe. The way she went about meeting him was impressive. Keith knew the hefty price that he paid for the Lexus would be worth it in the long run.

"My name is Selina," she said as she stuck out her hand. "And yours?"

"Keith," he said shaking her soft hand. "But I prefer KB."

"KB," she repeated. "That name fits you. It's...strong. Ya know?"

"So what you got up for tonight?" Keith said, tired of beating around the bush.

She said, "I rented me a motel room. I'm gonna relax, sip on some Alizè, and just enjoy this night without my son."

"By yourself?" Keith was anxious to hear her response.

"Yep, and I'll be all alone," she teased.

"Hmm. Why don't you take down my number? You know, just in case you get lonely or something."

"OK," she said as she turned toward her car. "Let me get a pen."

Keith got a peek at the bottom of her ass cheeks while she bent over into her car.

She turned back around with the pen and paper in hand. "What's the number?" she asked.

"555-1799, KB."

"I'll call you," she said when she finished writing.

Keith watched until she pulled off. When he got back inside of his car, Kevin had a frown on his face.

"What's wrong with you?" Keith asked.

"Nothing," Kevin said. "Was she Puerto Rican?"

"Sound and look like one."

"I don't trust that ho."

"You don't trust no bitch if she ain't black," Keith said. He cranked his beat up and whipped out of the car wash lot.

* * *

About an hour later, Keith was cruising down Prospect alone, listening to his favorite Levert CD when his phone rang. He unclipped the cell phone from his hip and flipped it up. "Hello," he said over the loud music.

"Can you turn that down, please?" A female voice screamed.

He grabbed the remote from the passenger seat and turned down the volume. "Who dis?"

"Selina," she said in a sexy voice. "I hope you ain't forgot about me already?"

"Hell nah," Keith said, forgetting to hide the excitement in his voice. "I was just thinking about you."

"Were you? Are you alone?"

"Yep. Just turning a few corners."

"Why don't you turn my way."

"Which way is that?"

"The Amercan Inn on Nolyn Road."

"American Inn, American Inn," Keith repeated to himself. "Where's that?"

She gave him the address and the room number.

"I'm on my way."

"If you can't handle it, don't come by," Selina said in a serious tone. "'Cause I will make you get up, and get out.'"

Keith smiled at her smart remark. "I'm on my way," Keith repeated and hung up. He made a right, got on 70 Highway and let the SC's .400 engine open up, chanting, "I'm go'n to get me some puuussy," along the way.

* * *

It took Keith all of twenty minutes to reach the motel and find room 206. It was on the far side of the motel near the check in office.

Keith spent another five minutes waiting for a minivan to leave so that he could park in front of the room, which was right next to Selina's car. He cracked open the bottle of Hennessy that he had been drinking earlier, and drank what was left. He wanted to be good and drunk before he went in. Judging by her words, it was obvious her pussy was a challenge that he intended to conquer. He grabbed his Glock .40 from the glove box and headed for the door. Just before he knocked on room 206, he heard his car alarm self-activate. His car was secure, and so was he.

"Who is it?" Selina asked after hearing two short knocks.

"Mister Lover Man."

Selina opened the door wearing a blue short t-shirt. Once again, Keith could see her crotch. But this time her camel toe was pantiless. Her curly pubic mound stood out like the hump in a camel's back.

"Come in," Selina stepped aside.

The room was a single. The TV was off and slow music was playing softly out of a portable radio on the floor beside the bed. Keith noticed a brand new package of Trojan condoms on the nightstand. He took a seat on the bed.

Selina picked up a full cup of Alizè on ice from the table, then sat beside Keith. "So what's up?" she said with a slur in her voice.

"Nothing," Keith replied. He watched her down half of her cup in one swallow. He imagined what else she could swallow like that.

Selina sat her cup on the floor, then laid back on the bed. "Whew," she hollered. "This Alizè's got me a little tipsy."

Keith's eyes traveled up her smooth legs to where her puffy pussy lips were clamped together. He could see now that her pubic hairs were shaved into a rectangular shape.

Selina caught him staring at her. "Just 'cause I'm naked under here don't mean you're getting any pussy," she stated.

"Umm-hmm," Keith murmured. He knew from their earlier phone conversation and the box of rubbers on the stand that he was hitting tonight.

Selina got up suddenly and took her shirt off on the way to the portable radio. Her body was flawless and her ass jiggled slightly as she walked. She bent over as she slipped R. Kelly's CD into the deck and started it from the beginning.

While R. Kelly began singing, "12 Play", she rocked her hips from side to side to the soft beat.

"Damn," Keith said to himself as Selina danced like a stripper while he looked on.

Selina did a spin which showed Keith her palm-sized, perky brown titties. Her nipples stood erect, like they belonged to a childless woman. Her small muscular frame started to perspire as she heated up the room.

Selina ran her hand over her body, from her breast to her pussy, freaking herself while Keith watched. Slowly, she played with her clit, looking him directly in the eye.

"You want to smell *mi chocha, papi?*" she asked in a seductive whisper. Selina's hands were folded over her head now, and she was rocking to the beat.

Keith reached out and pulled Selina close. Gently, he tongued her pierced navel while massaging her butt cheeks.

"Yes, *papi*," Selina said as she faked deep, slow breaths. She backed away from him and climbed onto the bed on all fours. Her pussy was so fat, it hung like two nuts on a man. She rotated her ass from side to side, inviting Keith.

"Eat me from the back, *papi*," she said.

Without hesitation, Keith jumped out of his clothes. He eased his face into the back of her, licking from her pussy to her asshole.

"Ooh, *papi*," she moaned. "Stick your tongue in it."

Keith parted her cheeks and stuck his tongue in and out. Slowly Selina began to push back, making sure he got a mouthful. "Don't stop, *papi*," she howled. "Oh please...don't...stop."

Selina uttered words Keith couldn't understand as the tingling sensation of his tongue worked in and out of her *culo*. Selina reached back and inserted two fingers inside her pussy. She wanted double the pleasure.

Keith's dick grew its full length when he heard the sweet gushy sound that her hand made inside her pussy. Selina smoothly worked her fingers in and out of herself.

"Put it in *mi culo, papi*," Selina hollered.

Keith stood up and glanced around the room for something to lubricate her ass with.

"Fuck me, *papi*," Selina said impatiently. Her ass was high in the air, ready and waiting.

"I can't find no lubrication."

Selina slobbered on her fingers, then reached around to rub the saliva around her asshole. "There," she said, "it's lubricated. Put it in me, now, *papi*." She wanted that big dick inside of her.

Keith pulled her toward him and prepared to go in. He looked down and saw Selina looking back at what he was working with. Obviously she was impressed with his size; he saw a hungry look in her eyes while she was licking her lips and staring at his dick.

Keith entered carefully. Selina let out a howl that could have woke Keith's dead homie. After a few strokes he felt himself about to come.

"Oh shit I'm 'bout to come," Keith moaned. He felt Selina's ass tighten on his dick. It felt like she had locked him inside of her.

Selina wrapped her feet around the back of his legs, squeezed her ass tighter, then started backing up on him, hard.

"Oh shit, I feel it in my stomach," she hollered. "Please, don't come yet, *papi*."

Keith felt himself coming, and started to fuck her harder. Selina was moaning something he couldn't understand, but she was taking all eight inches inside her ass with ease. It wasn't long before he pulled out and came on her ass crack. "Damn, I didn't know ass was that good," he said out loud.

Selina rolled over onto her back. "You ain't through, are you, *papi*?" she asked with a worried look on her face.

"Nah," Keith replied, "It's getting hot in here."

"Turn on the air, and hurry back over here."

On his way to the air conditioner Keith cursed himself for the three nuts that he used on his girlfriend Tukey that morning. He fumbled with the controls and saw Selina sneaking up on him out of the corner of his eye. She had a wet towel in her right hand. She pushed him against the wall and dropped to her knees.

"What you doing?" Keith asked, confused.

Selina lifted his dick with one hand and cleaned him up with the wet rag. She finished and threw down the towel.

"I want to taste..." She stuffed him into her mouth before she finished speaking. Selina moaned with pleasure as she took him in and out of her mouth.

"Suck it," Keith said softly. He looked down and his dick had vanished into her mouth. That made him moan even louder. He didn't even feel a tooth. Selina wiggled her tongue inside of her mouth with each stroke.

"I'm 'bout to come," Keith barely spat out. His dick began to throb. She kept it in her mouth, waiting for his sweet nectar to flow.

"Hmm," Selina moaned as she felt his warm come run down her throat. "*Slurrp.*" She kissed his dick after she finished then headed for the bathroom. She knew he was finished.

"She's a beast," Keith said to himself as he sat back on the bed. Five nuts for the day were enough for him. He laid back and drifted off to sleep.

The annoying sound of his cell phone woke him. Day light had arisen. He looked over and saw Selina's pretty face sleeping soundly. He reached on the floor, found his pants and answered the call.

"Hello," he said in a sleepy voice.

"Ya t'ink ya ca'an sleep at home sometime, huh?"

He snapped wide awake when he heard that Jamaican accent that he knew too well.

"Yu hear me?" Tukey asked impatiently.

Tukey was his Jamaican-American girlfriend with whom he shared his home with. She had been his friend and lover since high school. She was very sexy, cool and totally loyal to him. Tukey was tall; she stood five-foot-ten with no shoes on. Her long beautiful dreadlocks hung down her back and her skin was smooth and shiny, like a piece of sucked-on chocolate. At a hundred and fifty pounds, of which forty were tits and ass, she could have been a supermodel.

"What's up with ya, baby?" Keith tried not to sound suspicious.

"Don't yu 'what's up baby' me," Tukey yelled. "Yu must t'ink me stupid or sum'ting."

"What are you talking about?" He looked over at Selina who was waking up.

Tukey said, "Don't yu t'ink it time ya stopped playing games?"

Normally Tukey's patois would've turned Keith on, but she had fire in her voice this morning. While Keith sat there trying to explain himself to his girlfriend, Selina eased under the covers and nibbled at his crotch.

"Baby, I ain't playing no...ummm shit." Keith moaned as he felt Selina's warm saliva on his dick.

Tukey was silent for a moment. Then she hollered, "Me know

yu not fuckin' some bitch while me on the phone, mon?"

Keith pushed Selina's head away. "Nah, baby, I ain't...I'm putting my cloth...ummm." He felt Selina gargling with his balls. He reached under the covers and smacked her face, hard. "Meet me at our spot. You know where." He hung up and stared hard at Selina. "What the fuck is wrong with you?"

Selina came from under the covers, holding her face. She said, "Sorry!" in an innocent, child-like tone.

"Don't ever do no shit like that again, bitch!" Keith snarled. "You ain't my damn woman." He got out of bed.

Selina rose to her knees. "I'm sorry, *papi*. I promise, I was just playing around. Do you love her?"

Keith slipped into his boxers. "That's my woman. What you think?" he said in a harsh tone.

Not if I can help it, Selina said to herself.

Keith dressed, put his gun into his pocket, and left without saying goodbye.

* * *

Tukey had a huge frown on her face. She stood with her arms crossed next to her Range Rover as she waited on Keith in the Denny's parking lot. She heard Keith's music before she saw his Lexus pull into the parking lot and stop next to her.

"Trifling muthafucka," she said, staring at him through his closed window.

Keith read her lips but ignored the comment. He was trifling. Not that long ago, he had his tongue stuffed in a bitches ass whom he didn't know. Now he was about to get out of his car and kiss Tukey's ass.

Keith exited the car with his arms stuck out. "Hey, my little Jamaican cuisine," he said, trying to hug her.

"Don't yu 'hey baby' me, yu tramp," she replied as she turned away from him.

Keith mocked her accent. "Me sorry me didn't mek it home last night, mon." He embraced her from behind.

Tukey looked him in the eye. "Me not gonna always be here

for yu to seh sorry." She sounded distressed.

Keith placed a gentle kiss on her cheek and said, "I'd die if ya left me, boo."

"Umm-hmm," Tukey mumbled as they walked through the entrance door.

They found a quiet booth by a window. Tukey ordered eggs and bacon for Keith and a muffin with orange juice for herself. Keith usually did the ordering, but the waiter couldn't seem to keep his eyes off Tukey long enough to notice him.

They held hands and looked at each other the way lovers do after a fight. Keith gave her the "I'm sorry I won't do it again" look, while Tukey gave him the "I know you won't" look.

The waiter broke their silence when he spilled Tukey's orange juice onto her lap. He picked up a stack of napkins and started to wipe up the mess. "I'm so sorry," he said as he patted her leg with the napkins.

"Shit like that wouldn't happen if you focused on what you was doing, instead of focusing on my woman," Keith said in an angry voice. He was trying to score some brownie points with Tukey.

The young waiter ignored Keith. He looked at Tukey and apologized profusely.

Tukey was glad to receive attention from somebody. It was obvious that Keith was giving his to someone else; he was staying out all night with different whores.

She looked at the boy with flirtatious eyes and said, "Ya t'ink ya ca'an get me some more juice, please?"

"Yes Ma'am," the waiter said nervously. He turned and rushed to the back.

Keith stared at Tukey's beautiful chocolate face, perfect set of white teeth and those soft dark eyes that he loved so much. That Serena Williams body was calling him. He wanted to crawl up under the table and suck her pussy right where they were.

Tukey noticed him checking her out and blushed. "What yu looking at?" she asked.

"You," he answered. "You think you sexy, don't you?"

She flung her dreads over her shoulder and said, "Me don't t'ink. Me know me sexy." She winked at him. "Although, sometime me can't tell. Ya choose all them street whores over ya black beauty queen."

"I'm not perfect," Keith grabbed her hand, "but I do know I love you."

The waiter returned with Tukey's juice. He told her that their meal was on the house, and then went on about his business.

"Aw yeah," Tukey said with a mouthful of muffin. "Me uncle called."

"What did he say?"

"He she dat yu need to send me out dere soon as possible. He going on vacation or sum'ting."

Keith chewed a piece of bacon. "You feel up to it?"

Tukey looked at him like he was stupid, and said, "Yu t'ink me gonna keep riskin' me freedom for a mon dat don't love me? So yu ca'an trick all our money off wit' ya whores? Me don't t'ink so."

Anger flashed on Keith's face. Keith knew he tricked off money on some of his hos, but a trick hated to be called one. Like the old saying went, "the truth hurts."

"I ain't trying to hear that bullshit every five minutes," Keith yelled, getting defensive. "If you gonna do it, do it. If not, fuck it, I'll get somebody else."

Tukey didn't hear what he said. Her attention was focused on his neck. She cocked her head to get a better angle for what she was seeing. "What is dat?" She pointed at his neck.

Keith grabbed his neck. "What?" he asked, as if he didn't have a clue. Common sense told him that somehow, he'd ended up with a hickey.

Tears began to run down Tukey's cheeks. She stood up and said, "Me hate yu!" She picked up her juice and threw it in his face.

Keith jumped up as the juice ran down his face. "Aw bitch, you done snapped," he cursed.

Tukey flinched and backed up when she saw the hell in his pretty face. She knew it was time to leave.

"Yu should check the mirror 'fore yu leave ya bitches house," Tukey yelled. She was crying as she stormed out of the restaurant.

Keith dashed into the restroom. His reflection showed three suck marks on his neck. "That scandalous ass bitch," he hollered. "Damn that bitch! Must've did it while I was sleep," he ranted as he threw cold water on his neck, hoping the marks would disappear.

Keith ran out to the parking lot to catch Tukey. He was near panic. Her uncle Ben had called to say it was time for business. Tukey was the key to his small fortune, his negotiator, his mule, not to mention that he loved her.

When Keith didn't have a dime, Tukey stole clothes and ran check scams so that they could go places and do things. When she grew tired of nickel and diming, she took him out to California to meet her uncle Ben. Ben was large in the dope game. He hooked Keith up and he hadn't looked back since.

Tukey was rummaging through his Lexus when Keith got outside.

"Where is it?" she cried when she heard him come behind her.

"Where's what?"

"The place where yu keep dere numbers." Tukey hollered. Now she was in his glove box. Damn, Keith forgot that she had a key to that, too. "Come here, baby," he said as he attempted to pull her from the car. Tukey snatched away from him. Her titty jumped out of her shirt.

"Who put the marks on ya neck?" she said in between huffy breaths. She fixed her top, folding her arms across her chest. "Seh sum'ting! Tell another lie." Tukey yelled.

Keith looked Tukey straight in the eye and said, "You did." His tone was convincing. He knew that he and Tukey didn't have sex often. The fact that they just had sex three times yesterday morning, before he left, gave him reason enough to try to fool her into believing that she had done it. He was trying to manipulate her mind.

"Shit, I fucked the hell out of you three times yesterday morning. Remember, you was licking and biting on me like a fucking animal?"

That got Tukey's attention, and for a moment she wasn't sure if she did or not. "Me didn't even suck on ya neck yesterday," she said in an even tone.

"Yes, you did. Shit, even if I was fucking around, do you think that I would be stupid enough to let another bitch suck my neck?" Keith wrapped his arms around her waist. "Come on baby, think."

Embarrassed by the mistake she thought she made, Tukey hugged him back. "Me sorry, baby." She wiped her tears and runny nose on his shirt.

"See there, you tripping for nothing."

Tukey forced a smile. "Yu t'ink me crazy, don't ya?"

"No. I think you're a bit insecure. With a face and body like you've got," Keith paused, looked her over and whistled, "girl that's the last thing that you should be worried about." He removed his arm from around her waist and kissed her on the forehead. "Now go home. I got to run by mama's house. I'll be there in a minute."

"OK," Tukey fished through her purse. She took out her keys and shades and put them on as she walked to her truck.

Keith watched her soft ass jiggle all the way to her Rover. He smiled to himself as he got into his car, thinking he had her completely fooled.

* * *

Tukey watched Keith drive off before she pulled out of the lot behind him. She waited until he was completely out of sight, then removed her cell phone from her purse and dialed some numbers. She laughed at herself, wondering why she waited until he was out of sight. It wasn't like he could hear her.

"Hello," a female voice said.

"Hey girl, it's Tukey."

"Tukey? I don't know no damn Tukey," the girl snapped.

Realizing she wasn't talking to who she called for, Tukey said, "Me sorry. Ca'an me speak wit' Anitra, please?"

"Hold on," the girl said in an aggravated tone.

It only took a few seconds for Anitra to come on the line.

"Hello," Anitra said.

"Girl, what wrong wit' ya friend? She act like her got an attitude problem," Tukey said.

"Who, Diamond?" Anitra said. "She's just jealous of your accent. I told her you don't do the girl on girl thing, so she don't have to worry about you and me doing nothing behind her back."

Tukey changed the subject, "Guess who showed up dis morning wit' suck marks on him neck?"

"Who, Keith?" Anitra said in shock. "Girl, I know he didn't!"

"Dat's the same t'ing me said, girl. Him even try to mek me believe me did do it."

Anitra loved to hear bad shit about Keith. "Girl, I told you he wasn't shit a long time ago. You need to try something different." Anitra threw out the bait.

"Come on, mon. Yu know me strickly dickly." Tukey knew what Anitra was getting at. Anitra had been trying to turn her out for a while now.

Anitra had been her best friend through high school. She was the one whom Tukey ran to about her problems with varsity football player Keith, when he used to get caught skipping school with her so called friends.

Anitra was attractive and always had been. She was a petite redbone with green eyes and short sandy brown hair. She still had her high school track star figure. Tukey just wasn't attracted to her like that. It seemed to Tukey that Anitra was always trying to catch her when she was vulnerable.

Chapter 2

Tukey sat on her leather sofa with her legs open. Mi'kelle, her daughter, rested her head between them. Tukey was taking rubber bands out of Mi'kelle's hair and dumping them into a jar full of barrettes and ponytail holders.

They were watching *Casper* on their sixty-inch television when Keith came in, carrying a black gym bag. He dropped it on the floor.

"Get your uncle on the phone," he said to Tukey as he took off his shirt. He picked up the bag, kissed Mi'kelle's forehead and went into the kitchen.

Mi'kelle said, "Can I have some juice, Daddy?" Her hair was half done.

Keith could already see how well his daughter was gonna be shaped, and she was only six. *Kids grow up fast,* he thought. He hated the thought of her growing up and becoming like the women that he ran through and manipulated on a daily basis.

Keith removed a carton of HiC fruit punch and he handed it to her. "Now go back in the front room," he said in the calm voice that he always used with her.

While Mi'kelle left the room, Tukey was entering with the cordless phone in her hand.

"Here." She handed it to Keith.

Keith took the phone and said, "Big Ben, what's happening?"

"Ya t'ink ya ca'an send Tukey out here tonight?"

Keith looked up at the clock. It wasn't noon yet.

Keith said, "That depends on her, and if she can get a plane on such short notice."

Keith was out of dope anyway, and needed to go shopping bad. "Hold on a minute, Ben," Keith took the phone from his ear. "Tukey, you got to make that move tonight, if you're gonna do it." He gave her a serious look.

Tukey hesitated before saying, "Me guess. If ya need me to."

Keith put the phone back to his ear and said, "I'm gonna try and get her out on the next flight."

"Good! Let me know when and I'll meet her at LAX."

Keith hung up the phone. "Get ready, baby." He called the airport next.

While Keith took care of that, Tukey took Mi'kelle upstairs to her room. After talking Mi'kelle into playing quietly by herself, she went into her own room.

She undressed down to her panties and bra and smiled at her gorgeous reflection in the mirror. "*Him don't know how lucky him is,*" she said to herself. She massaged her firm breasts until her nipples became erect. Then she went back downstairs.

Keith damn near dropped the phone when Tukey walked into the kitchen. He loved the way she fit into her panties.

"OK, thank you," he said into the phone, then hung up.

Tukey put her hands on her hips. "Yu still t'ink me sexy?" Slowly, she turned around, pulling her hair up over her head. She made her soft butt cheeks clap in his face.

Keith contemplated throwing her on the counter and fucking her real good for that attitude she had earlier. Instead he left the table and came up behind her. She could feel his dick pressing up against her ass.

Keith gently kissed her neck while he massaged her swollen nipples. He slid his hand into her panties and parted her with two fingers.

"Ummm," Tukey moaned as she felt his long fingers enter her

crevice. He worked his fingers inside of her until she became moist. Keith took his fingers out and sucked her cunt juice off them.

"Taste good," he said in a soft whisper.

Tukey reached around and grabbed his hand. "Let me taste," she said. She closed her eyes and enjoyed her own sweet juice.

Keith pulled away. "We ain't got time right now, baby," he said seriously.

He wiped sweat from his forehead and walked back to the table where the money was. He reached into the side compartment on the bag, pulling out a roll of duct tape.

He rolled out a long piece, breaking it off. He asked, "You ready?"

She hesitated. Tukey remembered losing her leg hairs last time she took off the tape. She shaved her legs, but still didn't like the feeling of her hairs being ripped off.

Keith hollered, "Come on, baby! We ain't got all day. I got you booked on a one o'clock flight."

Tukey said, "It ain't dat me scared. It hurts so bad when us take the tape off."

He felt her pain and thought about the situation for a moment. "I'll tell you what. Go upstairs and put on your long john pants and shirt."

"OK."

It took her a few minutes before she came back wearing a tight-fitting long john under pants and shirt.

"That better?" he asked with attitude.

Tukey knew Keith was becoming frustrated with all her whining, so she just nodded her head. She stood in front of him with her legs apart. Keith taped five ten-thousand-dollar stacks around each of her thighs, and ten stacks around her waist. Each stack was in hundreds, so that the money would be easy to carry and wouldn't bulge out of her clothes.

"Now take a few steps around the room. Tell me how it feels."

Tukey walked to the living room and back. She said, "Me

cyaah feel the tape, but me pants feel like dey 'bout fi fall."

Keith thought some more. "Hold on." He got four safety pins out of the kitchen drawer. He carefully fastened Tukey's shirt to her pants on the sides, back and front. "That better?"

"Ca'an we use a couple more?"

"No. We don't want to chance that the metal detector might go off."

Tukey walked back into the living room and back. "It'll do," she said.

"Good." Keith smacked her on the ass. "Now, go get dressed."

Twenty minutes later, Tukey came downstairs wearing a loose-fitting business suit. She carried a black briefcase to look like she was on a business trip.

Keith gave her the usual inspection to make sure that the money couldn't be seen bulging through her clothes. He bumped into her just to see how it would feel. Kansas City Airport was always crowded this time of year, and she could easily bump into an off-duty officer or a citizen doing a cop's job. He didn't feel anything when he bumped her. That part was done. The hard part was for her to successfully touch down in LA, with the cash.

Someone knocked on the door. Keith jumped. "Who the fuck could that be?" he snapped. He didn't receive visitors without them calling first.

"Relax, baby," Tukey said. She walked past him to the front door. "Me called Mummy to watch Mi'kelle for a few days."

"Hey, y'all," Arie, Tukey's mother, said as she came through the door. "What's up, Keith?"

"What's up, Arie?" Keith replied as he picked up his keys and glasses from the table.

Arie was an older version of her daughter, only she was about two inches shorter and very petite. She sat her bags down and gave them both a hug.

Tukey said, "Mi'kelle's upstairs sleeping, now. And, she need yu to finish her hair."

"OK," Arie nodded.

"T'ank ya," Tukey said.

Tukey grabbed her briefcase and stood in front of the door. Keith was walking in her direction when Arie stopped him.

"Me need to talk to yu in private," Arie said.

Keith looked at Tukey and said, "Go on out to the car. I'll be there in a minute."

"Don't be long," Tukey walked out the door.

Arie waited until Tukey was gone before she said, "Let Mummy get a few dollars."

Keith reached into his pocket, pulled out two fifties, and handed them to her.

Arie gave him a hug. "T'anks, son-in-law," she whispered into his ear.

Keith broke her embrace, and said, "A'ight, I'll see you later."

* * *

Tukey was unusually quiet the whole ride to the airport.

"You having second thoughts?" Keith asked her in a calm voice.

"No," Tukey replied in a low voice. "It's not dat. Yu know me not afraid to do anyt'ing for yu."

Keith reached over and ran his fingers through her locks. "What's wrong?"

Tukey stared at him for a brief second. "Me t'ink us should get married," she finally said.

Keith saw the seriousness in her dark eyes, eyes that didn't want to be lied to. He shifted in his seat and sighed.

Tukey focused her attention out the passenger window. She knew what the silence meant.

Keith finally said, "We'll talk about it when you get back."

She smiled and grabbed hold of his hand. "Yu promise?" she said, thinking he was about to let her tie him down, at the age of twenty-two.

Keith leaned over and kissed her soft lips. "I promise," he said softly. "Now get out of here and take care of Daddy's business."

Tukey smiled and said, "OK, Daddy." She picked up the briefcase and stepped out of the car. "Me call yu when me touchdown, 'kay?" She waved goodbye, then went into the airport entrance.

A wicked smile flashed on Keith's face as he pulled out of the lot. Not every man could get his woman to do his dirty work; especially carrying two hundred thousand in cash on an airplane.

He fired up a stick of light green and turned the volume up on his Kenwood. He inhaled the smoke and let his mind drift. He thought about something Tukey had told him after they had finished going one on one. As she lay naked in his arms, she told him that it was in her Jamaican blood to please her man. That included risking her life. Even though Keith wasn't Jamaican, she loved him that much.

Keith believed her words. Since that night, he'd been making her live up to them. Tukey was his queen. As in a game of chess, she'd gladly risk her own life in order to protect her king. With her on his side, he'd never be checkmated.

His cell phone rang and interrupted his thoughts. "Hello," he answered.

"Keith. Dis Big Ben, baby. What's the word?"

"She's getting on a plane as we speak."

"Good. Real good," Ben replied. Keith could see the smile on his face through the phone.

"I'll pick her up from the airport," Ben said, then hung up.

As soon as Keith hung up with Ben, he called his little partner, Nukey.

Nukey was a sixteen-year-old boy from Keith's neighborhood. Keith used him to sign for the dope after it was delivered by Fed Ex. He figured Nukey's mother's house was the safest place to get a package delivered, especially since she was always ordering stuff through Fed Ex. She was a regular customer.

Nukey's mother, Brenda, was an attractive single parent of five. She suffered from a bad case of thinking that she was all that. Obviously she wasn't; after men had gotten her pregnant, they just disappeared.

Brenda's lack of marketable job skills made her glad to accept the five grand that Keith gave her every month to accept the delivery at her house.

Brenda answered the phone. "Hello," she said in a sleepy voice.

"Whassup, Brenda?" Keith said. "Where Nuke at?"

"He ain't here," Brenda yawned into the phone.

"I just wanted y'all to know that I'm expecting some mail in two days."

"OK, sweetie," Brenda said. "I'll be sure to pick it up for you."

"Cool." Keith pushed the button that disconnected her.

Chapter 3

When Tukey's plane landed at LAX, she nervously stood up and removed her briefcase from the overhead compartment.

"*Relax, girl,*" she said to herself as she made her way down the aisle. "*Ya gotten away wit' dis plenty time.*"

As Tukey walked through the crowded airport, she got plenty of unwanted stares. Husbands with their wives gave her their full attention. Even with two hundred grand taped to her body, she couldn't hide that Coke bottle body.

Any other time, Tukey would've loved all that attention. Not today. She just wanted to get out of there safely. Her stomach started getting queasy as she neared the exit.

She was still shaken from an incident that happened at KCI. She was standing in line at the security checkpoint before she boarded the plane to LA.

"Next," a short Vietnamese man in a security uniform said to her.

Trying to look conservative, she sat her briefcase on the conveyor belt, to go through the X-ray machine. Then she walked through the metal detector.

Beep. Beep. Beep. The loud sound of the metal detector going off echoed in Tukey's ears. She just about jumped out of her skin. She'd remembered the safety pins she was wearing and what Keith said about not wanting the metal detector to go off. She tried hard to keep her body from trembling.

The little man eyed her suspiciously. He ran the handheld detector up and down her body. It beeped at her chain on her neck.

"Your chain, Ma'am," the guard said in a suspicious voice. "Take it off."

"Huh? Oh." Tukey grabbed her neck. "Me so sorry." She took it off. "Me did not know."

She put her chain in the little tray. This time she walked through without a sound. Without delay, Tukey took her chain back, snatched her briefcase off the counter, and moved on. She didn't look back as she calmly walked to her plane.

Now that she had landed in LA, Tukey wondered if there'd be any more obstacles to go through. She was relieved when she saw her Uncle Ben waiting for her at the exit, instead of the police. "Uncle Ben," she yelled, and sped up in his direction.

Ben saw the spooked look on her face as he hugged her. He knew that look well, so he didn't ask any questions. He took her briefcase and followed Tukey out the door.

* * *

They were headed down Century Boulevard in Ben's *S600* Benz when he noticed that his usually talkative niece hadn't said a word since they left the airport.

"Ya alright?" Ben asked. He threw his arm across her shoulders. "If Keith's hurtin' yu, me ca'an arrange for him to go to a better place, mon. Huh?"

Tukey said, "Not'ing's wrong. Me just shook up from the plane ride. Dat's all."

Ben took a half-smoked spliff out of the ashtray, fired it up. He jumped into the right lane and floored the pedal.

Ben turned into the driveway of his huge home in Ladera Heights. His house looked like it was owned by a Hollywood movie star. He parked behind the Corvette in the circular driveway.

He lived in a newer model two-story home. It had four bedrooms, three baths, an underground pool and a guest house.

The thick plush white carpet didn't impress Tukey as she entered his home. The living room was huge with black round leather sofas, glass tables and black art on the walls. There wasn't a TV in sight, but sitting on a long oak wood table were nine small security screens. In one of them she saw herself, looking around.

Ben led Tukey downstairs into his private room. The carpet downstairs was dark brown. There was a large desk in the corner, and a long conference table in the middle of the floor.

Ben said, "Yu can go to the bathroom over dere, and take the money off." He pointed to an open door on the other side of the room.

"Right here is fine," Tukey said, as she unbuttoned her jacket. "Ya seen me naked before."

Ben had a surprised look on his hard face. He said, "Yeah. Dat was when ya was a likkle gyal."

Tukey looked at him. "Ain't not'ing changed," she said and winked. "Me body parts just got bigger."

Ben felt uncomfortable. He didn't know what was wrong with his niece. He felt stupid after she finished undressing and he saw that the money was taped to her long johns, instead of her naked flesh.

Tukey laughed at the relief in his eyes. "Did yu really t'ink me was gonna get naked?" She bent over and carefully unwrapped the money from around her thighs. She threw each bundle onto the table after she finished.

"Two hundred t'ousand," she said. "Dats what him owe yu."

"Yep," Ben picked up a stack from the table.

"It wasn't a question," Tukey said seriously. Ben was her uncle, but this was business. Keith sent her out there to handle it for him, and that's what she planned on doing. "Count it."

Ben smiled. "Ya just like ya old uncle, girl," he said as he dropped the stack back onto the table. "Me trust yu."

Ben opened up the closet door and removed a screw driver from his pocket. He started taking screws out of the closet wall, then he removed the false wall. He stepped into another room with steel walls. In the middle of the floor sat a neatly stacked pile of individually wrapped bricks of cocaine. It took him three trips to haul twenty of the duct-taped bricks into the other room. He set them on the table next to the money.

Tukey looked around the room and noticed a tall stuffed dinosaur that sat alone in the corner. "What dat?" she asked.

Ben didn't have to look to know what she was talking about.

He said, "Dats a mechanical stuffed animal. It has a motor in him belly dat makes his arms and legs work. Me gonna take the motor out, and the dope goes in."

"Me see," she said shaking her head. "Let me go use the phone. Me got to call Keith." She walked fast up the stairs.

Keith was standing at the bar, ordering his second bottle of Moët, when he felt his cell phone vibrating in his pocket.

"Hello," he yelled over the music.

Tukey heard the music in the back ground. She decided not to mention it. She'd whined enough for one day. She said, "Me made it, baby."

"Hold on a minute." Keith took the phone from his ear, handed the Moët to Kevin and went to he bathroom where he could hear. "I'm back."

"Me just wanted yu to know, me touchdown safe," Tukey said, she hoped that Keith was proud of her.

"That's my girl," Keith replied. "Make sure y'all get that mail sent out first thing tomorrow."

"Me know what to do," Tukey snapped. "Have ya t'ought about what me said earlier?"

"What?" he stalled, trying to avoid the question.

Tukey said, "Me said, ya—" The line went dead in her ear.

Keith stuck the phone back in his pocket. He'd hung up in her face on purpose. He didn't have time to be tied down to no one bitch. He didn't give a shit what she did for him.

He splashed some warm water on his face, ran his hand over his waves. "I'm a fine muthafucka," he said looking into the mirror. His two-carat earrings shone in the mirror. He wiped his hands and left.

* * *

R. Kelly's "Sex Me Baby" was playing when Selina walked through the door. She was wearing a black tight skirt with the sides and back cut out. She hit the dance floor, popping like she'd been in the club for hours.

Keith and Kevin were sitting at their table when Kevin saw Selina on the dance floor, freakin' herself.

"Ain't that the little Puerto Rican bitch you met the other night?" Kevin asked, as he pointed in her direction.

Keith saw Selina. "Um hmm," he said. "You was right, she's a scandalous muthafucka."

"I said that?"

Keith took a sip of his drink. "Umm hmm," he said with a mouthful of alcohol. "You said you didn't trust the bitch."

"What she do?"

"I went and fucked her that night, right? When I fell asleep, the bitch put suck marks on my damn neck. Funky bitch."

Kevin laughed. "Man, I told you about laying up with these hos. You gon' get fucked up one of these days."

They watched Selina turn down every dude who tried to join her. The floor was hers. She worked that thang like she was a stripper trying to earn a living.

Keith wondered to himself what she was doing here. He noticed how she kept cutting her eyes his way. It was obvious she knew he was in here.

Selina bent down and lifted her skirt, twerking that thang. She wore a pink thong, with a drinking panther tattooed on her right butt cheek.

"Damn!" Kevin exclaimed, keeping his eyes on her. "You ate *that* pussy?"

Keith just smiled and sipped his drink.

Selina put on a show for six songs before she got tired. When she was done, there were a bunch of dollar bills scattered around her feet. Hatred came into her face when she saw Keith pour a drink for a white girl. Selina ignored the money beneath her feet as she strutted over to Keith's table.

"*Perdóneme. Qué pasa?*" she said in angry Spanish.

Keith looked up at her through drunken red eyes. "What the fuck you say?" he snapped.

Selina put her hands on her hips. "Get this bitch outta here. That's what I said."

Keith looked over at the white girl, who was now pissed off. He grabbed her hand and said, "Why don't you excuse me for a minute, baby. You can take the drink with you."

The white girl bumped Selina as she walked by.

"Aw bitch, you tripping," Selina yelled and drew back her little fist. She hit the white girl upside her head, and dragged her back to Keith's table. The white girl hollered something no one understood.

"Shit!" Keith jumped up from the table.

Selina and the girl were locked into a fighter's embrace when Keith stepped in and broke it up. The bouncers glanced their way but didn't move. They were used to young girls fighting over Keith and his brother. They also knew that Keith would gain control, before it got too far out of hand.

At least one Saturday a month, Tukey would storm in the club and catch Keith tricking with some young ho. Knowing it wasn't the girl's fault, Tukey would go upside her head, anyway. She couldn't try to fight Keith and win. Every time, Keith would handle the situation, plus drop a few hundred in the pockets of security.

After Keith split up the two cat fighters he picked Selina up by the waist and headed for the door.

"Why you grabbing me?" Selina screamed.

Keith told Kevin to tighten up the bouncers before he went outside with Selina. She was kicking and trying to break loose all the way out to the truck. He popped the locks on the Rover and threw her in.

"What about my car?" Selina yelled.

Keith waited until he was in the driver's seat before he said, "It ain't going nowhere." They took off in Tukey's Rover down Blue Ridge Road.

Selina got what she wanted, but remained quiet; she didn't know what kind of mood she had put Keith in. She knew that fire head that she'd given him last night had him fiending. That was just a taste test. What she'd do to him tonight would seal the deal.

"Am I spending the night with you?" Selina asked timidly.

"Listen," Keith said as he ignored her question. "You're gonna have to check you'self. You ain't my bitch, my woman or my mama. And you ain—"

"I ain't," Selina cut in, "yo woman yet."

Keith's eyes got big. "Yet?"

Selina reached over and rubbed his leg. "Let's not trip on petty ass shit like that," she whispered. "I want you to have some of this hot *chocha, papi*. I already let you fuck me in my *culo*. Now I want to give you the real thing. Fuck me, *papi*."

Keith knew that after that conversation, he should've kicked her ass out. Selina was a home wrecker out to fuck his life up. Foolish as he was, he ignored the thought and depended on dick control.

Selina saw a 7-Eleven. "Ooh, baby," she yelled. "Stop and get some Jolly Ranchers. I want to try something."

She waited until Keith went inside the store before she started rummaging through the truck. She figured it was his girl's truck by all of the club pictures of Tukey and her friends over the door. Plus, there was a brand new package of pantyhose on the back seat.

Gotta get this bitch outta our lives, Selina thought to herself. She checked the glove box and only found Keith's gun, then slammed it closed. A picture of Tukey, taken at Glamour Shots, fell from the visor.

Selina picked it up. "*Damn, she's fine.*"

While she was prowling, Keith had come out of the store and was nearing the truck. All she could do was put the picture in her purse.

When Keith got into the car with the sack, Selina was leaning back in her seat with an innocent look on her face. "You didn't forget the candy, did you, *papi?*" she asked in her little girl voice. He handed her the bag. "Good! Now let's hit the freeway and ride."

Selina rummaged through the CD case until she found Usher. She put the CD in, found her song, then lay back again in the soft leather seat. Keith got on the freeway, set the cruise control on 65 mph, and let it ride.

The sound of Usher's voice got Selina aroused. Her nipples hardened. She eased out of the skirt she was wearing and threw it in the back seat.

Keith looked to his right and saw hard nipples and a pink thong. If he had a camera, he would've taken pictures. He liked Selina. She wasn't afraid to let him know that sex was her intention tonight. Wasn't no playing hard to get with her. He couldn't leave her as a one-night stand if he tried.

Selina reached into Keith's lap and unbuttoned his jeans. Keith lifted himself so she could get his pants down. She popped two Jolly Rogers in her mouth and sucked on them until they began to melt.

Keith's dick was soft when Selina took it into her mouth. It was at full length when she slid her lips off of him. Gently, she bobbed her head up and down, sliding the candy along his thick shaft. Keith's eyes closed for a second, then popped back open. He could feel the sticky candy juice running down to his balls. She pulled him out of her mouth and licked the juice off of his balls.

Keith grunted.

Selina looked up at him through seductive green eyes. "You OK, *papi?*" she asked him.

Keith shook his head.

Selina sat up. She slipped off her thong and threw it out the window. She removed one of Keith's arms from the wheel, slid into the driver's seat on his lap. The wheel jerked, but Keith regained control.

Selina hit the button that slid the seat back. "Let me steer it, *papi*," she whispered. "You just sit back. Let me and the cruise control do all the driving."

Selina rotated her hips in a circular motion. "Umm, *es grande*," she moaned. She felt Keith relax, letting her take control.

The thought of having a wreck popped into Keith's mind and just as quickly popped out. He sat back moaning, while she worked her *chocha* on him and steered at the same time.

Keith thought that Selina did this act like she'd done it a hundred times. She had to have plenty of practice, to be doing this on the freeway.

"Can...you...feel it, *papi*," Selina grunted, switching her rotation in the other direction.

"Yeesss. Yesss," Keith hissed. Her warm pussy had him so relaxed, he'd forgotten that they were in a truck.

Selina rode him around four curves and fifteen miles. Her legs began to shake and jerk out of control with orgasm.

"Ooh, pull over, *papi*," Selina screamed. "Hurry, *papi*!"

Keith took control of the truck and pulled it over on the side of the road. The truck hadn't stopped a second before Selina hit the flashers. She grabbed hold of the wheel for support, and started to buck like a horse as she reached her climax.

"*Danelo papi chulo*," Selina cried as she felt her vaginal walls release fluid. "Damn that was a fat ass nut!"

Keith didn't say a word. He came with her. He just sat there and panted as sweat dripped down his face. He finally said, "Girl you...you got some fire."

There was a loud sucking noise as Selina slid off of his dick and hopped over into the passenger seat. Keith didn't care if she got come juice stains on the seat or not. Soft leather was easy to clean.

Too exhausted to pull up his pants, Keith turned off the flashers and eased back into traffic. He never even noticed the white Toyota Camry that had been following him since he left the store.

Chapter 4

Tukey woke up panting, in a cold sweat. Her head turned from left to right. She calmed down when she saw the warm California sun coming through the window. She had been having a nightmare. Keith and some Mexican girl had been trying to kill her.

She was relieved to wake up under fresh crisp sheets. She got up and hopped across the cold floor to the bathroom. Her eyes looked puffy; she looked at her reflection and brushed her teeth. She and Ben had been up half the night packing the dope in the stuffed animal.

After she took a hot shower, Tukey slipped into a tight-fitting khaki shorts outfit and a pair of sandals. She styled her dreads, then went into the living room.

Ben was sitting on the large sofa, smoking a joint the size of a small dick. He was in the middle of playing himself in a chess game when he heard her walk in.

"Hey, pretty girl." He said and turned in her direction. "Did yu sleep good? Me t'ought me heard yu screamin'."

Tukey took a seat next to him on the couch. "Me OK," she said softly. She could smell the burning herbs, and wanted a hit. She didn't smoke weed, but she knew how it mellowed Keith out. "Let me have some," Tukey reached for the joint.

"Yu smoking now, huh?" Ben smiled to himself as he thought

about how much she'd grown up. It seemed like just yesterday when she was begging for dollars for the ice cream truck. Now she was smoking weed and smuggling money on airplanes.

"Me need sum'ting to calm my nerves," Tukey said with a forced smile.

Ben took a long puff then passed it to her awaiting hands. Tukey took too long a puff and she jumped up, coughing.

Ben said, "Yu have to take it easy."

Finally, Tukey stopped coughing long enough to try it again. This time she took it easy. She tried to look cool and take the smoke in from her mouth to her nose, like she'd seen Keith do many times. "Damn," she said through a light cough. "Me feel it already."

Ben took the joint out of her hands. "Dat's me Jamaican funk," he said proudly. "Me got a t'ousand pound of dis shit."

* * *

Tukey went into the bedroom to get her stuff. She stuffed her suit into the briefcase along with her hygiene products. Her cell phone rang inside her briefcase. She took out the phone and answered it. "Hello," she said in a frustrated voice.

"Hey girl, this Anitra."

"Hey! Me out here enjoying dis California sun," Tukey said. The weed had her feeling good now.

"California?" Anitra hollered. "What you doing out there?"

"Sum'ting for Keith."

"Figures," Anitra said sarcastically. "When you coming back?"

"Me have to run by Fed Ex." Tukey said. "Me plane leave at noon."

"Hmmm," Anitra thought out loud. "Why don't you call Keith and tell him that I'm gonna pick you up at the airport."

"What for?" Tukey asked suspiciously.

"So we can hang out together for a while. We can go out to dinner, or something."

Tukey thought about it for a moment. "OK! Meet me at the airport around five. Don't be late, Anitra."

"I won't," Anitra said excitedly before she hung up. Tukey clipped her phone on her hip, closed her briefcase, then left.

Tukey and Ben stopped at Fed Ex and sent the package to Kansas City under one of Tukey's fake names. She called Keith on her way to the airport. He didn't answer, so she left him a message, saying that he didn't have to pick her up. She put the phone back on her waist then laid back, enjoying her high.

Ben's fire-ass weed had Tukey thinking negatively. Whenever she would take trips for Keith in the past, he would call her every hour. Now he wasn't even answering his phone.

She got on her phone again and called her mama. Even she hadn't even heard from Keith. *I've got to get my nigga back on top of his game,* Tukey thought.

Ben said, "Did yu get in touch wit' Keith?"

Tukey shook her head. For the rest of the ride, she promised herself she wasn't gonna worry. She was acting like a stressed out old lady.

Ben pulled up in the front entrance and slammed the Benz in park.

"Tell Keith him owe me t'ree hundred grand on dis one." He put his cigarette out in the ashtray.

Tukey made a quick calculation in her head. She frowned and said, "Dat's fifteen grand a key. Too much!"

"Me know what it is."

"Well us can't be paying dat much for twenty bricks. Where's the deal?" Tukey's tone was serious. She was no pushover. She knew that once the shit got to Kansas City, Keith would be stuck with the price if she didn't straighten it out now.

She'd been hip to the dope game since she was young. Tukey used to sit in the back of her daddy's car while he discussed deals with people. After he was murdered, she and her mama moved to Missouri to start over.

"T'irteen five a brick sound cool?" Ben said.

"Me can work wit' d'at." Tukey shook his hand to seal the deal.

Ben reached over, pinching her cheek. "Ya drive a hard bargain," he smiled.

"Me got it from me mudder," Tukey waved goodbye as she got out of the car. Ben watched her disappear into the crowd.

On the flight back to Kansas City, Tukey imagined herself walking down the aisle in a wedding gown. She wondered what it would feel like to actually be married to Keith. He'd just be hers, and no one else's. Tukey hoped that when Keith got out of the game he'd take her to Jamaica and start a new life, have another child and be happy.

Anitra was waiting at the front gate when Tukey got off of the plane. Her eyes lit up when she saw Tukey's tight khaki outfit. *I'm gonna turn this bitch out*, she thought as Tukey came toward her.

Tukey didn't recognize Anitra with her hair cut short, and almost walked past her.

Tukey looked at her with a shocked look on her face, and said, "Anitra?"

Anitra smiled.

Tukey said, "What ya done wit' ya hair, gyaal? Me t'ought yu were gonna grow locks like me?"

"Girl, please."

"How long yu been here?"

"Don't matter. I'd wait all day for you," Anitra gave Tukey a hug and took Tukey's briefcase like a gentleman. They walked her to Anitra's car.

"When did yu get dis?" Tukey said as they approached Anitra's white Camry.

"This ain't mine. This Diamond's car. She took my truck down to the Ozarks for the week."

While they were headed south on I-35, Tukey tried to call Keith again. No answer. Then she checked her messages.

No messages.

Tukey slammed her flip phone closed as Anitra tried to suppress a smile. She already knew what Tukey was so frustrated about. She couldn't get in touch with Keith, and Anitra knew why.

"Where're us gonna eat?" Tukey said, trying to occupy her mind.

Anitra looked into her rearview mirror, then changed lanes so that she could get off at the next exit. "We're going to Applebees's. But first, I want to make a quick stop."

"Take me to pick up Mi'kelle before us go eat."

Tukey rode in silence watching the scenery. It was a sunny day. Young cats cruised the street in their old school and new school rides. If Tukey wasn't able to find Keith, she was gonna ask Anitra to go with her to the Jamaican Cuisine.

She and Anitra use to go there on Friday nights and freak dance with each other, which made the men go crazy. Tukey was an attention freak, like Keith. But she didn't like it enough to leave the club with some dude. All of the ballers tried to get in her pants behind Keith's back, but none ever succeeded. Most of the guys who tried to get at her became hostile after buying countless drinks for her with no luck. Not even a phone number at the end of the night.

Tukey became confused when Anitra made a right turn into the Relax Inn Motel parking lot.

"What is us doing here, An—" Tukey's voice trailed off when she saw her silver Rover parked in front of one of the rooms. She didn't really believe that it was hers, until she saw the license plate that read, 2-KEY. "Stop! Now!" she shouted.

Before Anitra could come to a complete stop, Tukey was already exiting the vehicle. Anitra slammed on the brakes and put the car into park before Tukey hurt herself.

Anitra got out of the car and tried to catch Tukey before she got to her truck. She already knew what Tukey was going to get.

She was too late. Tukey had already took out her key and opened up the door to the gas tanks. The place where she kept a loaded black .25 automatic. Tukey had it cocked and ready by the time Anitra caught up with her.

Anitra put her hands up and yelled, "Don't do it like this, girl. Please!" This was going further than Anitra had planned.

Tukey pointed the gun straight up in the air and held it too high for Anitra to reach.

"Ain't dis what yu wanted me to find out?" Tukey yelled. Now she understood the real reason why Anitra wanted to pick her up. "Huh, Anitra?" Tears were rolling down her face.

"Yes!" Anitra admitted. "But you can't handle it like this."

"Watch me."

Tukey pushed Anitra out of the way and walked up to the door in front of which her truck was parked. *Boom. Boom. Boom.* She banged on the door.

The loud knocks on the door woke Keith. He didn't know what was happening. He'd checked his messages hours ago and found out Tukey was gonna get picked up by Anitra, before he re-rented the room. *It couldn't be her. Had to be the manager,* he thought to himself.

Boom. Boom. Boom. "Open dis fuckin' door!" Tukey shouted.

Damn, it *is* her.

Keith hopped out of bed and slid on his clothes. He peeked out the curtain. He saw Tukey yelling, "Open dis mutha fuckin' door, now!" Now she was beating on the window.

"How in the fuck—" he started to ask himself. Then he realized how when he saw Anitra's yellow ass standing behind her.

All of the commotion woke Selina up. "Who the fuck is that beating on the damn door?"

Keith was still peeking out of the curtain. "That's my girl."

Selina saw the perfect chance to fuck shit up with him and Tukey. She got up and slipped on her skirt. She was about to look for her thong until she remembered throwing it out of the truck's window.

Selina hollered, "Yo bitch got me fucked up if she thinks I'm gonna hide in here like some punk," Selina hollered.

"Shee't, you better," Keith said seriously. "'Cause I can see a gun in her hand."

"I don't give a fuck about her gun," Selina snapped. "You're with me, and she's just gonna have to accept it."

Keith ignored her last comment. "Take your ass out there and get fucked up, if you want to."

Selina snatched open the door. Tukey reached a long arm in and grabbed her by her hair. Selina screamed in pain as Tukey pulled her out the door and threw her down on the concrete.

Tukey pointed the gun at her and shouted, "Bitch, what de fuck ya doing wit' me man?"

Selina looked up at the taller woman while she held her head in pain. She thought about rushing Tukey, but the barrel of the gun staring at her made her think otherwise.

"Put the gun down, bitch...and fight me head up," Selina pleaded.

"Head up?" Tukey snapped. "Bitch, yu ain't said not'ing." Tukey handed her gun to Anitra and kicked her sandals off. "Get up, bitch!"

Selina got up and rushed Tukey with wild swings. It didn't do her any good. Tukey extended out her long arms and struck the smaller woman in the face. Selina grabbed her face and saw blood on her hand.

Without mercy, Tukey stepped forward and hit Selina with a barrage of punches to the face. Suddenly, Selina wasn't tough anymore.

"Get her off of me!" Selina cried. Tukey had her on her back, with a knee in her chest. "I can't...breath."

Keith got tired of watching Selina get punished. He stepped in and snatched both of them by their necks. "Break this shit up," he snapped. Tukey tried to resist. He gave her a cold stare. "I said stop, Tukey."

Tukey looked up at him with a shocked look on her face, as if to say, who's side are you on?

Keith got them to calm down and told Selina to go over by the truck.

Tukey yelled, "Nah, dat bitch ain't gettin' in me truck." She tried to get loose from Keith's hold.

Keith let go of Selina and locked both of his hands around

Tukey. "I'm just gonna take her home. Now calm the fuck down."

Tukey was still trying to get loose. "Yu ain't taking dat bitch nowhere."

A crowd began to gather. People stepped outside their rooms after hearing all the commotion. Sirens were screaming from a distance. It was time for Keith to go. He put Tukey in a head lock with one hand and slid his keys out of his pocket with his other.

He pushed the button that unlocked the truck. Selina hopped in. Tukey slid out of his hold and struck Keith on the side of his face.

Out of reflex, he turned and smacked Tukey across her eye.

Anitra ran at Keith. Keith grabbed her by the neck and the arm that held the gun. He took it out of her hand, then pushed her into Tukey. They both fell to the ground.

"Bitch, don't you ever try to put your hands on me," Keith snapped. He put the gun into his pocket and took off in the truck.

Anitra ran to her car. She pulled over to where Tukey was still on the ground, crying.

"Why dis happen to me, huh?" Tukey screamed. "What did me do?"

Anitra got out of the car and ran to her friend. She picked Tukey up by her underarms. "Come on, girl. Get up. We got to go." She helped Tukey into the car.

An older woman who was watching the scene said, "Is she gonna be alright?"

"She's gonna be fine," Anitra said as she walked to the driver's side.

The motel manager yelled, "I called the police!"

Anitra didn't hear him. She slammed the car into drive and rolled out.

* * *

Keith was deep in thought as he sped down Blue Parkway. He was trying to figure out what the hell just happened. Why the fuck did he stay at the motel instead of taking that bitch home, anyway? Had Tukey finished taking care of business before she found out? He had a whole lot of unanswered questions popping up in his mind.

He saw that Selina's nose was still bleeding. He took some Kleenex out of the console and handed them to her.

"Thank you," Selina said in a soft voice. She was embarrassed about getting beat down in front of him. She shouldn't have gone out there like she was tough. Tukey was just too tall and strong for her. *I'm gonna get that bitch*, she thought to herself.

Keith couldn't help but smile. He thought about how confident Selina had been before she opened up the door. She must be feeling damn stupid after that ass-kicking that she took.

"You laughing at me?" Selina asked, already knowing the answer to her question. She was thinking the same thing he was.

"Nah," Keith lied.

"Umm hmm," Selina threw the bloody Kleenex out the window. "Go ahead, laugh at me."

Keith shrugged. "I told you not to take your tough ass out there. Didn't I?" Keith laughed. "Yo' dumb ass wouldn't listen."

"Shut up," Selina snapped, folding her arms across her chest. "If she was just a little shorter," she indicated with her fingers, "I would've smashed that bitch."

Keith didn't hear her. He was thinking again. That bitch Anitra! He promised himself that he'd get at her ass before it was all over with. Dyke bitch! He knew that she wanted to get with Tukey. Bitch should try to pull Tukey on her own, he thought. Why hate on me?

Hitting Tukey in front of Selina was bugging him. He should have handled the situation better. Bitch's pussy wasn't that damn good. Keith decided to wait until the situation died down before calling Tukey.

Selina could see that Keith was deep in thought. "You still mad at me, *papi?*" She wanted to see where his head was.

"Ain't yo' fault," he said evenly.

"I was just asking," she said softly. She threw her long hair over her shoulders and just sat there looking at him.

Selina saw a yellow parking ticket sitting on her windshield as Keith pulled into the club's parking lot, where she'd left her car last night.

"*Ain't that a bitch,*" she said to herself. Keith stopped beside the car. She could see that he was still thinking to himself.

Selina said, "You think its over between you two?" She pretended to sound sincere.

Keith didn't say a word, he just shrugged his shoulders. She tore a piece of paper off the 7-Eleven bag and wrote down her number. She placed the paper on the dashboard.

Selina said, just above a whisper, "I want to be your girl. I know I could do everything that she does for you."

Keith's hand twitched. He wanted to smack the shit out of her. It almost made him think that was her plan from the jump.

He was about to check her until he saw her beautiful face staring at him, like a helpless puppy. Her big green eyes took the anger right out of him. "You want to be my girl, huh?" he quizzed.

"Umm hmm," Selina said. "You can train me to be the woman that I need to be, to keep you happy. It'll be like teaching a young dog new tricks." She cracked a smile.

"Why you want to be my girl?"

She put her hand on his shoulder. "'Cause you seem ambitious." She rubbed his shoulder. "Ambition makes me horny."

Keith read her face. Her seriousness almost made him feel better about what he'd done to Tukey. Maybe it was time for them to take a break from each other. They'd been together nonstop since high school.

Fuck that, he thought. Ben was his source of income, and Tukey was his niece. He was down to a simple decision between money or a bitch. Money outweighed a bitch on any scale, in his book.

Keith said, "Let me think about it." He didn't want to let Selina go just yet. He wanted to fuck her a few more times first.

Selina leaned over and kissed his cheek. "Don't think long, *papi,*" she said seriously. She got out of the truck. "Bye, *papi.*"

Keith dialed Ben's number as he pulled back out into traffic.

"Speak to me," Ben answered. Keith could hear him puffing on something.

"Beanie Man," Keith said coolly. "What's up, baby?"

Ben seemed to be in a serious mood. "Tukey make it back OK?"

His words let Keith know that the business had been taken care of. "Yeah, she made it back OK," Keith said. He didn't want no trouble with Ben, so he decided to keep the fight he and Tukey had to himself. Tukey was Ben's only niece and he made it clear to Keith that he would be cut off if he ever put his hands on Tukey.

Ben said, "Everyt'ing's criss. Me sent yu some mail dis morning."

"Good!" Keith said. "How much is the postage?" That was code talk for "how much money do I owe you?"

Ben blew out a cloud of smoke. "Well...me upped ya dosage. Me added five to what ya got last time. So ya owe me two hundred seventy t'ousand."

Keith took a moment to figure out how much that was per kilo. He smiled and said, "Cool. You gave me some justice this time."

"Ya caan t'ank me niece for dat."

"I will," Keith said. "I'll hit you up when I'm ready. Have a nice trip."

Ben's face was full of smoke. He nodded his head, then hung up the phone.

Chapter 5

"Me goin' to take Mi'kelle to Kansas wit' me for the weekend," Arie said to her over the phone.

"Dat's cool," Tukey said. "Tell me baby me love her." She hung up the phone.

Tukey was soaking in Anitra's bathtub when Anitra walked in with a fresh bar of soap.

"Is Mi'kelle alright?" Anitra said, as she opened the soap.

Tukey propped her feet up on the edge of the tub.

"Her alright," Tukey said. "Her gonna spend the weekend wit' Mummy."

After they left the motel, Anitra talked Tukey into going home with her. Tukey didn't object. Her mama would've flipped her wig if she'd seen the scar over her eye. Arie would have hopped right on the phone and called Ben. Tukey knew that she'd most likely end up forgiving Keith, so she left her family out of it.

Anitra's home was a nice place for her to relax for a while. Her house was plush with glass tables, leather sofas, a big screen TV, and a thick carpet. Anitra inherited the house from her dead husband. He was believed to have been killed by one of his flunkies.

After he died, Anitra made a promise to herself that she'd never mess with another man. That was supposed to be out of respect for him. Ever since then, she'd only dated women. It turned out that she liked being with women more than she did a man.

Anitra watched lustfully as Tukey ran the soapy towel over her chocolate body. While she looked, she wondered just how vulnerable Tukey was right now. She wanted to make a move on Tukey, but she didn't want to blow it.

"Ouch," Tukey hollered when the towel touched the fresh cut over her eye.

"Here let me help you." Anitra knelt on the side of the tub. She took the towel out of Tukey's hand.

Tukey tensed up as she felt Anitra run the warm towel over her breast.

"Relaxxx," Anitra hissed softly. Her green eyes concentrated on Tukey's body. She noticed that Tukey's breathing had sped up.

Tukey was trembling slightly. Soon she began to relax at Anitra's smooth touch. Gently, Anitra ran the towel over her breasts, down to her navel, and finally, between her legs.

Tukey snapped her legs closed on Anitra's hand. The feel of the towel rubbing between her legs started to arouse her. "Me caan't," Tukey whispered.

"You need this," Anitra said. She eased Tukey's legs apart. "Just relax."

Tukey started to pant from the sensation.

Anitra dropped the towel into the water and traced her smooth fingers up Tukey's thigh. Before Tukey knew it, she felt Anitra's fingers slide into her crevice. Tukey's head fell back, with her mouth open.

Anitra skillfully worked her fingers in and out of Tukey. The pain from the cut on her eye had vanished. It started to feel good. The tender touch of a woman felt different from a man's touch. Tukey spread her legs wider so that Anitra could do her work.

While Tukey was being pacified with Anitra's two fingers, Anitra leaned over and slid her tongue into Tukey's open mouth. At first she resisted, but Anitra persisted until Tukey gave in and started to kiss her back.

"Ummm," Anitra moaned as she ran her tongue down to

Tukey's soft breast.

"Yesssss. Bite me," Tukey moaned in return she felt Anitra's teeth gently bite her nipples. Her moans encouraged Anitra to proceed.

Anitra ran her tongue down to Tukey's throbbing pussy. Tukey pushed her pussy out of the water so that Anitra could get a mouthful. She sucked and licked Tukey into an orgasm. Tukey came so thick, that it looked like she had lathered herself with Ivory soap.

Anitra was ready for the next step. She dried Tukey off and led her into the bedroom. Once a woman had let Anitra get this far, she was pretty much hers for the taking. She was an expert at this.

Tukey stretched out naked across Anitra's queen-sized bed to await whatever was about to happen next.

Anitra opened up her closet door and faced her huge selection of dildos. They ranged from two- to twelve-inch rubber dicks, some strap-on, some manual. Anitra decided to go with the two-inch anal worker and the ten-inch strap-on.

Tukey watched Anitra undress and strap on the huge black dick.

Anitra was sexy as hell. The fake dick fit snugly against her sandy brown pubic hair. Her titties were small and firm, with small freckles around pink nipples.

As Anitra approached, Tukey spread her legs wide, ready to take the massive fake dick into her crevice.

Anitra put Tukey's legs on her shoulders and entered her. "Oooh! Ooooh! Shiiittt," Tukey moaned and groaned as she felt Anitra hit the bottom of her pussy.

Anitra stroked her slow until Tukey loosened up, then she sped up and gave her deep, penetrating thrusts.

"Yess! Yess! Yess!" Tukey hollered. "Fuck me harder! Harder!"

Anitra jammed in and out of Tukey making her come twice, before she pulled out. They lay side by side, breathing each other's sexual fumes, until they drifted off to sleep.

* * *

Kevin and his two-year-old-son, Kevin Jr., were in their drive-way washing his black Lexus coupe when Keith pulled up in the Rover. Kevin noticed how stressed out his brother looked when he got out of the truck.

"'Sup, big bro?" Kevin said. He rinsed the soapy water off his car.

"Shit," Keith said as he bent down to pick up his nephew. "I just stopped by to see what y'all were doing." Keith looked into the eyes of his half-naked nephew. "What's up, ole bad-ass boy?"

Kevin Jr. smiled. He stuck his soapy hand in Keith's face.

"You little fucker," Keith yelled jokingly. He sat Jr. down.

Kevin dried off his car while Keith stood there in a daze.

Kevin said, "I hope you're thinking about getting some more dope. 'Cause we're out."

Keith shook his head. "I took care of that yesterday."

"Good! I got this cat coming in from Decatur to get three of 'em tomorrow."

"Decatur, Georgia?"

Kevin shook his head. "Illinois. It's a drought up there. I'm charging him twenty eight a piece."

Keith whistled.

"That ain't the worst of it," Kevin said with a smile. "He want it already rocked up."

"Damn. We gon' make over fifty Gs profit off that one serve." Keith thought for a moment. "He ain't the police, is he?" His tone was serious. "You know how the dudes don't be buying keys like that. The undercovers up there be buying more dope than the real dealers."

"Nope. Been fucking with him for a while now." Kevin turned off the water hose. "Let's go inside for a minute." Kevin pointed to Kevin Jr. "Grab your nephew."

Kevin led Keith inside. Kevin's baby mama, Kim, was sitting on the living room couch, flipping through channels on TV.

Kim jumped up when she saw Keith and pulled down her too short t-shirt. "Hey Keith," she yelled on her way to her room.

Keith couldn't help but sneak a peek at her well shaped thighs as she ran through the house.

"Hey Kim," Keith said as he sat little Kevin down.

Keith took a seat on the couch in front of Kevin's sixty-inch screen. He fished out a half smoked blunt from the ashtray. Kevin fired it up, hit it for ten seconds, then passed it to Keith.

"It's been a fucked up day, man." Keith blew the smoke out.

"I can tell."

"How?"

"That fucked-up look on your face," Kevin replied. "I've been knowing you all my life. I know when you fucked up." Kevin waited until his brother finished off the blunt. Then he asked, "What happened?"

"I had to smack Tukey's ass this morning," Keith said as he put the blunt out in the ashtray.

"No shit!" Kevin laughed. "What happened?"

Keith spent the next half hour giving Kevin the rundown on everything that happened, starting with the club last night. Kevin began to get irritated by Keith's story. From what he was hearing, Keith might have fucked up their meal ticket, all because he was tricking off with that Puerto Rican bitch.

They'd still be pedaling nickels and dimes if it weren't for Tukey. It was because of her hookup with her uncle that they owned homes, cars and had over two hundred grand stashed away. Sure, they could buy their own dope out of the city. But why pay twenty or better for a kilo of dope when they could get it from Ben for fifteen or less? Sometimes, Kevin wished that Tukey was his instead of Keith's. Keith was in the game for the fame and attention. He wasn't thinking about the possibility of things falling apart.

"You falling the fuck off, man," Kevin said harshly as he pointed his finger at Keith.

"Fuck you mean?" Keith shot back.

Kevin stood up. "I mean, you should've had yo' ass at the airport waiting on Tukey, instead of laying up with that ho." Kevin shook his head in disgust. "I knew that bitch was trouble the minute I laid eyes on her." Kevin stared at his brother. "How do you know if the shit got sent?"

"I called Ben on my way over here."

"And he said it was all good?"

"Yeah," Keith said with frustration in his voice.

Kevin put his hand on his brother's shoulder. "Tukey will be alright in a few days. That girl loves the shit out of your ass." He patted Keith on the shoulder. "Go in my room and find some clean clothes. We got to make some runs."

Keith took a hot shower while Kim got him some of Kevin's clothes. She brought him a pair of heavily starched jeans and a new Stafford t-shirt.

Keith dressed and was brushing his waves when someone knocked on the door. He opened it to find Kim standing there with a bottle of Chrome cologne in her hand.

"I like the smell of this stuff," she said. Their fingers touched as she handed it to him. "You ought to try it." She admired him for a moment, then turned and swayed away.

* * *

They decided to stop by Pete's Lounge to unwind for a minute. They hopped in the Rover, taking Highway 71 to Grandview.

Keith felt better after the hot shower and change of clothes. He counted the wad in his pocket and felt good again. The weed had kicked in and he was on cloud nine as he drove the seventy-thousand-dollar truck up the highway.

He had almost forgotten that he had twenty keys of dope coming in tomorrow. More dope meant more money. The way Keith figured it, this time next year he'd be playing with a hundred keys or better.

Happy hour was almost over when they got to Pete's. It was a place were all the ballers went to chill out, have a few drinks and pick up a few honeys. The crowd usually consisted of people between the ages of twenty-five to thirty. The place wasn't huge, but it had a bar, a pool table and some of the sexiest waitresses around. It wasn't packed, but there were enough pretty girls in there for a player to have a good time.

Pete, the owner, shook their hands as they came through the door. Pete noticed that they were dressed for happy hour, but he hoped the big spenders stayed until nightfall. The dress code didn't apply to big spenders.

Pete personally led them back to the pool table. He grabbed the arm of a waitress passing by, and instructed her to bring them their usual bottle of Moët.

While Keith and Kevin chose their cues, Toya, the sexy black waitress, strolled up with a bottle of Moët and two chilled glasses. She eyed Kevin as she opened up the bottle, and filled their glasses. She had spent the night with him two weeks ago and hadn't heard from him since. She knew he had a girl. She'd seen them come in together, many times before. She didn't care. She just wanted to continue to sleep with him.

"Your usual," she said as she handed Kevin his glass.

Kevin took the drink out of her hand. He noticed how she kept staring at him. "What's up, baby?" he said in a cool tone.

"Will you be needing anything else?" she asked, trying to fake a smile. She'd hoped he'd say something more than, "What's up, baby."

"We're good," Kevin replied. He knew that she wanted more conversation out of him. He was playing hard to get, for a minute.

The champagne dribbled down Keith's chin. The waitress grabbed a napkin and wiped his mouth. "Call me if you need anything," she said seductively.

Kevin watched with lust as she strutted her sexy ass back over to the bar. He remembered how sexy she looked laying naked across the motel bed.

Keith said, "Bitch ain't bad. Her pussy as good as it looks?"

"She cool," Kevin lied. "Rack the balls up."

They were in the middle of their third game of nine ball when their partners, Tee and Andre, walked up to the pool table.

"Players, players," Kevin greeted as they all shook hands.

Tee and Andre were brothers. They grew up in the same neighborhood as Keith and Kevin. When Ben put Keith on, Keith put them on as well. That was their circle – just the four of them.

Tee and Andre were of medium build and wore their hair in corn rows. To girls, they were pretty boys. To niggas on the streets, they were gangsters. They both had a body or two under their belts. To those who knew them, they were considered not to be fucked with.

Tee had a problem that Keith didn't like. He preyed on less fortunate dudes' girls. Niggas with no money ain't got nothing to lose, was Tee's theory. To Keith, that was inviting unwanted trouble that men of their status didn't need.

Whenever Keith dropped the dope off to them, he'd give it to Andre. Tee was a trick and sometimes spent beyond his means. That's why Andre kept their money separate. They were brothers, true enough. But Andre was in the business to stack and get out. Tee, on the other hand, spent every dime he made.

Keith still tried his best to keep money in Tee's pocket. He couldn't stand for anyone around him to be broke. They grew up together, so he felt obligated to look out for Tee. "If your whole crew is getting money, there won't be no reason for y'all to fall out with each other," Keith always said.

Kevin yelled for the waitress. "Toya! Get us another bottle over here."

The DJ put on "Back That Ass Up" by Juvenile. Every bitch in the club went wild as they hit the dance floor. Keith grabbed him a cutie and hit the floor, too.

"What you niggas doing here?" Kevin asked as he bobbed his head to the music.

Tee said, "I'm trying to find me something to take home."

Andre added, "I just came to have a few drinks."

Toya, the waitress, brought them another bottle and two more chilled glasses.

Kevin, Tee and Andre had finished two bottles of Moët and

were on their fifth game of side pocket when Keith came over with the cutie with whom he had been dancing.

The three men undressed the girl with their eyes. She was a redbone chick with long red hair. She was squeezed into a tight pair of red slacks and a black blouse that showed too much cleavage. Her outfit was expensive; you could tell she had money, or had a nigga with money. Right now she was digging Keith, so it didn't matter. Alexus was her name and judging by her rear end, the name fit her just right.

Alexus stood next to Keith and danced in place while Keith hit his drink. Her ass brushed up against Keith and got him going. He threw his hands up and grinded behind her.

"Heeyyy! Get low, get low," Alexus hollered as she bent over and shook her thang.

A big black dude with a big gold chain around his neck and a jheri curl walked over and stood in front of Alexus. She was too busy backing it up to notice him.

Keith's face went from a smile to a frown when he saw the big guy standing there. The mug on the other man's face was a sign of trouble.

"Alexus? What the fuck are you doing?" the big guy yelled angrily.

Alexus's eyes got big when she looked up at him. "I-I-I...we was just dancing," she stammered. She grabbed him by the arm. "Teddy, come on. Let's go."

By then Kevin, Andre and Tee had stepped up. Teddy ignored them and kept his mug on Keith. "Find your own woman to dance with," Teddy commanded.

Keith was harsh when he said, "You better listen to your bitch and get your big ass somewhere else." Keith was itching to steel on him, right there.

"Baby, let's go," Alexus pleaded. She pulled at Teddy's arm.

Kevin added, "Make it easy on yourself, big Teddy. All the talking is through."

Teddy accepted defeat and backed up, following Alexus out of there. He made a pistol out of his finger and pointed it at Keith, as he walked out.

Keith asked, "Y'all strapped?"

Tee said, "You know I keeps mine."

"Cool," Keith said. "Just in case we have to hand his hat to him."

Andre picked his stick up again. "Let's shoot some pool."

The club was closing. Toya picked up their empty glasses. They'd punished seven bottles of Moët. They put up their sticks and got ready to leave.

"Who's paying for this?" Toya asked in a sassy voice.

"How much is it?" Kevin licked his lips, trying to seduce Toya so that they wouldn't have to pay.

"Four hundred. Plus my tip." Toya stuck her hand out. "You got it, big baller."

Kevin counted out four c-notes and handed them to her. Toya looked at the money as if it had been shat on first.

"Where's my tip, Kevin?" Toya asked with a frown.

"You want a tip? Stop fucking with niggas like me," Kevin retorted as he headed for the door.

Tee pulled out a hundred dollar bill and handed it to Toya. "You should've gave me the pussy." He laughed as he trailed behind Kevin.

The warm night air hit Keith in the face and he broke into a sweat. He had forgotten all about the confrontation that they'd had with big Teddy earlier. They walked right past two guys sitting in a red Volvo with the lights out, who watched the foursome leave the club.

"I'll give y'all a call as soon as the shit touches down tomorrow," Keith said. They shook hands goodbye.

Keith was hoping that the alcohol would've stopped his pain. It did for a while, but now that he wasn't drinking and having a good time anymore, reality set back in. His mind was back into thinking mode as he stepped into the Rover.

Keith wanted to smack himself every time what happened earlier flashed in his mind. He couldn't undo what had already happened.

Before they pulled out of the parking lot, Keith told Kevin to get the Glock out of the glove box. Kevin smiled when he saw Tukey's little .25 in there, also.

Keith was creeping down Blue Ridge, listening to Tukey's old message on his cell phone. He stopped at a red light.

He still hadn't noticed the red Volvo that was now following him.

When the two dudes in the Volvo saw them stop at the red light, they prepared to make their move. The one on the passenger side pulled a Tech .9 from underneath his seat.

"Let's twist these niggas' caps back," he said as he rolled down his window.

The Volvo crept alongside of the Rover's driver's side.

"Shitt!" Keith hollered. He hit the gas after he saw, out of the corner of his eye, the Tech sticking out of the Volvo's window. He didn't bother to look over to make sure that that's what he'd seen.

Wop! Wop. Wop! was the terrifying sound that echoed in the dark night. Bullets ripped through metal and tore through the Rover's interior.

Suddenly, Keith felt a sharp pain in his side. Without panic, he made a quick right turn onto a dark street. He pressed the pedal to the floor, going full speed down the street. He had a plan.

"Kevin," he yelled over the loud gun shots. Kevin had his head between his legs, ducking slugs. "As soon as we get over this hill, I'm gonna stop. It's gonna take them a minute to slow down. Before they get a chance to turn around, I want you outta this truck and gunnin' at they asses. You hear me?"

Kevin shook his head. He looked down and saw that his brother was hit. "Damn! You hit?"

"Yep, but I'm OK. Ready?"

Kevin shook his head again while he cocked the gun.

The Volvo was coming up alongside them fast, Keith saw in his rearview mirror.

Keith hit the brakes. *Errrrrrk* was the sound that the tires made as the truck swerved to a stop.

When the driver of the Volvo saw what was happening, he hit his brakes, too. He had his mind set on the occupants of the Rover dying tonight.

Without hesitation, Kevin jumped from the truck, nine drawn, letting loose rounds. Empty shells jumped out the chamber so fast, Kevin was running into them.

Keith watched in triumph as the bullets slammed into the Volvo. The driver did a 360 and took off down the road.

Kevin almost panicked when he got back to the truck and saw Keith slumped over the wheel.

"Big bro...talk to me," Kevin said as he smacked Keith's face to revive him.

"I'm hi—" Keith mumbled before he passed out.

"You gon' be alright," Kevin hoped. He helped Keith to the passenger side, got into the driver's seat and smashed out to Research Hospital.

Chapter 6

Anitra woke up after hearing an annoying sound in her ear. It was Tukey's cell phone. She eased out of the bed and went for Tukey's purse on the dresser. She took out the phone and answered it. "Hello," Anitra said in a sleepy voice.

"Let me speak with Tukey," a man said in a hurried voice.

"Who is this?" Anitra asked with attitude.

"This Kevin, bitch. Now hurry up and put Tukey on the phone. It's an emergency."

Anitra was about to hang up in his face, until she heard him say, "emergency." Quickly, she ran to the bed and started to wake Tukey.

"Hmm. What!" Tukey mumbled.

"Get up, girl," Anitra yelled, shaking her. "Kevin's on the phone, talking 'bout it's an emergency."

Tukey's eyes popped open at the mention of Kevin's name. She snatched the phone away from Anitra "Hello?"

"Tukey, this is Kevin," he said calmly. "Keith's been shot."

"No!" Tukey yelled as the phone dropped to the floor. She slid off the bed, crying. "Please, don't do dis to me, God."

"Tukey, what's wrong?" Anitra said, concerned.

Tukey didn't respond. She sat there crying her heart out. Anitra picked up the phone and put it to her ear.

"Kevin, what's going on?" Anitra asked. She listened quietly while Kevin gave her the rundown on everything that happened. Then he instructed her to get Tukey together and get her down to Research Hospital.

As soon as Anitra hung up with Kevin, she rushed over to Tukey and tried to calm her down. "It's going to be alright," Anitra threw her arms around Tukey's shoulders. "But you've got to get up so we can go to the hospital."

Tukey nodded her head. "OK," she sniffled.

Anitra threw on a pair of jogging pants and a white t-shirt. Then she helped Tukey, who was still on the floor crying, up from the floor and into some clothes.

On their way to the hospital, all Tukey could think about was how stupid she was for having sex with Anitra. Anitra took advantage of her while she was weak and finally got what she wanted.

Having sex with a woman was just as bad as having sex with a man, in Tukey's book. If she could do something as bad as having sex behind Keith's back, what else was she capable of doing? She didn't enjoy it, and the only reason why she did it was because she was vulnerable at the time, she told herself.

When Anitra and Tukey arrived at Research Hospital, they rushed into the emergency room. Kevin was sitting beside his mother, holding her hand.

Mary looked much younger than the thirty-nine years she'd spent on this earth. She was short like she wore her hair. She loved both of her sons and stood by them whether they were right or wrong. They were all she had, besides her two grandchildren and grumpy husband.

She attempted to dry her eyes when she looked up and saw Tukey and Anitra. She stood up and gave Tukey a warm embrace.

Tukey asked, "Are ya OK, Mama?" Tears started rolling again.

"I'm OK, baby. The doctors are patching him up, right now. The bullet went in and out of his side."

"When caan me see him?"

"They told us to have a seat and they'll send him out when they're through."

Anitra felt odd as she saw Tukey sit down with Keith's family, like she was one of them. Jealousy started to kick in. Now she wished she'd never answered the damn phone. She knew that somehow Keith would use this to make up with Tukey. She thought about telling Keith that she fucked his girl.

Anitra rolled her eyes when she saw Kevin eyeing her suspiciously.

They waited for almost an hour before Keith came limping into the visiting room. Everybody, except for Anitra, ran over to him.

"Ouch! Y'all hurting me, now," Keith complained. The pain medicine was just now starting to kick in.

"You need to stay yo' ass outta trouble," his mother lectured him.

Keith said, "I am, Mama." He gave her a hug and a kiss.

"Ya OK, baby?" Tukey asked softly.

Keith didn't respond immediately, he just stared at her for a moment. He was giving her his "I'm sorry" look that Tukey knew too well.

Tukey reached out and hugged him.

Keith whispered into her ear, "I'm sorry, baby." He tried to sound as sincere as he could.

Tukey broke the hug and stared at him. "Are yu gonna leave dat bitch alone?"

"Already have," Keith said, then kissed her lips.

"Well," Kevin said, "Let's go home."

Anitra got pissed off as Tukey walked past her, hugged up with Keith. Acting like she didn't see her.

"What you gon' do, Tukey," Anitra asked hotly. "You riding with me, or what?"

"Hell naw," Keith said, pushing Tukey toward the exit. "She goin' home with me."

Not really knowing what to do, Tukey left, not saying a word to Anitra.

Keith's mother dropped them off at home. Tukey helped Keith

into bed, then got into the shower. She set the water as hot as she could stand it. She washed and scrubbed Anitra's smell off her.

Tukey felt as if she'd betrayed Keith. Even though she'd caught him at the motel with another girl, she felt that what she did was wrong.

She got out of the shower and rubbed herself down with some apple-scented lotion. Slipping on her black nightgown, she snuggled up in the bed next to Keith.

Keith felt her warm body next to him. He wrapped one arm around her neck and threw his right leg on top of hers, like he always did, and drifted off to sleep.

"Owww! Ouch! Ouch!" Keith screamed, waking up. The pain medicine had worn off. He reached over and shook Tukey awake. "Get up, Goddammit!"

Tukey wiped her eyes. "What's wrong, baby?"

"The medicine wore off," Keith cried. "I need the pain pills." He pointed at the bottle on dresser.

Tukey tossed the covers off her legs and went into the bathroom. She came back with a cup of water, retrieved the pills from the dresser and brought them over to him.

"Sit up, baby. Take ya pills."

Keith sat up and let her feed him the pills, like a baby. "Thank you, baby," he said in a soft tone. He leaned back and let the pain medicine take its course.

When the pain eased, Keith limped to the closet and took out a Phat Pharm jogging suit and a pair of Air Maxs. Then he limped over to the drawer for socks and underwear.

Tukey watched him grimace in pain. "What are ya doing?" she asked, as she watched him disappear into the bathroom. She heard water running.

"About to wash up," he said loud enough to be heard through the closed door. Pain shot up his body every time he lifted his arm to wash under it.

Tukey's sexy ass appeared in the doorway. "Want some help?" she asked.

Keith looked at her reflection in the mirror. Damn, she look good. He shook his head.

Tukey took the towel from him and began at his neck.

Keith cried out in pain as she touched the left side of his body. The bullet had pierced just above his left hip, going straight through his flesh. After countless efforts by the police to get Keith to tell them who shot him, they gave up. The doctors stitched him up, wrapped him in gauze and sent him on his way.

Tukey finished washing him up and helped him into his clothes.

Keith was brushing his hair when Tukey walked up behind him. She put his Glock in his pants pocket. Kevin had given it to her when they were dropped off last night. She had loaded it for him while he was getting dressed.

"Ya want me to drive ya?" she asked softly.

Kevin shook his head. "Nah, Kevin's gonna meet me out there."

Tukey stood in silence as she stared at his reflection in the mirror. She felt shameful.

Keith looked away when he saw the scar above her eye where he'd hit her. After all she'd done for him, he couldn't understand why he'd reacted like that. Especially behind a girl that he'd just met.

Tukey was lost in her own thoughts. Flashes of she and Anitra making love kept popping up in her mind. Like a ghost, it was haunting her. She'd dreamed about it last night. Now awake, she was daydreaming about it. How long would the guilt last? If it was a good or bad sign, she didn't know. She could only hope that she could put that experience behind her.

Keith took a small bankroll out of his sock drawer. He split it into what he thought was half, and handed one of the halves to Tukey. He put the other in his pocket.

"What me do wit' dis?" Tukey asked as she held the money toward him.

Keith replied, "The dealership won't be able to get you a rental car until Monday. So take that, call your mama and tell her to take you to Enterprise before they close."

"OK."

Keith gave her a hug and kiss before he left.

* * *

Keith was speeding down Highway 71 when his cell phone rang. "Hello."

"Be careful," he heard Tukey say on the other end.

"Always," Keith replied, then they both hung up.

Keith was flirting with two light-skinned honeys in a red Honda when his phone rang again.

"Damn it," Keith huffed, reaching for his phone. "Hello."

"Where you at, bro?" It was Kevin.

"I'm on the highway, headed your way," Keith said, still flirting with the two girls, who were trying to get his attention.

"Cool. I'll meet you in front of Nukey's."

"Alright." Keith hung up.

The two girls were waving and honking for Keith to pull over. Any other time, he would've done so. But he was on business at the moment. He smiled, put up a peace sign and hit the gas.

He saw the "fuck you" fingers that they gave him through his rearview mirror. He shook his head and zoomed up the highway in his Lexus SC400.

Kevin was sitting in front of Nukey's house when Keith pulled up behind him. Instead of waiting on Keith's slow ass, Kevin grabbed the half-smoked blunt from his ashtray and got in the car with Keith.

"You late, nigga," Kevin said, as he shut the passenger door.

"It's only eleven forty-five." Keith looked at his watch.

"Suppose to be here at eleven thirty."

Keith looked at his brother like he was crazy. "Fuck you. How about that?"

Kevin shrugged and took a hit from the blunt.

Keith's Movado read 12:10 p.m. when they saw the white Fed Ex truck stop in front of Nukey's house. They looked around, watching for anything suspicious as the delivery man wheeled the package up to the door.

He knocked twice before Brenda opened the door. She was wearing tight jean shorts and a cutoff shirt that showed off her pierced navel.

Kevin said, "Remind me to get me a shot of that old pussy." He noticed how well she was shaped for her age.

"For what?" Keith asked curiously, eyeing the delivery man.

"If I start fucking her, then maybe we won't have to pay that five grand every month."

Keith ignored Kevin. He watched carefully as Brenda signed for the package. For a second he thought the DEA agents were gonna jump out of nowhere. But they didn't. Through the mail was a risky way to transport drugs. You never knew who might show up along with your package.

Brenda stepped out of the way so that the man could wheel the package in.

Reading Brenda's lips, Keith saw her say "Thank you," as the delivery man was leaving.

Keith and Kevin waited until the Fed Ex truck was out of their sight before they went inside the house. Brenda was waiting with her hand stuck out.

The house was clean, yet had a musty smell. Clothes and kids' toys were scattered around the room. A hard-looking middle aged man was laying on the couch with his feet up, watching TV.

"Who's that?" Kevin pointed at the man.

"That's my brother," Brenda said, as if he should've known.

"Get him out of here," Kevin said with calm authority.

For a minute, Brenda looked at Kevin like he was crazy. Then she realized why it was so important for her brother to leave. It wasn't his business what they had going on. She walked over to her brother. "Ronnie. Why don't you go down to the store and get me some beer and cigarettes?"

"I ain't got no damn money," Ronnie said harshly.

Brenda reached into her pocket and handed him a twenty-dollar bill. "Bring back my damn change, Ronnie!"

Ronnie threw on a dusty ball cap and left.

Kevin asked, "Is there anybody else in here that shouldn't be here?"

"Just the kids. I already told them to stay in their rooms."

Keith was locking the front door when Nukey came from the kitchen, carrying a box cutter.

Brenda stopped him. "Hold on, Nuke." Brenda took the box cutter away from him. "Where's my money?"

Kevin reached into his pocket and pulled out a wad of money wrapped in rubber band. He handed it to Brenda. Keith watched as Kevin gently brushed his hand up against hers, in an attempt to seduce her.

"Satisfied?" asked Kevin.

"Very," Brenda said, then handed him the box cutter. "Ain't nothing personal. It's just business."

After Kevin opened up the box, they both grabbed hold of the animal, took it out of the box and sat it on the floor. The animal was laying face down when Keith opened him up with the box cutter. He took out all of the stuffing until he came across a bunch of carefully stacked, duct taped bricks of cocaine.

"Bingo." Keith held up one of the bricks. He was as excited as a child who found the golden Easter egg.

Nukey stood next to his mama and watched Keith pull out the twenty bricks and sit them on the floor.

"Run out to my car and get those two gym bags," Kevin said to Nukey. He handed young man the keys to his Lexus.

When Nukey returned with the bags, Keith packed ten bricks into each bag and handed one to Kevin. "Let's go."

They loaded the bags into Kevin's trunk. "Stay on my tail," Kevin said, as he climbed into the driver's seat.

"I got you covered, bro," Keith assured him. On the way to his car, Keith signaled Nukey to come on.

Bumper to bumper they got onto the freeway and headed for Keith's house. They followed the same plan as always to get the dope home safely. Whoever was trailing the car with the dope in it had to be the one to create the diversion if the police ever tried to stop the carrier car, even if it meant running into the police car to make it look like an accident. By all means necessary, they were not going to get caught with any drugs.

Keith noticed a brand new Cadillac parked in front of his house as he followed Kevin into the double driveway. He hit the garage opener on his key ring as they slipped inside without drawing attention from his nosy neighbors. They were old and prejudiced. Keith didn't want them to start becoming suspicious. It was bad enough that he had to wear a work shirt when he left the house on weekdays, trying to make them believe that he had an actual job. That was his way of making them believe that he earned a living the same way they did. Honest.

Once they got inside, they headed straight for the kitchen. Keith wasn't surprised to see that Tukey had everything already prepared. Clean glass beakers and fresh baking soda were on the table and a pot of boiling water was on the stove.

"Just sit the bags on the floor," Keith commanded Nukey and Kevin.

They both got on their cell phones and called up every one of their people, letting them know that the dope had touched down. After they finished taking orders, it was time to shake and bake.

Keith said, "Did you talk to your boy from Decatur?"

"Yeah. He's already in town," Kevin replied. "I told him that I would hit him after we finished putting the bake on it."

At that moment, Tukey came into the kitchen with a triple beam scale. "Me almost forgot about dis," she said as she placed the scale on the counter.

"Whose Cadillac is that parked out front?" Keith asked curiously.

"Oh, dat's me rental car dat me mama take me to get today," Tukey chirped. "Do ya like it?"

"It's cool."

Kevin frowned. Tukey hadn't even acknowledged his presence.

"What's wrong, Tukey, you ain't speaking to your brother-in-law, today?"

Tukey gave him a warm smile. "Ohh, me sorry, baby." She held her arms out toward him. "Come over here and give me a hug."

Kevin resisted. "I don't want one now, it's too late," he said in a childish tone.

"Boy, ya better get over here and hug your sister." Tukey put him in a head lock. "Ya know me mind be goin' sometime."

While they were embracing one another, Keith went into the bags and removed three bricks of cocaine. He cut away the duct tape with a razor. Careful not to spill any of the powder, he dumped one of the bricks into a wide-mouthed beaker. He weighed fifteen ounces of baking soda on the scale and dumped it into the beaker with the cocaine. Keith went to the cabinet and retrieved an old blender, into which he poured the contents of the beaker. He plugged it up, put the top on and pressed "blend." Nukey watched carefully while Keith went to work. He wanted to be like Keith and was determined to learn all of his methods.

When Keith figured that it was fine enough, he poured the powder back in to the beaker. Then he sat the beaker in the boiling water, added a few tablespoons of the water into the beaker, and stirred until the powder turned oily.

"Hand me that cake mixer out of the drawer over there, Tukey," Keith said.

Tukey obediently plugged the mixer into the wall and handed it to him. Keith put the mixer on low, stuck it into the oily mixture and rotated it slowly. He wanted the soda and coke to blend as evenly as possible. When he was satisfied with the mixture, he took the beaker out of the pot and sat it on the counter to harden.

It took about twenty minutes for the dope to get hard. Using a butcher's knife, Keith popped the huge solid cookie out of the beaker. On the scale it weighed 1,420 grams. That was 420 grams more than what he started with. Satisfied with the outcome, Keith repeated the same process with the other two bricks.

By the time he finished cooking the three bricks, Keith came up with 4,260 grams out of a base product 3,000. He used three zippered plastic bags to put the 3,000 grams in, for Kevin's partner from Decatur.

Keith handed the bag to Kevin. "Here you go." He took four more bricks out of the bag and sat them on the table. "You see how I just done that?" Keith asked Nukey, who was still watching his every move. "I can take all extra dope and do what I want with it."

Keith considered himself to be Nukey's mentor and father figure. He taught Nukey the ins and outs; the what to do and what not to do in the game. He took care of Nukey, from his school clothes to his doctor bills. Keith first came in contact with the young fella a couple of years back; the boy looked like a bum as he stood at the school bus stop. That evening Keith was parked at the bus stop waiting on Nukey to get home from school. When Nukey hopped off the bus, Keith walked over and introduced himself. After a brief conversation, Keith persuaded Nukey to let him take Nukey shopping for new clothes. Ever since, he found himself taking a liking to the young fella.

Keith said, "Help me take the rest of this shit downstairs, Nukey."

They both grabbed a bag and walked downstairs to the basement. Off in a dark corner they came to a three-foot-tall, steel combination-locked safe that was bolted to the floor. Keith sat the bag down, kneeled over and began to spin the dial on the lock.

Nukey stood behind him and peered over Keith's shoulder. "35-0-10," Nukey said to himself, trying to remember the numbers.

The safe opened. Keith neatly stacked the remaining 13K inside the safe and relocked it.

"Tukey!" Keith yelled from the basement. Nukey and Keith went back upstairs.

Tukey came running with Mi'kelle in her arms. "What?"

When Keith saw that Mi'kelle was home, he quickly reached out for her. "Hey, baby!" he said with excitement.

"Hi, Daddy," Mi'kelle said in a sleepy voice.

Keith gave her a big hug and several kisses before giving her back to her mother. "Give me the keys to the Cadillac and you take my Lexus."

"OK, baby," Tukey said, eyeing Mi'kelle's nappy head. "The keys are on the table."

Kevin was in the kitchen putting the rest of the crack into a plastic bag, when Keith came in. "Leave it on the table for Tukey. She's got some people of her own that she needs to get with today." Keith took a brown grocery bag from the bottom cabinet and placed the four bricks, plus the three thousand grams of crack, inside. "Carry this out to the car, Nukey."

As they were leaving, Keith kissed his family goodbye and followed Nukey and Kevin out the door.

Chapter 7

The smell of new leather filled their lungs as Keith and Kevin took the freeway in the brand new Cadillac STS. The car was jet black, equipped with a heated peanut butter-colored leather interior, CD and tape player, dual air bags and a North Star engine.

The streets were heavy with the evening traffic as tired workers headed home from a hard day's work. The traffic was a good disguise for a person riding with something illegal. Kansas City had its share of rush hour traffic accidents, but Keith would rather travel while the streets were full, instead of being the only one on the streets with the prejudiced police. He figured that he was a target at which bored cops liked to take a shot.

Keith made a right turn and got off at the 87th Street exit. "Call your boy from Decatur up, Kevin." Keith said. "Have him meet us at the Motel Six."

Kevin opened his cell phone and placed the call. The phone rang twice before someone picked up.

"Hello."

"Lil Wayne. What's up wit' you?"

"Who dis?" Wayne asked curiously.

"Nigga you need to start learning voices," Kevin demanded. He hated to say his name over the phone during a business deal. "This Kev, nigga. Where you at?"

"Aw, Kev," Wayne said. "I didn't know it was you. I'm

around."

"Good," Kevin said. "Meet me at the Motel Six on 87th Street. I'll be sitting in the back in a black STS."

"On my way," Wayne hung up the phone.

Just hearing their conversation made Keith's stomach turn. He didn't like dealing with out-of-towners. They could get busted, rat on you and run right back to their home town like nothing happened. Even though Wayne was one of Kevin's regular customers, Keith felt his pocket for his gun. Not only was he cautious about Wayne being the police, he was prepared in case it turned into a robbery. Anybody that was stupid enough to pay $28,000 for an already rocked-up kilo was stupid enough to put a pistol in your face.

"Where you meet this nigga Wayne at?" Keith quizzed.

"Through this bitch," Kevin answered.

"I know this ho?"

Kevin shook his head. "You know Nicky."

"Nicky, Nicky," Keith repeated as he searched his memory bank. "The one with the Escort?"

"Yeah, that's her," Kevin said. "She introduced him to me at a Halloween party last year."

Kevin thought for a moment. "Can she be trusted?" He made a left into the motel parking lot. He circled the lot once, making sure there was no sign of a setup. Then he found a low-key spot to park in the back.

"I'm vouching for 'em both," Kevin said.

"Remember you said that. How long do you think he'll—"

"There he is right there." Kevin pointed his finger at a blue Yukon.

Wayne saw Keith flick the Cadillac's lights on and off. He parked, got out of his truck with a blue Nike gym bag, and walked toward the Cadillac. Keith popped the locks so that Wayne could get into the back seat. Nukey was glad that the car was so roomy, so that the six-foot-two big man wouldn't be all over him.

"What's up, dog?" Kevin shook Wayne's hand.

"Tryin' to make a livin'," Wayne answered.

While they were talking, Keith kept a close eye on Wayne in the rearview mirror.

Wayne asked, "You got the shit here or somewhere close?"

"Nah, I got it right here," Kevin said. He opened the grocery bag and removed the three zip-closed bags, handing them back to Wayne.

Wayne took a moment to carefully examine his packages. He opened one of the bags and removed a chunk. Satisfied, he put the chunk back into the bag and re-closed it.

"You straight?" Kevin asked.

"Yeah." Wayne opened up his gym bag and pulled out a JC Penny bag full of money and handed it to Kevin. Then he placed the three zippered bags into the gym bag.

Kevin went through the JC Penny bag and counted out eighty four stacks of cash. "These all thousand-dollar stacks?"

"Yeah. Go 'head and count it."

Kevin closed the bag. "That ain't necessary."

Wayne opened up the door to exit the car. "I'll be getting back at y'all."

"Do that," Kevin said seriously. "Next time I'll do something about that high ass price for you."

Keith pulled out of the parking lot with caution and looked in all directions for signs of the police. He made everybody in the car put on their seatbelts as he crept through the back streets to Tee's house.

A green Neon that resembled Selina's pulled away from Tee's house in a hurry as Keith pulled up in front. *I know that ain't Selina's car?* Keith thought to himself. What the fuck would she be doing over here?

The three of them walked up to Tee's door with Nukey carrying the grocery bag with the remaining four bricks in it. Kevin had locked the money up in the trunk of the car.

Tee showed up at the front door with a Polo towel wrapped around his naked body. "Why did you wait until you was around the corner before you called, saying you were coming?" Tee stepped aside so they could come in. "I had just hopped in the shower."

Tee's house was a typical bachelor pad. It was small, with only two bedrooms. In the living room sat a three-piece set of black leather sofas, glass end tables and dingy white carpet. All of this sat in front of a 45-inch TV screen, with a PlayStation and DVD player hooked up to it. In the middle of the dining room floor was a pool table where a dining table should have been. Judging by all of the empty food wrappings on the coffee table, you could tell where Tee did most of his eating.

They all took seats on the couches. "Where's Andre?" Keith asked.

Tee said, "I ain't seen him since this morning."

Keith thought about the Neon that he saw pulling off when he arrived. "Tee, don't you got a baby by a Puerto Rican chick?" Keith asked, figuring that Selina might be her.

"Yeah. Why?"

Keith shrugged. "I'm just curious of why you ain't got no pictures of her or why we ain't never saw her?" Keith said. "Or the baby."

Tee stared at Keith for a moment. He couldn't figure out what the man was getting at or why. "I ain't got no pictures 'cause we don't get along. She don't even let me see my son." Tee tried his best to sound upset about it, but Keith could see right through him. Tee only thought of himself. He didn't even spend time with his kids with whom he was in touch.

"What's her name?" Keith quizzed.

At that moment Kevin knew exactly what Keith was thinking. He, too, had seen the Neon speeding away when they pulled up.

Tee said, "Jennifer. What's up with all the stupid questions?"

Keith shook his head. "Nothing's up. I just thought I knew her."

Now that the interrogation was over, Tee excused himself to go put on some clothes. Kevin was talking on the phone and Keith and Nukey were playing *John Madden Football* on the PlayStation when Tee got back.

Keith hit "pause" on the game when Tee signaled for him to follow Tee to the kitchen. Keith rose and grabbed the grocery bag and followed Tee's lead.

"What you bring me?" Tee asked as he cleared the kitchen table.

Keith sat the bag on top of the table and removed four bricks. Tee picked one up and examined it.

Keith said, "That one's yours. The other three are for Andre."

Tee stared at the one brick in his hand, then he looked down at the three on the table for Andre. "Why I only get one?"

"What you mean, why you only get one? It takes you too long to get rid of that," Keith said seriously.

"You don't even trust your partner," Tee complained.

"Man, don't start that shit."

"I'm just saying, man. I think I'm ready to move up a step." Tee threw his arm around Keith's shoulder. "I promise, I'm gonna stop tricking off so much."

Keith said, "You can show me better than you can tell me."

"You'll see. I'ma have this baby gone by tomorrow."

"Alright. Tell Andre that he owes me fifty-eight grand. Just give me nineteen for the one you got." .

"So all together that's what...seventy-seven thousand?" Tee said, doing the math in his head.

Keith left the kitchen. "Just call me when y'all ready."

It was getting dark outside when the three of them left Tee's house. "Where you want me to drop you off at, Nukey?" Keith asked.

"At my uncle's, on 41st."

"Cool." Keith drove off. The night air felt good as it blew on his head through the large sunroof. The smooth ride felt more like he was floating on the air, rather than riding on concrete. He felt relaxed now that he had rid the car of drugs. He turned on the radio and floored the North Star engine. "I've got to get me one of these," he said to no particular person.

Two middle-aged men were sitting on the porch, drinking Wild Irish Rose, when a new Cadillac pulled up in front of their house. Nukey's Uncle Ronnie watched as his nephew emerged from the back seat of the car.

"I'll catch y'all later," Ronnie heard Nukey say to the occupants of the Cadillac.

Nukey was walking toward the men as they watched the Cadillac quietly pull off. Ronnie was finishing what was left in the bottle when Nukey joined them on the porch.

"Whose new car is that?" Nukey asked. He pointed to a green Ford Tempo that sat in the driveway with a temporary tag in the back window.

"Mine," said Uncle Ronnie. "'Course it ain't nothing like that new Cadillac that you just stepped out of."

"That's what I've come over here to talk to you about."

Ronnie threw the empty wine bottle into the yard. He stood and stretched. "Just what are you getting at, boy?" he asked curiously.

"Let's go inside," Nukey said. "This ain't for everybody to hear."

* * *

"OK baby," Kevin said, "I'll be home in a minute. I know, bye." He hung up the phone.

"Who was that?" Keith asked.

"Kim. She's crying about me not being at the crib enough."

"You tell her that we were on our way to my house to get yo' car?"

"Yeah," Kevin yawned.

The motion sensor lights came on as Keith pulled into his driveway. The only lights that he saw in the house came from the living room. He grabbed the bag of money before he got out. A sharp pain shot up his left side as he stood. The pain pills that he'd popped earlier were beginning to wear off.

"You gonna be alright, bro?" Kevin asked after seeing the

painful expression cross Keith's face.

Keith frowned. "Yeah, I'll be cool. Just gotta pop me a few more pills, that's all."

"Alright then. I'll holla," Kevin said, as he walked toward his car. "I'll get up with you tomorrow."

Keith limped up to the door, almost dropping the bag of money. He'd hit the ground before he'd let the bag fall, he thought to himself. It took him several minutes to reach into his pocket and locate his key.

Tukey heard keys jingling and her man grumbling at the door, trying to get the door unlocked. She jumped up from the couch to help him inside.

"Yu alright, baby?" she asked, concerned. She took the bag then helped Keith to his favorite chair. Quickly she took the money downstairs, put it in the safe, and returned to Keith's aid. "Let me relax yu, baby." Tukey removed his gun from his pants pocket.

"Mi'kelle," Keith yelled out. He grunted as Tukey took off his shoes with care.

Mi'kelle was up in her room, playing with her dolls, when she heard her daddy's call. She dropped her toys and ran to the top of the stairs. "Yes, Daddy," she yelled back.

"Bring me those pills off my dresser," Keith instructed. He could hear her tiny feet moving around upstairs as she ran to get the pills.

One step at a time, Mi'kelle came down the stairs in her Tweety Bird house shoes, careful not to drop the pill bottle.

"Here you go, Daddy." Mi'kelle handed the pills to him. Keith opened his eyes and took the bottle from her. "Be right back." She spun around and went into the kitchen. Soon she came back, carefully carrying a Mickey Mouse cup of water. She handed it to him. "Drink."

"Where did this water come from?" Keith asked.

Mi'kelle looked confused. "The kitchen."

"You sure you didn't scoop this out of the toilet?"

"Daddy," she laughed, "Just drink it."

Keith popped two of the pills and chased them with the warm water that Mi'kelle brought him. After he finished he sat the cup down and she climbed into his lap.

"What are you doing wearing these tight-ass pajamas Mi'kelle?" Keith asked.

Tukey smacked Keith on the arm. "Don't yu talk about me baby's pajamas. Her love her Tweety Bird pajamas."

"She need to throw 'em away, 'cause that shirt's fitting her like a damn turtleneck."

"Yu need to quit," Tukey said. She popped in a DVD, grabbed the remote, then found a comfortable spot on the armrest of the chair in which Keith sat.

Keith sniffed. "Umm, you smell good. What you wearing?"

"Me," Tukey said in a sexy voice. "Ya like it?"

"I love it." Keith leaned over to kiss Tukey on the lips. "And you taste good, too."

"Stop it, Daddy," Mi'kelle said, feeling jealous.

Keith looked at his daughter, who was sitting with her arms folded and lips stuck out. "You don't like to see me kissing on your mama?"

"You didn't give me no kiss," Mi'kelle whined. "I'm the one who got you the water."

After seeing the seriousness in her daughter's face, Tukey decided to tease her. "Mi'kelle is jealous. Mi'kelle is jeal—" She was interrupted by the phone ringing.

While Tukey went to get the phone, Keith noticed for the first time tonight that she was wearing a transparent night gown, under which she wore a black thong. His dick jumped as he watched her sexy long legs walk over to the phone. He wanted to fuck, but he knew the pain in his side wouldn't let him perform the way he wanted to.

"Telephone, Keith." Tukey walked toward him with the phone in her hand.

Without taking his eyes off her, Keith took the phone.

"Hello."

"What's up, nigga? This Andre."

"Dre dog. I dropped that package off with your brother 'bout an hour ago."

"Forget about that shit, man," Andre said. "What happened after we left the club the other night?"

"Aw, man, just a fender bender. Wasn't nothing."

Probably over Tee trying to steal somebody else's girl, Tukey thought as she stood there and listened. She didn't ask, but she just knew that whatever reason Keith got shot, Tee had something to do with it. She knew that Tee had been jealous of Keith ever since high school. Tee was the one who had started dating Tukey first. Even though they weren't a couple, Tee became outraged when he heard that Tukey had been seen skipping school with his friend Keith. His pride was hurt. He was one of those cats who thought that he was too cute to have a girl taken from him.

"Me not ya girl, Tee," Tukey told him after he'd confronted her about what he'd heard.

"But that's my friend," Tee pleaded, hoping that she'd change her mind about seeing Keith.

"So?" Tukey's tone was harsh.

"So we through or what?"

"Yes." Tukey walked off and left Tee standing there, looking stupid.

Tukey heard Keith hang up the phone and came back to reality. She returned the phone to its charger.

"Me don't like yu hanging out wit' Tee," she said. She squeezed into the chair with Keith and Mi'kelle.

"Why not?"

"'Cause sum'ting always happen when yu go out wit' him." Worry laced her tone. "Ya got too much going on right now to be getting into stuff."

Keith frowned. He hated getting into conversations with Tukey about his friends. Who he fucked with on the street was none of her business. He ignored her and kept his attention focused on the TV, until he drifted to sleep.

* * *

Keith awoke when he heard Mi'kelle's Sunday morning cartoons blasting out of the TV. He winced from the pain in his side. After a quick shower and shave, he threw on a pair of Nike sweats and a Stafford t-shirt. The screen of his cell showed five messages. Tee called about some business, a couple people had called trying to get some dope, and Selina had called twice. She wanted to give him her number in case he'd forgotten it.

To his surprise, Keith felt himself get a little excited that she called. He had to fight back the desire to call her while Tukey was in the house somewhere. He slipped the phone into his pocket and limped downstairs into the basement, where his safe was bolted to the ground. Keith took two kilos out of it for the two people who left the messages on his phone.

Tukey was standing at the top of the steps with her hands on her hips, when Keith came running up. "Yu gonna eat before yu leave?" she asked.

"I ain't got time." Keith walked around her. "I got a few runs to make."

Furious, Tukey slammed the basement door shut and followed him into the living room. "Why don't ya try to spend some time wit' me and ya dawta, instead of the streets?"

Keith turned toward her with a frustrated look on his face. "I owe yo' uncle $270,000, baby; that's a lot of money to be owing somebody. Ben may not do nothing to you, but he sure as hell come lookin' for me." He kissed her on the head. "We understand each other?"

"Yes," Tukey replied softly.

Keith walked past Tukey to the closet taking out one of Mi'kelle's old backpacks. He put the two kilos inside it and threw it over his shoulder. "What you do with that shit I left with you yesterday?"

"Me sold it to Gary for twenty-six t'ousand. Me put the money in ya sock drawer."

Li'l Gary was one of her Uncle Ben's old customers from when he stayed in Kansas City. After Ben plugged Keith with the dope, Tukey made contact with some of Ben's old customers to get the business started for Keith. Now that Keith had his own clientele, she used Ben's old clients to make some money on her own. The fact that she was a woman made it easier for her to hustle. Guys called her to get dope, just to have her in their presence. They also had hopes that one day she and Keith would break up so that they could have a chance. They thought that Tukey was hustling for Keith. What they didn't know was that what she made on the side, she kept.

"Cool," Keith said. He kissed Tukey on the cheek. "Catch you later."

A white envelope was stuck underneath his windshield wiper when Keith stepped outside. Curious, he walked over to his Lexus and snatched it off. It was a letter.

The letter read:

Dear Keith,

I have this insatiable craving that can only be tamed by your thick heavily veined shaft. Lately, I've been haunted by fantasies of a freakish nature, causing lust and a bunch of uncontrolled emotions to rise, forcing my chocha to moisten. I'm anxious for you to give me some long, hot and most kinkiest sex that you are able to give.

I have one question before I end this letter. Do you think I'm nasty? Good!

Love always, Selina

Cautiously, Keith looked back toward the house while he balled up the letter. He hoped that Tukey hadn't seen him.

"How in the hell does she know where I stay?" he asked himself. He shook his head and jumped into his Lexus before he took off down the road.

Keith removed his cell out of his pocket, dialing Selina's number.

"Hello, *papi*," Selina said answering on the first ring. She already knew who it was.

"How you know where I live?" Keith asked hotly.

"What? I didn't hear what you said."

"You heard what the fuck I said."

Selina became quiet. "I saw you out, and I followed you home last night."

"I was driving a rental car last night," Keith said with suspicion. "I wasn't even in my car."

"Boy, I saw you in that car at the Motel Six yesterday. I thought that you saw me following you."

"Listen, man." Keith sighed. He was beginning to get fed up with Selina hounding him. "You gon' have to cut all this bullshit that you pullin'. Straight up, man."

Selina became silent again. "I'm sorry, *papi*," she finally said in a soft tone.

It was something about the way that Selina said, "I'm sorry," that made Keith soften up.

Keith changed the subject. "So what you got up for the day?"

"Waiting on your fine ass," Selina purred in a sexy voice.

"Trying to see me, huh? Well, ahh, I'm a make some stops and I'll get up wit' you when I get through."

"Aw, man," Selina pouted. "I was hoping to see you right now, *papi*."

Keith thought about it for a moment. "Where you at?"

He could hear the excitement in Selina's voice when she said, "I'm at my grandma's house. She lives in those apartments down on 19th and Highland. Just pull up to the front gate and you should see me out front."

"On my way."

Chapter 8

Tukey opened Keith's sock drawer and removed six of the twenty-six-thousand dollars that she put in there yesterday. Then she took it to Mi'kelle's room, where she stuffed it into a small safe inside the closet. That's where she kept the extra money that she made off Keith's dope.

Tukey figured her money to be somewhere between forty or fifty thousand dollars by now. She had to be smart and save money, just in case Keith went sour on her. She remembered how Michael Beach did Angela Bassett in *Waiting To Exhale*.

Mi'kelle was playing by herself on the living room floor when Tukey came downstairs. Tukey was just about to get on her about the mess that she'd made when she heard the phone ring. Disgusted, she ignored Mi'kelle and ran to get the phone.

"Hello," Tukey said.

"Why haven't I heard from you?" Anitra snapped.

"What yu talkin' bout, Anitra?"

"I'm talking about how you've been acting," Anitra yelled angrily. "One minute I'm fucking the shit out of you, and the next minute you're back swinging from Keith's nut sack." Anitra sighed. "Don't try and act like nothing ever happened."

Immediately Tukey became embarrassed by Anitra's last words. Once again she regretted having the sexual encounter with Anitra. The last thing she wanted was for Keith to find out. She allowed herself to be violated and now she was paying for it.

Tukey said, "Me can't...us need to forget about what went on between us."

"So just fuck me and leave me. Is that it?"

Tukey sighed. Anitra was her best friend and she didn't want to ruin their friendship. "Me sorry, Anitra. Me....." She was at a loss for words.

The phone was silent.

Finally Anitra spoke up, "Well don't come crying to me the next time he slaps the shit out of you over a hoodrat."

"Anitra, please don't act like dat," Tukey pleaded. "Ya supposed ta be me best friend. What happened between us was an accident. Me love Keith regardless of what him do."

"Well whatever, fuck it," Anitra said. "What you gonna do today?"

"Me and me pickney is going shopping."

"Will it be asking too much of you to stop by my house and pick me up?" Anitra said sarcastically.

"Ya still me best friend. Us be over after us get dressed."

"Hurry up," Anitra said before she hung up.

* * *

Selina was sitting on the trunk of her car with her legs crossed, reading a magazine when she saw Keith's Lexus pull into the parking lot. She looked like a young model in a cream-colored sundress and tan flip-flop shoes. She focused her attention back on the magazine, and pretended not to notice him.

Keith turned his music down as well as his window as he came to a stop. "Excuse me," he said. "But do I know you from somewhere?"

Selina decided to play along with him. "I don't think so. I only date ballers."

"Aw, you only date ballers, huh?" Keith got a kick out of that. "I guess I'll be on my way then." He pulled the car away slowly.

Selina quickly jumped off the trunk of her car. "Boy, you better stop playing." She stuck her small arm through Keith's window to prevent him from rolling it up.

Keith stopped the car. "Wait wait," he laughed. "A minute ago, you only dated big time ballers. So why you stopping my car? I ain't no baller."

"I think that I'll make an exception this time." Selina leaned over to kiss his cheek. "Hold on a minute." She took her keys from her purse, locked her car and hopped into his passenger seat.

While they rode up Paseo Boulevard, Keith popped in a Levert CD and let the sunroof back so the wind could play with Selina's dress. He watched her get comfortable so that she could finish reading her magazine.

Kids were playing and getting wet by a busted fire hydrant when Keith turned onto Highland Street. He rolled up the window so that they wouldn't get wet as they drove by. He pulled into the driveway of a small yellow house with bars on the windows.

He didn't get out of the car because it was the house where Big Willie Jones sold dope. He'd have a better chance getting away on the outside than he would being in the house, if the police came. The front door opened and a short, dark chubby man came out. He was wearing heavily starched jeans and a red button-up shirt, with a fresh new hair cut.

Keith stepped out of the car and moved the front seat up so that Big Willie could squeeze into the back seat.

"What's up, Will?" Keith said as he shut his door.

Big Willie didn't answer in a hurry. He was too busy staring a hole through Selina. Keith wanted to smile after he looked through the rearview mirror and saw Big Willie leering. He always enjoyed being seen with fine-ass females like her. He loved to be envied by his friends. That's why he didn't have a problem with her riding with him to make the run.

Big Willie finally snapped out of his daze and said, "Damn, man I'm trippin." He laughed to himself. "I'm chillin' man, my mind just went blank for a minute."

"I feel ya," Keith said to let Big Willie know that he knew why his mind went blank. Selina sat there reading and didn't have a clue as to what they were talking about.

Keith reached down on the floor between Selina's legs and grabbed the backpack with the dope in it. He unzipped it and checked it, out of habit, then handed it back over his shoulder to Big Willie.

"What's the price on this shit?" Big Willie asked.

"Forty grand." Keith watched Selina out of the corner of his eye. Even though she knew that he was in the game, he was still trying to impress her. He liked to look like a big man in front of women. It hadn't been a week and already he found himself falling for Selina. In the past he never minded his bitches fucking around except for Tukey. But Selina was different, and some kind of way he was gonna make her fit into his life. Right next to Tukey.

Big Willie took out a razor and cut into one of the duct-taped kilos. Evidently he liked what he saw, because he got on his cell phone and called inside. The call was to have one of his brothers inside to bring out forty grand for Keith. Keith frowned up when he heard Will tell the guy on the phone to only bring out forty grand. He still owed five grand from the last time he bought some dope from Keith. He didn't want to front the man out in front of Selina, so he asked Willie to step out of the car.

"You know you still owe, nigga," Keith said after they stepped out of the car.

"I know," Big Willie said. "As soon as I make a few moves I'm a hit you right back."

Keith stared at him for a moment.

"Don't make this shit no habit, Willie man," Keith said, firmly.

At that moment, another short chubby dude who resembled Big Willie came out of the house carrying a black gym bag. Big Willie nodded his head toward Keith and the dude handed over the gym bag. Keith opened the bag, eyeing it quickly. It seemed to be all there. He shook Big Willie's hand and got back into his car.

"Don't forget to get at me," Keith told Willie through his window as he backed out of the driveway. His cell phone rang while he was pulling away. "Hello."

"I'm at the crib," Tee's voice said on the line.

"Give me 'bout ten minutes," Keith said, then hung up.

During the ride over to Tee's house, Keith and Selina finally took the time to get to know one another. Upon Selina's request they decided to stop by Applebee's after they left Tee's house.

Tee was sitting on the porch talking to a dark-skinned girl in a short skirt when Keith pulled up. Keith stuffed the bag of money under his seat and took the keys out of the ignition. He didn't trust Selina to be alone in the car with his money while he went inside Tee's house. She didn't budge while Keith was getting out of the car. He gave her a confused look.

"Come on," he said.

Selina looked up at the house like it was haunted. "Nah, I'm a stay in the car."

Keith thought about that for a minute. He had the keys, so she wouldn't get far if she tried to get out and run with the money. "Alright. I'll be back in a minute," he said.

As Keith approached the porch, Tee had his hand on the girl's ass while kissing her on the ear.

"I'll see you later, baby," Tee said, smoothly.

"I hope so," the girl said in a sexy voice.

Keith looked at her in fascination as she strutted past him to her car. He could just imagine how sweet that dark meat must be.

"Who was that?" Keith asked Tee as he returned to the porch.

Tee put his hand on Keith's shoulder. "That's a black stallion," Tee said. "And a straight freak, too." He smiled and enjoyed the view as the girl walked away. "Let's go in the house."

Andre was weighing up a bag of dope on the living room table when they came inside. He stopped long enough to shake Keith's hand. Keith took a seat while Tee went to the back to get his money. He returned carrying an orange Nike shoe box in his hand. Sitting down, he opened the box and started taking out small rolls of money. Keith watched him count out nineteen thousand, then slid it over to him.

"You want me to carry it out in my hand?" Keith asked sarcastically.

"Hold on, man," Tee said getting up. "Let me see if I can find you somethin'."

It took Tee fifteen minutes to come back, still empty handed. Keith's face frowned up after he saw Tee come back bagless.

"Damn, nigga, you been gone all that time and didn't find nothing?"

Tee threw his hands up. "Man, ain't nothin' back there to put it in."

Keith shook his head and thought for a moment. Then he took out his cell phone and called Selina out in the car.

"Hell-o," Selina answered sounding disgusted.

"Reach up under my seat, get that bag and bring it in here."

"I ain't tryin' to come in there, *papi*."

"Why?" Keith asked, curiously.

"'Cause I ain't tryin' to be around whatever it is you was doing."

"Girl, just bring me the damn bag, shit," Keith yelled into the phone, then hung up. Tee was standing next to him with a strange look on his face. "Fuck you looking so stupid for?"

"Man, I don't want that bitch coming up in here," Tee complained.

"Why?"

"Man, we don't know that bitch," Tee said seriously. For all I know she could be the police."

"Bitch ain't no police, you scary ass nigga," Keith said. He got up and walked over to the front door to meet her. She was opening the screen door when Keith appeared in the doorway.

She shoved the bag into his chest. "Here," she said, and quickly walked back to the car.

Keith didn't bother responding to her attitude. Instead he walked back over to the table where the money was. While he was putting the money in the bag, he noticed Andre staring at Selina out the window.

"Where you meet her at?" Andre asked.

"You know her or something?" Keith asked curiously.

Andre glanced over at Tee before he answered. "Nah, I was just wondering."

Keith zipped up the bag. "I'll tell you about when I got time, dog. Right now I've got to roll," Keith was on his way out the door.

When he reached the car he saw Selina sitting in the passenger seat with her arms folded across her chest, looking mad at the world.

"I'm hungry," she complained.

"We're headed to go eat, right now."

On the way to the restaurant Keith couldn't help but wonder if there was a connection between Andre and Selina. Something wasn't right. She didn't want to come into their house and they didn't want her in there. Keith glanced over at her.

The parking lot was full when Keith pulled his Lexus into it. He had to find a spot between an old Chevy wagon and a Ford Fairlane. He put the bag of money in the trunk before they went inside, making damn sure it was secure.

"Party for two?" A young black hostess asked when they entered.

"Yes, please," Selina said softly.

The young hostess grabbed two menus and led them to a booth in the back of the restaurant.

Once seated, she took their orders, then excused herself.

"So have you thought more about what we talked about the other day?" Selina said, looking Keith in the eye.

"What did we talk about?"

"About us," Selina slammed her fist down on the table. "You and me, silly."

Without answering her question Keith opened up his menu, and pretended to look through it.

"Well?" Selina's voice was firm.

Keith looked up from his menu and sighed. "No I haven't."

Slowly Selina shook her head back and forth, mad at herself for even believing that he would think about leaving his woman for her so soon. She was just about to say something when the hostess interrupted her.

"Your drinks," she said, sitting their drinks in front of them.

They both ordered Riblet Baskets. Selina waited for the waitress to finish, so that she could carry on the conversation. She wanted to get this settled before Keith and Tukey got a chance to make up.

"Why didn't you think about it?" she asked suspiciously. He seemed to be holding something back from her, she thought. "She's back, isn't she?"

Keith shook his head while stirring the ice in his glass.

"Umph," Selina grunted. "So where does that leave us?"

Keith stopped fooling around with his glass and looked up at her. "Where we started from," he said calmly. "Friends."

Selina got up and walked around the table, then slid into the seat next to him. She took a long sip of her Coke to clear her throat.

"I like you a lot," she said calmly. "And I guess I'ma just chill and wait in line until you decide to come around. I know it's not easy for you to just pick up and leave someone you love. Especially over someone you just met." Selina stared at Keith for a moment. "I didn't mean to fall for you so quick. It just happened."

Keith threw his arm over her shoulders, slid her closer to him. "So you gon' be content with being second, when a fine girl like you could have anybody that she wanted?"

"Evidently, not anybody." Selina took a deep breath. "But give it time, I—"

Keith's phone rang and cut Selina off.

He flipped the phone up and answered it. "Hello."

"Hey mon." It was Tukey.

"Hey," Keith said in a nervous tone.

Selina knew who he was talking to by the silly ass look on his face. She removed her arm from around him and moved back to her original seat.

Tukey said, "Me and ya dawta at the mall shopping."

"Ya'll pick me up something?"

"Here Mi'kelle," Tukey said handing the phone. "Tell ya daddy what us bought him."

"We bought, we bought you some shoes, Daddy," Mi'kelle said.

"Thank you," Keith said in a child's tone.

"Bye Daddy," Mi'kelle said, then handed the phone back to her mother.

Tukey said, "So what ya doing? Yu t'inking 'bout me?"

Keith glanced over at Selina, who was staring directly at him. He put up his index finger to signal her that he'd be off in a minute.

"I'm taking care of some business," he lied.

"Yu sure? 'Cause yu sound kind of funny."

"I'm positive," Keith said. "We been doin' good, now don't start with me."

"Me not, me not," Tukey lightened up on him. "Tell me sum'ting freaky real quick."

Keith sighed. He knew that after what happened the other day, Tukey was gonna be real suspicious and was gonna stay in his ass from now on. She wanted him to talk freaky to assure her that no other woman was around him.

He turned his face away from Selina's and began whispering. "I love you!"

"Dat's not freaky enough," Tukey complained. "Try again."

"I want to suck yo' pussy from the back." Keith almost laughed out loud.

"Dat's better. Now tell me yu want to kiss me booty."

"I ain't 'bout to say all that," Keith said loudly.

The rise in his tone of voice didn't faze Tukey. "Den yu must be wit' some bitch."

"I'm by myself."

"Den say it, now." Tukey warned.

Keith sighed again. "I want to kiss your booty."

Tukey found that amusing and was relieved to know that he wasn't with another girl. "Now ya see, how hard was dat?"

"I'll holla at you later, baby," Keith said trying to get her off the line.

"One more t'ing. Kevin came by our house and picked up a brick dis morning."

"Alright." He was anxious to get her off the phone.

"Bye."

The waiter had brought their food and Selina was putting sauce on her ribs when he finally hung up. She had a wicked smile on her face.

"What you smiling for?" Keith asked. He began to put salt and pepper on his ribs.

Selina said, "Ya'll sound so sweet and in love on the phone. I hate to be the one to break up y'all's happy home."

Keith ignored her and continued to prepare his food.

"I especially loved the part when she told you to say that you wanted to kiss her booty. That just goes to show how insecure she is."

"What about you?"

"What about me?" Selina asked in a sassy voice.

Keith finished chewing on a piece of rib before answering. "You have any insecurities?"

Selina sipped her drink while she thought about his question. "I don't have a reason to be insecure," she said arrogantly and stood. "Just look at me."

Slowly and real sexy-like, she spun around to show off her bad ass body. A group of young black guys sitting in the next booth got a glimpse of her thong through her damn-near-see-through dress. One of them gave Keith a thumbs up for having such a fine woman.

Selina slid into the booth next to Keith and kissed him on his neck and ear. He resisted.

"What you doing?" Keith looked around to see if anyone was

watching.

"I want you, *papi*," Selina whispered in a sexy voice. "I want you right now."

She stuck her tongue into his mouth, kissing him gently. "Umm," Keith moaned. He could taste the sweet barbeque sauce on her tongue. He grabbed her ass on purpose and pulled up her dress so that the youngsters watching could get a good shot of her ass.

"Excuse me," the hostess interrupted them. "We do have kids in here."

Selina stopped kissing Keith and cut her eyes at the hostess.

"We were just leaving," Keith said quickly before Selina got a chance to get out of line. He dropped a fifty on the table on their way out of the restaurant.

When they reached the car Selina grabbed Keith's arm and pulled him to her. "Let's go find a quiet park where we can fuck on the swings, *papi*," she purred. She looked down and saw a hump growing in his crotch area. Grabbing hold of it, she pushed his back up against the car and started kissing him again.

Keith stopped her after he saw the group of youngsters walk out of the restaurant. "Do *papi* a favor," he asked Selina.

"Anything." She looked up at him.

Selina listened carefully and nodded her head while Keith whispered in her ear.

"You are something else," she said after he finished talking.

"You said anything."

"And I meant it."

Selina turned around and strutted over to where the youngsters were standing, watching them make out. Nervously they looked at one another and wondered what she could want with them. The youngest one of the group, who was chubby, froze when he realized that she was coming toward him.

"Hi, *papi*," Selina said to the chubby boy.

He took a deep breath and tried to appear cool. "What's up?"

Selina stepped close enough to him that he could feel her firm titties up against his. Then she whispered in his ear. "You wanna smell my punanny, *papi?*"

Slowly, with his mouth open, he nodded his head. Selina looked over at Keith, who was leaning up against the car watching. She reached under her dress, and removed her thong. She handed it to Chubby. "Go ahead." Then she walked back over to Keith's car.

"Satisfied?" Selina asked as she got into the passenger seat.

"Very."

Keith winked his eye at the boys as he was getting into the driver's seat. Selina watched in fascination as the boys began to fight over her thong.

"That punanny must smell awfully good to 'em," Keith remarked as he pulled out of the parking lot.

Selina put one leg upon the dashboard. She stuck her finger inside her pussy and wiggled it around. Then she pulled it out and stuck it into her mouth. "Taste good, too," she said, licking her finger.

Keith looked at her sucking her finger and was instantly turned on. "Let me taste it."

She did it again, this time sticking her finger inside of his mouth. "Umm," Keith moaned.

"I need something big in me, *papi,*" Selina licked her lips.

"We're on our way," Keith said.

* * *

The mall was packed with young girls trying to get the latest outfits for whatever party they were headed to when night falls. It was Sunday and the skating rink was the likely place everybody was gonna be tonight.

Tukey was exhausted from running Mi'kelle from toy store to toy store. Not to mention, Anitra had her waiting in the sex toy store for hours as she looked for something new. Finally, they got tired and found a spot to eat pizza and take a load off their feet. Anitra waited until Tukey got Mi'kelle situated before she started with the questions.

"Do you think about what we did?" Anitra asked.

Tukey put her head down and picked the olives off her pizza. This was a conversation that she'd hoped to avoid. She wondered if she should tell Anitra the truth or lie to her. If Tukey told her the truth, it might make matters worse and persuade Anitra into proceeding with trying to make a relationship out of this. If she told her a lie, it might make Anitra feel like she just didn't get her good the first time and continue to try and hit it again.

"Yes, me t'ink about it sometime," Tukey admitted.

Anitra tried hard to suppress the huge grin that appeared on her face. She was in love with Tukey. A burning feeling came to her stomach whenever they were alone together. Now, after years of trying to sleep with her and finally seducing, Keith just had to come up with some way to reel Tukey back in. For all Anitra knew, he probably got himself shot on purpose.

"You miss me?" Anitra said.

Tukey swallowed a bite of pizza. "Me don't want to talk about it, OK."

"Well, I do," Anitra said firmly.

Tukey angrily wiped her mouth with a napkin and threw it on top of her half-finished pizza. "Come on, Mi'kelle," she snapped.

Mi'kelle spit out the pizza that she was chewing. "Me not finished yet, Mama."

Anitra grabbed Tukey's arm. "Let the baby finish eating. I promise that I'm through with it."

Tukey took a deep breath, then slowly sat back down.

"Look Anitra," Tukey said harshly. "Me enjoyed what us did together, OK? But dat's not what me want."

Anitra got pissed off. "You act like—"

"Act like what?" Tukey cut her off.

Anitra calmed down before speaking again. "You act like I don't have feelings or something." Her eyes began to water. You know that what we did meant something to me. Maybe not to you, but it did to me," she said with anger. "Now you acting like I don't have the right to say something. That is so selfish of you,

Tukey."

Anitra grabbed a napkin and wiped the tears that were flowing down her pale cheeks. She glanced over at Mi'kelle, who was too busy making a mess to notice Anitra's crying.

Tukey reached across the table to hold Anitra's hand. "Me sorry," she said in a low voice. "Me know how yu feel about me and me should not have let it go dat far. But it did. And dat was it. Now us have to get over it. Me still in love wit' Keith and dat's just how it is. Me hope dat yu understand and yu still want to be me frien'."

Anitra stared at Tukey through reddened green eyes. She cleared her throat and said, "I understand. But I'm in love with you and I can't help that."

Tukey said, "If it's meant to be, den it will be."

They both stood up and hugged. Anitra gave Tukey a quick peck on the cheek, then smiled, and said, "You'd better take me home. Diamond's supposed to be coming over tonight and I don't want her to get jealous."

"OK."

* * *

After she dropped Anitra at home, Tukey stopped by the liquor store and picked up a bottle of cognac. She wanted to make love tonight. After all that had happened she and Keith needed to sit back, unwind and talk over a few drinks. Then, have a long night of hot, passionate butt-naked sex. Just the thought of sex with Keith excited her. She accelerated and lip-synched with Mary J. Blige all the way home.

"Yes," Tukey said with excitement after she saw Keith's car parked in the driveway. She grabbed the cognac and Mi'kelle, then rushed inside the house.

All of the lights were out when she got inside the living room. Quietly, she tiptoed upstairs into Mi'kelle's room. Careful not wake her, she removed her daughter's clothes and put her to bed.

In the bathroom, Tukey took a quick shower to make sure she smelled good and clean. Keith was sleeping like a baby when she entered their bedroom with the bottle of cognac and two glasses. She smiled to herself, thinking how peaceful he looked laying there. She sat the drink down and quietly slipped Joe's CD into the player, then put it on song number two. "Somebody's Gotta Be On Top," sang softly out of the small stereo.

The music woke Keith. He opened his eyes and saw Tukey dancing naked around the room. She poured cognac in the glasses and handed one to Keith. Even though he was exhausted by the fucking Selina put on him earlier, he still couldn't resist the Jamaican goddess that stood naked before him. He could feel her heat as she slid her warm soft body into the bed beside him.

Looking into each other's eyes, they sipped their drinks little by little without a word to one another.

Tukey finished her drink and sat it on the floor next to the bed. "Now do ya t'ing," she commanded in a soft voice.

Keith sat up and ripped the comforter off the bed. Tukey lay in its center with her arms behind her head and her legs spread. He took another sip of the cognac to get his lips good and wet. The he poured what was left in his glass on top of Tukey's naked flesh. "Umm," she moaned and twitched when she felt the warm liquid hit her flesh. Gently Keith licked her from her freshly manicured toes to her cognac-soaked pubic mound. He lifted her legs and right on cue, Tukey grabbed hold of her ankles to lock her legs in place. She wiggled, moaned and screamed out in pleasure as Keith sucked and nibbled her sensitive pearl. Her screams turned into loud howling noises, loud enough to wake Mi'kelle. Realizing that, Tukey grabbed hold of one of her titties and shoved the nipple into her mouth to pacify herself.

Her pussy became so wet that Keith had to go in, now. He flipped Tukey around on all fours and slid his long erect pole deep inside her tight pussy. He started off gently, with a light smack on her ass cheek to start the horse to bucking. Before long, he was hitting her with hard, fast and long strokes, which caused Tukey to grip the pillow tightly while she bit down on her bottom lip.

Gently out and roughly in, Keith rode Tukey all through the

night. Neither her nor she knew that this would be their last sexual encounter with one another.

Chapter 9

The sun had not yet come up. Tiny pecking sounds came through the window as last night's rain finished up. Three guys sat in a basement, oiling and loading pistols and a shotgun. When they were through, they put the loaded the guns into a bag and sat them by the front door.

The oldest of the threesome fired up a stick of wet and took a few puffs before passing it around.

"Helps boost your courage," he said to the other two. "I don't want nobody getting scared on me." He pulled out a pack of Newports and fired it up to chase the wet with. He blew a big gust of smoke into this nephew's face. "Now tell me again. What time does he leave the house every day, pretending to be going to work?"

His young nephew's hand shook slightly as he took the stick from his mouth. "About seven or seven thirty," he said nervously. The wet had not yet taken effect.

"Good," the oldest one said. "We'll leave here at seven thirty. He should be gone by then."

* * *

The alarm clock buzzed loudly in Keith's ear. He moaned and cursed while fighting his way out from under the covers. He looked over at Tukey, who was fast asleep. He turned the alarm clock off and wondered why it never seemed to bother her. The sight of her laying there naked made Keith want to go one more round with her before he left.

Tukey grabbed his arm when she felt him easing out of bed. "Where yu going, baby?" she said in a groggy voice.

"You know where I'm going."

"When yu gonna stop getting up so early, pretending to be going to work every morning?"

"When I get a job and really start going." Keith snatched his arm away from her and got up. "Ow, shit," he hollered in pain. He immediately grabbed his side.

"What's wrong, baby?" Tukey jumped up with concern.

"Fucking wound is hurting again," Keith whined. He snatched up the pill bottle on his way to the bathroom. A quick shower and a quick run of the toothbrush in his mouth and he was back in his room, putting on his imitation work clothes.

Tukey sat up in the bed and admired the way Keith looked in those work clothes. She loved being with a hustler, but she also wouldn't mind it if she had to iron his work uniform every day and pack him a lunch to go to a real job. She hopped up and rushed to his aid when she saw him having trouble with his zipper. "Let me help."

Seductively she felt around his crotch until she found his zipper. She finally found it and zipped it up slowly. "Dat better?"

"Um hmm," Keith said.

Tukey pulled him close and kissed him on the lips. Keith picked her up and was about to sit her on the dresser, when he heard the door bell.

Tukey sighed. "Me get it." She snatched her red silk robe from the closet on her way down the stairs.

She looked through the peephole and saw Kevin standing there. Hard nipples were what he was faced with when she opened the door.

"Looks like I'm just in time," Keith smiled.

Tukey looked down at he chest and saw her nipples bulging out of her robe. An embarrassed look appeared on her face.

"It's not what yu t'inking," she said as she closed the door.

"Oh, yeah? Well, what is it that's got your sex drive so aroused this early in the morning?"

"Must be the cold air," Tukey joked. Then she headed back up to the bedroom.

Kevin couldn't help but look at her bouncing butt cheeks as she ran up the steps. "*Damn, that ass is fat*," he mumbled to himself.

At that moment, Keith came running down the stairs. "You lookin' at my girl's nipples, huh?" Keith asked.

Kevin shook his head. "Nope. They were lookin' at me."

They both laughed at that.

Keith picked up his gun and shoved it into his waistline. He eyed his younger brother with hard eyes. "We ain't never fell out over no bitch before. But I think we'd have to fight about that one."

"Let's take it outside then," Kevin walked toward the door.

"I'm right behind you," Keith said, trailing behind Kevin. They both jumped around with their guards up.

"First five hits, wins." Keith studied his opponent.

Kevin rushed in too soon and caught one to the jaw. "That's one," Keith said, still jumping around.

Kevin rushed in again. Keith was just about to swing, when he heard Tukey yelling, "Get out from in front of me house wit' dat!" Keith stopped and looked up at her, which allowed Kevin to creep up and hit him with five quick ones to the face, counting each one out loud.

"One two three four five," Kevin said, then threw his arms in the air in victory.

Keith stood there stunned. He looked up at Tukey, who was hanging out the bedroom window, laughing. "Ya got knocked the fuck out," she crowed.

Keith said, "Ya'll set me up. Y'all lucky we got neighbors or I'd shoot the shit outta both of y'all."

"Don't even try it, ba-by," Tukey yelled. "Yu lost fair and

square. Now both of y'all get out of me yard." She shut the window.

"Let's ride, dog." Kevin got into the driver's seat of the old Ford pickup that read, "Keith & Kevin's Roofing" on the door.

Keith said, "Let's go to Niece's and get some breakfast. We'll come back around noon and pick up the dope so we can get our money on."

Kevin put the pickup in drive and took off down the street.

* * *

Falling back to sleep was not seeming to happen. Frustrated, Tukey got up, walked over to the window to shut the blinds halfway. Then something caught her eye. A green Ford Tempo carrying three guys inside drove slowly up the block. The small guy in the back seat looked as if he was watching her house. She wasn't sure, but she could've sworn that she saw that same green Tempo ride by while Keith and Kevin were out there play fighting.

Tukey waited by the window to see if they were going to circle around the block. After ten minutes of watching and no sign of them, she began to relax. The sight of her purse sitting on the dresser made her think of her pistol. She took the gun out her purse and put it into her robe pocket, just in case. Then she called Keith.

"What's wrong, baby?" Keith answered.

"Me just wanted to ask yu did yu know anybody who drive a green Ford Tempo?"

Keith thought for a moment. "Not that I know of," he finally said. "Why?"

She sighed. "Not'ing. Me must be paranoid or somet'ing."

"You got your gun, don't you?"

"Yeah."

"Well, if something don't look right, you call me. If it goes down before I get there, you start dumping."

"OK, baby," Tukey said, feeling more secure now that she had talked to Keith. "Me love yu."

"You too."

They hung up.

Tukey slipped into a pair of tight-fitting stretch pants, a blue tank top and a pair of blue Air Max Nikes. She gave her near perfect body a glance in the mirror before going to the kitchen to fix Mi'kelle's breakfast.

Eggs were frying and bacon was sizzling when she saw Mi'kelle enter the kitchen out of the corner of her eye.

Tukey turned toward her. "Hey, boo boo," she said with her arms extended to her child.

"Me hungry, Mama," Mi'kelle said in a sleepy voice. "Me want somet'ing to eat."

Tukey picked her up. "Mama cookin' right now, sweetie. It'll be ready in a minute." She kissed Mi'kelle on the cheek and sat her down at the table. Tukey reached for the refrigerator door, when a sudden knock on the front door startled her.

"Somebody at the door, Ma—"

"Shhhh," Tukey hushed her. "Damn," she cursed, realizing that she'd left her gun upstairs in her robe pocket. The next best thing was the knife that she pulled from the kitchen drawer.

The knocking started again.

"Yu stay right here, Mi'kelle," Tukey whispered. Then she tiptoed into the front room and stood in front of the door. Normally she wouldn't have been scared to open her own door, but the guys in the green Tempo had her shaken up.

"Who is it?" she asked with the knife held tightly in her fist.

"Charley."

Tukey relaxed when she heard a familiar name come from the other side of the door. She unlocked all of the locks except for the chain. As soon as she turned the knob, the door crashed in on her and knocked her to the floor. Through teary eyes, Tukey looked up as three men wearing masks entered her house. The smallest one reached down and grabbed her by the throat. Suddenly, Tukey remembered that she still had the knife in her hand. Thinking quickly, she made a deep slash across the small guy's hand, causing him to release her neck instantly. Then she kicked him in his chest and sent him falling into the glass table.

Tukey attempted to get up when she felt a strong hand close around the back of her neck. She swung the knife but the third man hit her in the head with the butt of his shotgun before she hit her target. The knife fell out of her hand as she fell to the floor. The small guy got up from the frame of the broken glass table and kicked her once between her legs.

Tukey screamed loudly while tears ran down her bloody cheeks.

"Get somethin' to tie this bitch's hands up," the leader of the trio said.

The small one ran into the kitchen and was back in seconds with a roll of gray duct tape. Tukey was surprised and relieved that the small guy said nothing about seeing her daughter in the kitchen. She watched, horrified, as they taped her hands and feet, leaving her stuck in the middle of the floor.

The leader instructed the other two to go get what they came for while he kept an eye on Tukey.

Down in the basement the smaller guy led the other directly to where the safe was. It sat in a corner bolted to the basement floor. The small guy reached into his pocket for a piece of paper with the combination on it. As he read the numbers off the other guy twirled the knob accordingly. They held a collective breath as he pulled the latch that opened the safe door.

He turned his head toward the small guy grinning from ear to ear. "Jackpot."

"I told you," the small guy said excitedly.

Quickly he untied the laundry bag from around his waist and began filling it with the money and the bricks of cocaine. When they finished, they courteously shut the safe door behind them and shot up the stairs.

"Stoooopp! Stoooopp!" Tukey was screaming while the leader tried to cover her mouth with his hand.

Tukey's legs were wide open and all of her clothes except for her panties and bra had been ripped off when the two guys came up from the basement. Their leader had untaped her legs and was trying to force his way between them.

"Open up, you bitch," he yelled into her face, then slapped her viciously. He'd taken off his mask, but her eyes were too filled with blood and tears for her to identify anybody.

The small guy put his hand on the leader's shoulder. "We got the shit, now let's get the fuck outta here."

"You lucky bitch," the leader said before he spat on her. He stood up, breathing rapidly, then snatched the bag from his partner. "Let's go."

After she heard the door slam, Tukey jumped up and ran into the now smoke-filled kitchen. Barely able to see, she felt her way to the stove, slid the pan over to uncover the burning flame. She took a deep breath, then stuck her hand over the fire. As soon as the tape began to melt, she pulled her hands apart to break the tape. Her wrist burned a little, but it was nothing compared to what she'd just went through.

"Mi'kelle, Mi'kelle," she hollered. She was turning off the stove when Mi'kelle kicked open the cabinet doors under the sink. Tukey rushed over to her. "Me baby," she said, relieved that Mi'kelle was OK. She checked the girl for bruises, but there were none. "Stay here, OK," Tukey said, then took off for the stairs.

With great speed she found her gun, bolted back down the stairs and out the front door. She looked both ways, then decided to run in the direction that she saw the Tempo coming from earlier. She ran for almost a block before she realized that she was half naked, and that they were long gone.

"Shit," she cried. Then ran back down to the house to call Keith.

* * *

Keith was in the middle of writing down the phone number of a young waitress at Niece's when he heard his phone ring. He checked the caller ID before answering and frowned when he saw that it was only Tukey. *She don't want nothing*, he thought to himself. So he finished writing down the number.

The waitress asked, "So when are we gonna go out?"

"Maybe this weekend or something." Keith looked over at Kevin who was also talking to a waitress. Kevin took his phone out and at his caller ID. "Is that Tukey?" Keith asked.

"Yep."

"Don't answer it. She probably got a lie to tell that'll get me to come home."

While they were leaving the restaurant, they walked past a young kid trying to sell ceramics out of the empty lot next door.

"Excuse me," the boy said. "Would you like to buy one of my vases?"

Keith and Kevin both rudely ignored the young man and kept walking to their truck. Keith's phone rang again. This time the number that showed up on the caller ID belonged to his friend Chris.

Chris was one of his boys that Keith grew up with. Out of all the guys who lived in the 'hood, Chris was the first one to come up and stay up. Keith always respected the fact that Chris got where he was today starting from a fifty-dollar double-up. He stayed true to the game and the game stayed true to him. Every now and then Keith would buy a kilo or two from him, just to keep things cool.

Keith answered the call. "What's up, nigga?"

"Trying to see what's poppin' with you," Chris said.

"You know me. Trying' to fuck these hos and dodge the feds while I make ends meet."

"How you lookin' on the work?" Chris asked.

Keith paused for a moment to do some quick figuring in his head. He had to figure out how much he'd sold and how much he had left. "I got about ten of 'em left," he finally answered.

"Aw yeah," Chris said. "How much you gon' let me get five of 'em for?"

"Sheeit.....probably about ninety-five," Keith said with caution. He knew that Chris wasn't used to prices that high.

"Alright, cool. When you gon' go pick it up?"

"I'll call you in 'bout an hour." Keith hung up. "Take me to the crib."

Kevin slowed down and made a sharp U-turn in the middle of the street.

From down the street Keith could see two police cars and an ambulance parked in front of his house. Kevin stopped the truck dead in the middle of the street and quickly threw it into reverse. He backed up steadily for about two blocks before he slowed to a stop. Seeing the police cars parked in front of Keith's house spooked him. All Keith could think to do was get out of sight, just in case they were there for the wrong reasons.

"Why you back up?" Keith asked curiously.

"'Cause you never know what's going on. Call the house and make sure it's clear before we go walking into a trap."

"Good thinking." Keith took out his cell phone and nervously dialed his home number. His stomach was in knots as he waited for Tukey to answer the phone.

"Hello," Tukey answered the phone in a stressful voice.

"Baby, is everything alright?" Keith asked excitedly. "What the police doing there?"

Tukey was sobbing. "Somebody kicked in our door and robbed me. And one of 'em tried to rape me."

"Is Mi'kelle OK?"

Tukey nodded her head but Keith couldn't see her through the phone. He could hear cops in the background asking questions.

"Where's Mi'kelle, Tukey?" Keith yelled into the phone.

"What happened?" Kevin said, but Keith wasn't listening.

"Just come home, Keith," Tukey cried.

After hearing Tukey through the phone, Kevin put the truck in drive and burned rubber all the way to the house. The truck hadn't stopped before Keith jumped out and ran toward the house.

When Keith barged in, the paramedics were bandaging Tukey's head and a white policeman was standing over her writing on a small tablet.

The policeman put his hand on Keith's chest and stopped him in his tracks. "Who are you?"

"I live here," Keith said, in a hostile tone. He ran over and gave Tukey a hug. She cried while resting her head on his chest. She wasn't crying because of the physical hurt. She cried because the robbers had gotten the money. While she cried, she replayed the whole event back in her mind, trying to look for some familiarity in one of their voices.

"Are you finished here?" Keith asked the cop.

The cop slammed his tablet shut. "Yes. Just as soon as my partner finishes looking around."

"Where's Mi'kelle?" Keith asked Tukey.

Tukey raised her head and said, "Her asleep in her room."

"Can I ask you a question?" Keith asked the officer.

"Go ahead."

"If the guys who did this are gone, then why in the hell is your partner going through my shit?"

The paramedic sensed that Keith was about to get hostile, so they made an exit out the door.

The policeman eyed Keith suspiciously. "Who said there were guys who done this? Maybe you know something that we don't."

"If I—" Keith didn't say what he was about to 'cause there was no use arguing with the asshole.

After his partner finished his search, they left their business cards on the table and left Keith and Tukey alone. As soon as they were out of sight, Keith began to grill Tukey.

"What the fuck happened?" he hollered.

Tukey hesitated for a second. "Dey robbed us," she cried out.

"They got into the safe?" Keith asked doubtedly.

Tukey nodded her head. "Yes. Me don't know how, but dey did."

Keith looked up at Kevin, who was standing in the doorway, looking like death had hit him in the face.

Keith took a deep breath and said, "Tell me everything that

---

happened." They both listened carefully to every detail of the shocking story that Tukey told them. As Keith listened, he wondered how the fuck Ben was gonna react to this. With the money they had put away, plus what people owed him, he could pay Ben still. But that wasn't likely to happen. After all, they didn't rob him. They robbed Tukey. Her own uncle couldn't fault her for that.

When Tukey finished telling them what happened, Keith ran down into the basement to get a look at the crime scene. His hands were shaking so bad that he had to try the combination several times before he finally got it open. He was about to grab the latch to open it when he noticed a dried blood stain on the door behind it.

Keith thought about that for a moment. Whoever opened the safe must have been bleeding when he opened the door, because his cut left a slash of blood where his hand touched the safe door.

As a precaution, Keith used his shirt to pull the latch on the door. It was empty.

"Fuck!" he screamed loudly.

Kevin left Tukey and ran down into the basement when he heard Keith scream. Kevin approached him slowly from behind but didn't say a word.

Keith began kicking on the basement wall. "How in the fuck did they get into the safe?" He shook his head in disbelief.

"You suspect her?" Kevin said evenly.

Keith slowly shook his head again. "She didn't know the combination," he said in a low voice. Then he dragged himself up the stairs.

Kevin stood there shaking his head at the empty safe. Then he kicked it closed.

Tukey hated seeing the stressed out look that was plastered on Keith's face. She ran over and threw her arms around him. "Me sorry baby. Me tried to do sum'ting, but me couldn't."

"Shhh," Keith rubbed her back gently. "It wasn't your fault. Now go on upstairs and lay down." He gave her a kiss on the forehead.

Kevin came up from the basement just as Tukey was heading up to her room. He took a seat on the couch with his head between his legs. "So what are we gonna do about Ben?"

Keith stuck his hands into his pockets and leaned against the wall. He thought for a moment. "We got two choices," he talked slowly. "We can tell him what happened, and tell him that we ain't got the money to pay him. Or, we can give him the money that we got stashed and go on with business as usual."

"Why don't we sleep on it," Kevin said.

Keith took his shirt off. "We're gonna have to get to the bottom of this shit," he said seriously. He took his gun out and sat it on the table. "Whoever it was opened the safe right up. Let's lay on it a couple of days and see who tells on theyself."

"You stayin' here tonight?"

Keith sat down beside Kevin. "Yeah. I might take my family out or something. I don't want Mi'kelle to be shook up by this shit."

Kevin smiled to himself. "Mi'kelle ain't no fool. I'm glad that she was smart enough to hide when trouble came."

"Me too," Keith said smiling for the first time.

They both sat there quiet, deep in their own thoughts. Blood had to shed behind this, even if they had to give somebody a free case. If word got out about this and they didn't do anything about it, jackers would be trying them on the regular. One thing Keith wasn't going to let himself or his brother do was make a move until their heads were clear. Like Ben told him, "A killer makes at least twenty-five mistakes and doesn't realize them until he leaves the crime scene." Whether it was the truth or not, Keith listened to all advice that was given to him.

They both agreed on getting together after a good night's sleep, then they'd figure out the best thing to do. Before Kevin left Keith's house, he had to swear that he wasn't going to make any stupid moves on his own.

Mi'kelle was asleep in her mother's arms while Tukey stared up at the ceiling. Keith slid into bed and embraced the both of them. Silently, he thanked the Lord for not letting Mi'kelle get hurt. He kissed Mi'kelle on the head then watched her sleep peacefully.

Tukey turned toward him and looked him in the eye. She felt so helpless for a woman of her caliber. She was tough and knew that if they had to get the combination out of her, she would've died first.

Finding no words that would comfort her man, she lay there in his arms with her eyes closed, praying that they would find out who did this to them.

Chapter 10

Kevin and Kim lay naked on their bed after making love on and off since one o'clock that morning. Kim could tell that Kevin was stressed out when he came home. Without even asking him what's wrong, she undressed him, lay him down and tried to ride all of the tension out of him. Sex soothed the savage beast. That's why she had given it her all last night.

Her pussy felt swollen and her knees a bit weak, but somehow Kim managed to get out of bed. She pulled out her weed tray from under the dresser and twisted up a joint. She smoked half of it, then passed the rest of it to Kevin.

"You want to talk about it?" Kim asked with deep concern in her voice.

Kevin slowly blew the smoke out of his mouth. He sat there for a moment, then he hit it again. He was in no hurry to talk and Kim had all of the patience in the world for him.

"Some fucked up shit happened." Kevin put out the joint.

Kim didn't speak, she just lay there and listened to what Kevin had to say. "Somebody robbed Tukey for all our shit."

"All of it?" Kim asked in disbelief. Kevin nodded. "Don't y'all have some money put away? We can sell my car and pawn my jewelry and stuff, if y'all need the money."

Kevin smiled and gently kissed Kim's forehead. "We don't need to sell nothin' baby," he said. "We got enough stashed to pay

Ben. But if we do that, we gon' have to start all over again."

Kim held his hand. "What do you think he'll do if y'all don't pay him his money?"

Kevin could hear the concern and worry in her voice, so he didn't tell her what he really thought would happen. "I don't know," he said. "It was his niece who got robbed for the shit. Not us."

Kim wrapped her arms around him and hugged him tight. "I don't want nothing to happen to you out there in them streets." Her eyes began to water.

Kevin said, "Don't worry yourself about stuff like that." He rubbed her back while they held each other. "I'll kill that nigga 'fore I let somethin' happen to me or my brother."

"And what about Tukey?" Kim quizzed. "Do you think she's not gonna mind y'all killing her uncle?"

"Tukey better understand the game," Kevin said coldly.

Kim sighed. She didn't like what was going on one bit. It was too much for her nerves to handle. Raised by two Christian parents, she'd never experienced anything like this before. Suddenly, she wasn't able to stomach the conversation anymore. She slid out of Kevin's arms and onto the bed. Then she forced herself to sleep.

Kevin put the roach into the ashtray next to his bed. His body felt weak from the bomb ass sex that he had with Kim, and the bomb that Tukey had dropped on him yesterday. Stretching first, he wobbled on his weak knees into the bathroom.

A little while later, Kevin was dressed and sitting in front of the TV, eating cereal with his son.

"Ooops," little Kevin said, looking down at the cereal that he'd spilled on the floor.

Kim saw what happened from the stairs. "Ooops your ass," she yelled at him. "Go in the kitchen and get a towel. Clean yo' mess up."

Mad and pouting, Little Kevin got up in his soggy diaper and ran into the kitchen.

"Don't be hollering at my son like that," Kevin said calmly.

"He's my son too," Kim said as she walked over to the window. "It's too dark in here." She opened the blinds and filled the room with sunlight. She jumped when Kevin's pager suddenly vibrated on the living room table. "Marlet's wondering why you didn't come by her house last night."

"Marlet ain't got my pager number," Kevin picked up the pager. "She's got my cell number."

Kim narrowed her eyes at him. "You better take that back," she warned.

Kevin laughed. "Stop talkin' shit then."

"I know I bet' not find out that y'all fucking around again. This time, I won't be so lenient."

Keith's number showed up in his pager when Kevin checked it.

Kevin shoved his bowl into Kim's arms. "Take that in the kitchen for me."

* * *

Keith was sitting up in his bed, thinking, when his phone rang. Strangely, his gunshot wound wasn't bothering him.

"Hello," he answered.

"Waiting on your word," Kevin said.

Keith said, "I'm gonna round up all of our loose cash, then I'ma meet up with you later."

"Alright. You decided on anything yet?"

"Yeah." Keith yawned. "I'ma give you a holla when we get together later."

"Alright then." Kevin hung up. "I'm 'bout to go, Kim. I'll be back in a little bit."

Kim came running from the kitchen. "You're still gonna spend some time with us tonight, ain't you?" She was breathing heavily.

"Yep," Kevin replied. "Now give me some suga."

They kissed for almost a minute before Kevin vanished out the door. Kim locked the door up tightly then closed the blinds again.

Kim looked down at the table and saw that Kevin had left his pager. But by the time she got the door unlocked, he was gone.

* * *

Bob Jones moved his elderly frame slowly from behind the cash register to the Coke machine. His hands were shaking out of control as he inserted two quarters into the machine. The Coke came tumbling down and he grabbed it. He was cooling off with his cold drink when he saw Keith's Lexus pull into his parking lot.

Bob straightened his crooked bowtie when he recognized the car. He was fascinated by the tall black girl that called herself Tukey, who usually drove it. Lust filled his eyes as he watched her step from the vehicle and strut her way to the door. She was wearing a blue tennis skirt and a pair of white canvas shoes. So many times he wondered what it would feel like in between those firm thighs.

The bell rang and brought Bob back to reality when Tukey came through the door.

"Good morning," Bob said in his most pleasant voice.

"Hi, Mr. Jones," Tukey replied, trying to appear in a good mood.

"You sure are looking pretty today," Bob said. He pretended not to notice the bandage on her face.

She leaned over the counter so he could get a good peek at her titties. "Me look so pretty, 'cause me knew me had to come see yu today."

Tukey's accent made Bob's old Johnson stiffen. So many times he had wanted to proposition her, but couldn't build up enough nerve to do it.

"What can I do for you today," Bob asked as he put on his glasses.

Tukey reached over the counter and straightened his tie. "Me seem to have lost me key to the storage room, and me need another one. If it not too much trouble."

"Nooo, it's not too much trouble." Bob turned around and took key number 221 off the shelf before handing it to her. "Here you go sweetie."

Tukey frowned and said, "Me t'ought yu was gonna help me."

A worried look came over Bob's wrinkled face. His hard dick was poking through his slacks, and he didn't want her to see him like that. He glanced over her shoulder and saw Keith sitting in the passenger seat of the Lexus.

"You don't want your boyfriend to help you?" Bob asked hopefully.

Tukey turned around and glanced out the window. Then she turned back toward him and shook her head. "Him not me boyfriend," she said convincingly.

"Oh."

Tukey reached around the counter and took Bob by the arm. "Come on, Mr. Jones," she said as she pulled him toward her.

After little resistance, Bob came around the counter. Tukey looked down at his crotch.

"Dammmn," Tukey said, staring at his pants. "Yu kinda freaky, Mr. Jones."

Bob blushed. "I didn't mean for this to happen."

Knowing that he was embarrassed, Tukey decided to make him feel good about himself. "Me wish dat guy in me car was packing what ya packing," she said in a low voice. "Now come on."

They went outside and walked around back to storage room 221. The old man opened the lock and raised the door. Inside was a bunch of old furniture that Keith filled the room with to make it look good. Just in case Tukey's good looks didn't keep down the old man's suspicions.

Tukey stepped into the room. "Help me wit' dis TV."

Keith was cracking up inside when he saw Tukey and the old man struggling to get the TV to the car. He just knew that Bob would fall before they reached the trunk.

After they finished, Tukey gave Bob a kiss on the cheek, then told him to lock up for her.

"How's your boyfriend?" Keith asked her in the car.

"Him good," Tukey retorted when they pulled away from the storage place. "Where us headed?"

Keith glanced at his watch before he said, "Run me by Tee's house."

Bob Jones had just closed the door to unit 221 when he saw the shadows of two men come up from behind him. He turned around and saw two middle-aged white guys in dark blue suits. The taller of the two pulled out a badge that read "FBI."

With a stunned look on his face, Bob cleared his throat and said, "May I help you gentlemen?"

"I'm special Agent Browning," the taller one said, then pointed to his partner. "And this is special Agent Carter."

"We would like to search this unit," Carter said.

"You gotta warrant?"

"No," Carter said. "But it wouldn't be a problem for us to get one."

Bob finished locking the unit up. "Come back when you get one."

Browning said. "Do you mind if we ask you a few questions?"

Bob stood firm. "Go right ahead."

Agents Browning and Carter pulled small writing tablets out of their breast pockets.

Carter started first. "Do you personally know the young woman who came by here to—"

"That's enough questions," Bob cut him off. "You're getting a bit too personal." He walked away and left the agents looking stupid.

Kevin was speeding up Paseo when he noticed for the fourth time that a green Crown Victoria was following him. He wasn't sure the first three times, because the car kept its distance. Now that traffic had slowed, the car stuck out like a sore thumb.

Just to make sure, Kevin made a right turn, drove a block and made a left, then stopped. He waited, but there was no sign of the green Crown Victoria.

When it didn't show, Kevin felt that he was just being paranoid. He put the car in drive, continuing on his journey.

Kevin could hear blues blasting out of his mama's house when he pulled up. He went inside and headed straight for the basement. Off in a far corner was a stack of old tires, piled about five high. Kevin reached between the loops and pulled out a black bag. He opened it to ensure sure that it still had the twenty grand in it that he made off the kilo that he got from Tukey.

Kevin was walking through the dining room when the music suddenly shut off.

"Who is that in my damn house?" his mother yelled from the back room.

"It's me, Mama."

The old wood floor beneath the carpet squeaked as she made her way to the dining room. The black bag was the first thing that she noticed.

"What's that," she quizzed, pointing at the bag. She knew the answer and she knew that Kevin was gonna tell a damn lie.

"My clothes," Kevin answered.

"Why you gon' stand here and lie in my face?"

"What you want me to say, Mama? That I stashed a bag full of money in your basement?"

"It's better than straight out lying to your own mama." She walked into the kitchen. "You heard from your brother?"

Kevin followed her. He took a carton of orange juice out of the fridge and drank from the container. "I talked to him earlier today."

He saw the strange look on his mama's face that said, "what the hell are you doing?"

"What?"

She put her hand on her hip. "Is this your house?"

Kevin sighed. "Come on, Mama. Don't start." He put the juice back into the fridge.

She said, "When you do see your brother, tell him to call me, 'cause he don't seem to answer my calls."

"I'll tell 'em." Kevin kissed her cheek. "What day is the family reunion on?"

"Next Friday," she said seriously. "And y'all better be there.

You go upstairs and speak to your stepfather?"

"Nope. But I talked to him yesterday. We goin' fishing this Saturday."

She turned on the water faucet. "Just make sure you bring my grandbaby by when you come."

"I will," Kevin said over his shoulder as he left the house.

* * *

Tukey dropped the Lexus over into the right lane and passed a red Civic in her hurry to get to Tee's house. For some reason, she had the feeling that they were being followed. She was tired of bugging Keith and decided not to mention it to him. She just kept a close eye on all three of her mirrors as she weaved in and out of traffic.

For the last thirty minutes, Keith's cell phone had been ringing off the hook. But that wasn't what irked her. What pissed her off was that every time it rang, he would look at the caller ID first, then hang it up. This was something that she planned on bringing back up, when this was over.

Keith knew that if his phone kept ringing and he didn't answer, sooner or later Tukey was gonna snap. Selina kept calling back to back, like she knew that he was with Tukey. Out of all his bitches, she was the only one that didn't respect the fact that Keith had a woman. She was becoming a pain the ass that he didn't want to get rid of.

When they got to Tee's house, Keith told Tukey to wait in the car and watch Mi'kelle, who was asleep in the back seat. Tee's door was open, so he stepped in without knocking. Two girls were cleaning house when he came through the door. One vacuumed while the other dusted the furniture. The duster looked at Keith and smiled.

"You looking for Tee or Andre?" she asked.

"Either."

"Tee's gone, but Andre's in the kitchen." She pointed in that direction.

Andre was counting money on the kitchen table when he

heard Keith walk in. He saw Keith out of the corner of his eye but didn't look up until he finished counting the stack.

"What's up, playboy," Andre asked. He was still focused on what he was doing.

Keith didn't answer right away. Instead, he took a seat for a moment. For a minute he thought about telling Andre what happened. Then he quickly dismissed the thought when he remembered that it was an inside job.

"You alright, dog?" Andre asked.

"Yeah, man I just....I'm trying to lay my hands on as much bread as I can, by tonight."

Andre rubbed his chin. "Shit, I still got plenty of dope left. But I can give you that fifty grand I owe you right now if you need it."

"I do, man," Keith said anxiously. "You know I wouldn't hound you for it if I didn't need it."

Andre sensed some trouble, but decided not to ask. If Keith wanted him to know, he would have told him.

Andre stopped what he was doing and left the kitchen. It wasn't long before he came back carrying a Dillard's shopping bag. "Here you go." He handed the bag to Keith.

Keith nodded head. "Thanks, man. I don't like pressuring you about nothing you owe m—"

"Don't worry 'bout it, dog," Andre cut him off. "Take care of your business. I know you'll tell me what's up later."

"Right on."

Three men sat in a white van five houses up, snapping pictures of Keith coming out of the house carrying the shopping bag. Keith called Kevin as soon as he got into the car.

* * *

Tukey, Kevin and Keith sat at the table at Keith's house counting up all of the money that they gathered. The TV they got out of the storage unit contained two hundred thousand dollars in the guts of it. The TV money, all the other money that they collected, plus the fifty thousand that Tukey had stashed for her personal use, came up to three hundred twenty-eight thousand dollars.

Kevin said, "So we gon' pay Ben or what?"

Keith smoked a blunt as he stared out the patio doors. Blowing smoke out of his nostrils, he walked over to the table.

"First I'm gonna tell him what happened. If he don't get upset about it and takes it as a loss, then we won't pay him." Keith sat down. "If he does trip, then we'll pay him the two seventy."

Tukey shook her head. "Bad idea," she disagreed. "If ya tell me uncle dat us don't got him money, what ya t'ink him gonna do? Laugh it off? Me don't t'ink so."

Keith jumped up. "Well what the fuck do you want me to do, Tukey," he yelled at her. "Just hand him over all my fuckin' money?" He pointed his finger at her. "You're the one who got robbed, not me. And now that we're on the subject, how did they talk you into unlocking the damn door?"

Tukey stood and straightened her tall frame. She looked Keith dead in his eyes and said, "Me told yu everyt'ing dat happened," she said hotly. "If yu don't trust me, of all people, den fuck yu."

Already mad, Keith's reflexes jumped and he grabbed Tukey by the throat. He was pulled back his fist to hit her when Kevin jumped up and grabbed his arm.

"We don't need this shit right now, Keith," Kevin said in a serious tone. "Let her go."

With a crazy look in his eye, Keith maintained his grip on her throat.

"Bitch, you don't ever talk to me like that," Keith said harshly. "You hear me?"

The anger in his eyes let Tukey know that he meant business, and she didn't want to take it any further. She slowly nodded her tear-soaked face. She stormed out of the kitchen as soon as he let go of her throat.

"Don't fuck up and lose her," Kevin warned him.

"Fuck that bitch," Keith said, loud enough for Tukey to hear. "I don't trust her no more, no way."

Kevin took a deep breath. "So, we gon' pay him or what?"

Keith fired the blunt back up and took a long drag. "Fuck her uncle. She's the one who lost his money." He took another puff, held it for a while, then blew it out. "Let her pay him."

Keith's sudden I-don't-give-a-fuck attitude made Kevin nervous. But regardless of whether he agreed with Keith or not, he was gonna stand behind him, one hundred percent.

Keith said, "I've got some Mexicans on the Westside I can call up if Ben gets to talking crazy."

Kevin stood up and removed his car keys from his pocket. "I'm supposed to take Kim and my son to the show tonight. I'll get up with you tomorrow."

"See ya," Keith said nonchalantly.

Kevin stared at his brother for a minute. Then he left.

Chapter 11

Keith stood over his kitchen stove, adding water to a pot that he was rocking up a kilo in. He made a call to his Mexican friends that morning. Then he met them over on the Westside to buy a kilo, for starters. The price was nothing in comparison to Ben's, but it was below what they were going for in the hood.

Keith didn't really want to end his business with Ben, but he couldn't see himself just handing over all of his money, especially when it wasn't his fault. Shit like that happened in the game. Tukey wouldn't like the idea, but she was gonna have to deal with it.

If Ben wanted to trip, then fuck it, it'll be on. Educated in the cold streets of Kansas City, Keith was no stranger to gunplay. *Even a coward don't know the evil he might do*, Ben always told him.

A huge rock began to form in the beaker, so Keith took it out of the pot and placed it in the sink. He waited for the beaker to cool a little, then ran cold water on it to help cool it faster.

Two soft arms slid around his waist. Keith knew that it was Tukey, so it didn't startle him, nor did he look around. A ticklish feeling surfaced on the back of his neck. He could feel the wetness of a tongue running down his neck.

"Me sorry, baby," Tukey whispered into his ear.

Keith turned the faucet off, then turned to face her. "Who's side are you on?" he asked in a serious voice.

"Ya side," Tukey said in a firm tone. She tried to kiss Keith, but he turned away.

"Get your uncle on the phone," Keith ordered.

"OK." Tukey looked into his eyes then she walked slowly to the phone, and dialed Ben's number.

"Hi, Uncle Ben." Tukey put false cheer into her voice. "Hold on, let me put Keith on."

Keith took the phone from her. Tukey took a seat and sat down quietly while the two of them talked. Her stomach was in knots because she knew her uncle, and she knew how he was gonna take the bad news, regardless of whether she told him that she was the one who got robbed or not. Ben was gonna think that she was lying for Keith, because that's how she was raised: to protect the one who takes care of you.

"What's up, Ben?" Keith prepared himself for the conversation that was ahead.

"Keith. Ya don't sound too good, mon." Ben heard the stress in Keith's voice.

Keith took a deep breath, and said, "We've got a little problem."

"What kinda problem?" Ben's voice had a trace of hostility in it.

"We...nah, Tukey got robbed for all your shit," Keith said. He ignored the hard gaze that she trained on him.

Tukey looked at Keith like he was a bitch.

"Tell me wha'appened."

Keith explained to Ben everything that Tukey had told him, word for word. The phone become quiet while Keith waited for Ben's response.

"Keith, ya dere?" Ben finally said.

"Yeah."

"Ya listen to me good, Keith." Ben's voice was cold. "Me don't give a fuck wha'appened. Ya get me me money."

"And if I don't, muthafucka?" Keith hollered.

"Me not gon' kill ya. Me gon' kill somet'ing close to ya." Ben laughed, then hung up.

The phone went dead in Keith's ear.

"When is your uncle due back in the country?" he asked Tukey.

"Saturday." Tukey could tell that the conversation had gone badly.

Keith threw the phone down as he walked out of the room.

* * *

He and Kevin were riding around, making moves in Tukey's rental Cadillac. They had about nine ounces left out of the kilo that they started with. It was so hot outside that the temperature felt like it was going up by the minute. Nobody that he'd served so far had called him with any complaints about the dope. Keith couldn't wait until Pedro, the head Mexican, got back into town so that they could negotiate a deal on some real work.

After hearing Ben's unsympathetic response abut what happened, Keith knew that he was gonna have to make a move first; paying him was out of the question. His plan was to fly out to California Friday night and be waiting on Ben when he got back in town on Saturday.

Keith's cell phone rang. "Yeah," he answered.

"Keith, this Nukey. Come by my house for a minute, my uncle is trying to get something."

"Give me a few minutes."

Keith parked in front of Nukey's mama's house and ran up to the front door. Nukey answered the door wearing a new Sean John outfit and a new gold chain.

"What's up, Keith," Nukey said. "Come on in, man."

Nukey's Uncle Ronnie was sitting on the living room couch, counting a small stack of cash, when Keith walked into the room. Immediately Keith became suspicious. If he remembered right, that was the same man that was here the day that the package came. The same man that borrowed money from Brenda to get something from the store. Now he was sitting here, counting a stack of money.

Nukey said, "My uncle's trying to get some work. How much you got on you?"

Keith lifted the Crown Royal bag that he held in his hand. "About nine ounces."

"Let me get 'em." Ronnie spoke for the first time.

Keith opened the bag and dumped the dope onto the table.

"How much?" asked Ronnie.

"Six thousand," Keith said calmly. He was trying not to show the anger that was building inside of him. The last thing he wanted them to think was that he was onto them.

Ronnie counted out six grand and tossed it near Keith like it was nothing. Without even counting it, Keith put the money into his pocket.

"Call me if you need some more," Keith said on his way to the front door.

"What you doing today?" Nukey asked as he followed Keith.

"Trying to make a living."

Nukey felt himself about to sneeze, so he lifted his hand to his nose. The bandage that he had around his hand disturbed Keith.

"What happened to your hand, dog?" Keith tried to sound concerned.

Nukey looked at it like he'd forgotten about it. "I got into a fight with this bitch."

It took everything Keith had not to steal on Nukey right there. He hadn't brought his gun in with him and he was sure he'd have trouble trying to take on all three of them. Plus, Keith still wasn't sure that Nukey did it. Or maybe he just didn't want to believe it.

"Give me a call later," Keith said. "I want to rap with you 'bout something."

Keith looked straight ahead on his way to his car. He didn't even glance over at the green Tempo that he noticed out of the corner of his eye. The one that he remembered Tukey telling him that she saw outside their house the day they got robbed.

He turned a few corners before he let Kevin in on what he'd discovered.

"I think I know who got us," he said to Kevin.

"Who?"

They were interrupted by Keith's cell phone. "Hold on a minute," he told Kevin. He answered the call. "Hello."

"¿Me gustaría pasar tiempo contigo?" Selina said.

Keith smiled. "Me speak no Spanish."

"I said, can I spend some time with you?"

"I wish I could, baby. But I'm busy right now."

"I miss you, *papi*," Selina pouted. "When can I see you, then?"

Keith made a right turn to avoid the patrol car that was coming up behind them. "I'm a call you as soon a I get a chance, OK?"

"You promise?"

"Yep. Peace!" He hung up on her.

Kevin was becoming restless while he waited on Keith to tell him what was going on. "Who you think got us, nigga?" Kevin said impatiently.

"I think Nukey and his uncle robbed us, man." He looked over at Kevin to get a look at his facial expression. "Nukey set us up."

Kevin gave Keith a strange look. He never thought that much of Nukey anyway. "How you find that out?"

"You see that green Tempo that was in the driveway?"

Kevin shook his head.

"Tukey called me that morning while we was at Niece's and told me that she saw three dudes circling our house in a green Tempo. That, plus he got a scar on his hand right where Tukey said that she cut one of them."

Kevin got upset. "Come on, nigga! Let's go back and get them muthafuckas."

Keith calmly fired up a half a blunt that they'd started earlier. He took a couple of puffs, then passed it to Kevin.

"Can't do it like that," Keith explained. "First, we got to make him confess. Then, we gotta find out what he did with the money. You see what I'm saying?"

"Whatever, man," Kevin said. "What you plan on doing?"

"I'm a have him come by the house tonight," Keith said. "Then we gon' beat it out of him."

They sat in Keith's living room drinking glass after glass of Rémy Martin V.S.O.P. Tukey's nerves were jumping. She wanted so bad to get back at Nukey for attacking her like he did. She'd been anxious every since Keith had called Nukey, telling him to come over. Now that she'd thought about it, his little hands and skin color should have given him up. Tukey knew that it was an inside job, but that it was Nukey, of all people, had never crossed her mind.

"Have a seat, girl, damn," Keith told her. "You making me nervous."

Tukey hit her left palm with her right fist. "Me can't wait to get dat little muthafucka."

For the third time, Kevin checked the clip to his 40 caliber. It pissed him off that Keith fucked with Nukey like that in the first place. Maybe now he'd stop trusting so many muthafuckas.

Nukey knocked on the door.

"Straighten your face, girl, and don't let on that we know," Keith said to Tukey. He looked at both of them until their faces were straight.

"Let him in, Tukey."

She opened the door greeting Nukey with a big warm smile. "Hey, Nuke Nuke," she said. "Come in."

The PlayStation was on and Keith and Kevin were playing boxing when Nukey came in with a fifth of Rémy in his hand. Tukey kept fixing drinks while the three of them played the game and got drunk. Nukey didn't notice that he was the only one getting refills. When Keith thought that Nukey was drunk enough, he cut off the game and invited Nukey down in the basement.

In the basement, Keith led him back to where the safe was at. Nukey's stomach began to bubble when he saw a chair sitting directly in front of the safe, surrounded by plastic.

Nukey stopped. "What's the chair for," he asked nervously.

Kevin appeared behind him. "That depends on you, Nuke."

"What you talking about?" Nukey frowned.

"If you don't tell us what we want to know," Kevin stepped closer to him, "then that's the chair we gonna torture your little ass in."

Nukey looked over at his friend Keith for help. Keith shrugged his shoulders.

"How you hurt your hand?" asked Kevin.

"I had a fight."

Kevin grabbed Nukey's hand and removed the bandage. When he finished, he pointed to the latch on the safe and said, "Grab it."

Nukey's small hand shook as he reached out to grab the latch. The scar that was on his hand matched perfectly with the line of blood that dried up on the safes door.

"You know what I think, Nukey?" Keith finally spoke. "I think you robbed the one nigga in this world who's ever looked out for you."

"I don't know what y'all talking about, Keith," Nukey pleaded. "I swear I don't."

Kevin grabbed him by the neck, and slammed him down in the chair.

"I didn't do nothin'!" Nukey began to cry.

Kevin smacked him across the face. "Shut the fuck up, liar!" Nukey started to fall out of the chair, but Kevin held him up.

"Where's our money, Nukey?" Keith asked calmly.

"I don't—" Kevin smacked him again before he had a chance to lie.

Kevin got real mad and repeatedly smacked Nukey across his face and head. "Talk nigga." *Smack. Smack.*

Nukey tried to protect his face from the hard slaps that Kevin gave him, but it didn't work. Kevin continued to punch and kick him until he looked like something ugly.

"Talk," Keith yelled in Nukey's ear but still got no response. "Aw, you a tough little nigga, huh? Tukey, bring my gun down here!" Keith spit on him. "We gon' see just how tough you is."

"I didn't do it," Nukey said through bloody, swollen lips.

Tukey came downstairs with a gun in one hand and a pillow in the other. She handed them to Keith. Seeing Nukey's mouth and face busted up made her feel good.

Gently, Tukey rubbed her hand over the scar that they put on her face when they robbed her. "How does it feel to be the bitch now, Nukey?" She reached into her bra and pulled out a switchblade knife, and opened it up. "Grab his arm, Kevin."

While Kevin held Nukey, Tukey kneeled and slowly pulled down his pants. Nukey watched in horror as she reached into his underwear and took out his little dick. "Tell us where the money is, Nukey. Me'll suck it if yu tell us." Tukey wiggled the little thing from side to side.

"I ain't got it, Tukey," Nukey cried. He knew what she was about to do with the knife. The kid inside of him was on its way out.

"Dat's too bad, Nukey. Yu could've got ya dick sucked." Tukey slashed the blade across his dick.

Nukey kicked and screamed louder than anyone they'd ever heard scream in their life. Tukey put her hand over his mouth to muffle his screams. "Ya know anyt'ing, now?"

Through all the pain and suffering, Nukey finally nodded his head.

"Who?" Kevin hollered.

"My uncle did it," Nukey blurted out as soon as Tukey removed her hand from his mouth.

"You a cold bitch," Keith told Tukey.

"One hundred percent Jamaican," she retorted in a cold tone.

Keith walked over and stood in front of the awful sight of Nukey. Kevin let him fall to the floor, where Nukey curled up into a ball.

"Where's yo' uncle now?" Keith asked.

"He....he left town this evening." Nukey held his bleeding dick.

"Where'd he go?"

Nukey shrugged his shoulders.

Tukey kneeled down beside him. "Tell us what's goin' on, Nukey."

Nukey sniffled. "They took the money and left town this afternoon after you left the house. They...they said that you was acting suspicious."

"How much did you get out the deal?" asked Keith.

"Only a couple thousand," Nukey murmured.

Tukey shook her head. She didn't believe what she'd just heard. "Dat don't make no sense. Ya fin' ta die over a couple t'ousand dollars, Nukey. Yu know dat?"

Nukey began to cry harder after hearing Tukey mention death. For some stupid reason, he thought the confession was going to save his life.

"Y'all gon' kill me," Nukey cried while snot ran out of his nose.

Keith said, "Nukey, that little stunt you pulled could cost one of us our lives in the future. And it for damn sure took yours."

Kevin picked up the gun and pillow from the floor. Nukey started kicking and screaming as Kevin forced the pillow over his face.

"Go on upstairs," Keith told Tukey.

Tukey shook her head. "Me want to see."

Never before had Keith seen such a wicked look in her eyes. He knew that Tukey was 'bout it, but he had never seen this side of her.

Tukey walked over to Kevin. "Use dis." She handed him the blade. "Ya gun will make too much noise."

Nukey's eyes bulged and his mouth fell open as the cold steel entered his stomach. Kevin put his hand over Nukey's mouth and began to stab him repeatedly in his stomach. He didn't stop until he felt Nukey's body go limp.

"Give me the knife," Tukey said. She took it and went up the steps.

Kevin wrapped the body in plastic while Keith went to get

some rubber gloves. When he returned he threw Kevin a pair.

"Grab his feet," Kevin said, putting on the gloves.

They carried the body into the garage and dumped it on top of the plastic that lined the trunk of the Cadillac. Tukey came into the garage and handed Keith the zippered plastic bag that had the broken-up knife in it.

"Me cleaned it and took it apart," she explained.

Keith threw it on top of the body. "Be back in a minute," he told Tukey. He and Kevin put on their seat belts and carefully drove off.

Chapter 12

Someone was beating loud on her front door. She'd been hearing the knocking for a while, hoping that whoever it was would go away. Brenda jumped out of the bed and stomped through the house.

"Hold on a damn minute," she said in a cranky voice. When she opened the door, she saw two sheriff's deputies standing on her porch. "May I help you?" she asked cautiously.

One of the deputies looked at a small legal pad in his hand. "Are you the mother of Fanuke Brown?"

"Yes," Brenda said slowly.

Her faced creased and tears immediately started falling down her face as she stood there and listened to what they had found. Nukey's body was seen floating naked down Brush Creek around six thirty that morning. Two kids on their way to school stumbled across the body while taking a shortcut. From what they could tell, he had been beaten and stabbed multiple times in the stomach. An autopsy would reveal the rest.

Brenda's body collapsed, but the two officers caught her in time. They helped her inside to the couch. They waited to make sure that she would be alright before they left. They knew that she wouldn't be able to answer any questions today.

Brenda lay askew on the couch and cried for over an hour. Guilt filled her heart because she knew why her son was killed,

and who did it. She should have known better than to let Nukey
and his uncles rob Keith. What mother in her right mind would
condone something like that? Now she knew the reason for
Ronnie wanting to leave town so fast. Somehow they knew that
Keith had found out and left poor Nukey to pay the price.

Hours passed before her tears began to slow. Brenda took a
cigarette out of her pack and fired it up. Something had to be
done about this. Either she was gonna go to the police and tell
them everything or...."Wait a minute," she said. She had an idea.
Call Ben.

She knew of Ben because she'd ended up spending the night
with him one day when he came over with Keith. After she threw
herself on him, he took her out to dinner, then to a hotel room.
During the little time that they'd spent together, Ben told her a lot
about his business with Keith.

Brenda knew that Keith owed Ben for the dope that Nukey
and her brothers stole from Keith. If she could persuade Ben into
thinking that Keith never got robbed and that the whole thing was
a scam, then Keith and Kevin would be joining Nuke shortly.

She removed her phone book from her drawer and searched
for Ben's number. As soon as she found it, she got him on the
phone.

"Hello," a man answered Ben's phone.

"Can I speak to Ben?" Brenda asked.

"Who's calling?"

"Tell him it's Brenda from Kansas City and it's important."
She could hear the man tell Ben that she was on the phone, in the
background.

Ben came on the line. "Hello."

"Ben it's me, Brenda." The stress was evident in her voice.

"Hey baby," Ben said. "Me haven't heard from yu in a while."

"Well I, *we*, got a problem," Brenda explained.

"How so?"

Ben listened closely while Brenda filled his head with a bunch
of lies about Keith. She told him that she'd overheard Keith brag-

ging about how he got Ben for twenty kilos of dope, using Tukey as an alibi. Then she told him about how Keith killed Nukey over a petty debt.

"You need to come down here," Brenda said. "He's planning on moving out of town in a couple of days."

"How do yu know dis," Ben asked suspiciously.

"Like I said, I was over his house when he and Kevin were talking about it."

Ben checked his Rolex. He still had an hour before noon. By coincidence he had flown home early from Jamaica with plans on going to Kansas City. But his plan wasn't to kill Keith, yet. He was gonna kill the one who meant something to him: his only sibling, Kevin. Now that Brenda was involved, things would be a lot easier to put into play. Ben would use her as bait. Even though she was thirty-eight, she still looked good enough to lure Kevin into his trap.

Ben said, "Me on me way down dere. Meet me at the airport around six."

"I'll be there," Brenda promised.

"OK." Ben hung up and prepared to leave.
* * *

Keith, Kevin, Andre and Tee went out to the Soul Bowl bowling alley with Selina and her friends. Kevin was all over her friend Maria, leaving the girl no room to breathe. Every chance they got, they would sneak away to a spot where they could freak each other like high school kids. Maria was tall for a Puerto Rican girl and hella sexy. Kevin just knew that he'd be hitting that by nightfall.

Every time Keith got up to bowl, Kevin would catch Selina and Tee giving each other funny looks. Not seductive looks, like they wanted one another, but looks of familiarity. He wanted to say something about it, but decided to wait until after he fucked Maria. He couldn't see himself blowing that ass over no bullshit.

Selina picked up her little bowling ball and stood at the top of the lane. Anyone who was looking couldn't help but see the pussy print that was bulging out of her tight-fitting capris. She bent over and used both hands to throw the ball down the lane.

"Aw, shit," Selina pouted when the ball rolled into the gutter. "I can't do it by myself, *papi*."

Keith walked over to show her how it was done. "Let me help you," he said. He got behind her and positioned her body for the proper stance. "You hold it like this. Draw back, and release it."

This time Selina threw the ball down and knocked over two pins. "Ooh, I did it, *papi*," She clapped her hands.

"You sure did," Keith said with sarcasm.

"Don't make fun of me." Selina hit him on the arm. "It won't be so funny if you don't get none tonight. Would it?"

Keith pulled her closer to him so that she could feel his dick bulging through his shorts. "You want this dick just as bad as I want some of yo' panocha."

"Maybe even more." Selina smiled and grabbed his dick.

"Girl, you need to quit," Tina, the girl who was there for Andre, said.

Selina took her tongue out of Keith's mouth and turned to face Tina. "Don't hate 'cause Andre ain't all up on you like Keith is on me."

"Hey hey hey," Andre said. "Keep me out of it."

The DJ of the Soul Bowl put on Usher's cut, "Nice & Slow", and the four *senoritas* went crazy.

"Hey, that's my song!" Selina grabbed Keith by the hand.

All eight of them got up, dancing and grinding on each other in the middle of the floor. White families gathered their kids and left so that they wouldn't be around the freaky couples. The girls that Selina brought along barely had enough clothes on to be out anyway.

As time passed, a friendly bowling game turned into a competition. The girls were on one team and the boys were on the other. The boys let the girls win in hopes of getting some pussy tonight. It was a little after nine when they finished and headed for the door. They huddled around Selina's car.

"So what y'all 'bout to do, now?" Kevin asked Selina.

"I'm 'bout to go home and wait on Keith to come over." Selina said. "I don't know what they gon' do."

Kevin looked at Maria. "So what you gon' do?"

"I'm sorry, but I have to be at work by eleven," Maria said bashfully. "But I'll be free tomorrow night."

Kevin tried hard not to let the disappointment show on his face. Even though he wouldn't be able to hit her tonight, there was always tomorrow. He gave her a hug and said, "I'll give you a call tomorrow, then."

Maria smiled; she was relieved that Kevin didn't get all bent out of shape because she had to work. She really wanted him to come over. But work was more important than dick.

"I promise that I'll make it up to you tomorrow," Maria said in a soft tone.

"We'll see."

Tee and Andre got turned down as well. The bitches were too cute for them to get mad and dog out. So they exchanged phone numbers with the girls and sent them on their way. Then all four of them jumped into Andre's Yukon Denali. The Westport area on Thursday night was normally packed with niggas and hos partying from club to club, so they headed in that direction. For the moment, Kevin couldn't get his mind off Maria.

"Damn, I'm mad I didn't get to fuck that bitch," Kevin complained.

"She couldn't fuck with that little bitch I was on," bragged Tee. "Bitch had me mad with all that faking and shit."

Andre said, "Of course she gon' act like she want to fuck when you was buying her all of them drinks."

"Dig it," Tee agreed. "I thought she was about to fuck me in the bowling alley, freaky as she was acting."

"That's enough of all that bullshit," Keith said, then cranked up Andre's radio.

People were gathered and walking in groups on the streets as they bounced from spot to spot, trying to be seen. Andre turned on his four TVs and let down his windows so the beat could be heard.

"Turn the music down for a minute," Kevin said. He could feel his phone vibrating in his pocket.

"Can't you see that I'm trying to floss?" Andre complained. He shook his head slowly while he turned down the volume.

"Man, fuck that shit," Kevin said. "Hello."

"Hi, Kevin. This is Brenda," she said in a low voice.

"Hey, Brenda what's up," Kevin said trying to sound sympathetic. "Me and Keith are gonna come by tomorrow and drop off some money for Nukey's funeral. You doing OK?"

"I'm alright, I guess. It's just....I'm here all alone and I don't think that I should be."

"Where the kids at?"

"They're over to their daddies'. They came and got 'em so they wouldn't keep getting on my nerves." Brenda sniffed. "Plus, I had to go identify the body."

"Aw yeah. What about the rest of the family?" Kevin asked, wondering where this conversation was headed.

Brenda cleared her throat. "They should be in town tomorrow."

"You want me to come over and keep you company?"

"If you ain't busy."

"Nah, I ain't busy. Give me about twenty minutes."

"OK. Bye," Brenda disconnected.

Keith was listening hard to the conversation, after he heard Kevin say Brenda's name. He couldn't wait until Kevin hung up before he came with the questions.

"What she say?" Keith asked curiously.

Kevin smiled. "She wants me to come by and keep her company."

"When?"

"Now," Kevin said. "I told her that we had the funeral covered. So she'll understand that we were about her son."

"Right, right," Keith nodded, liking that idea. "Give her my love. And tell her that I'll be by there tomorrow."

Kevin looked at the back of Andre's head. "Can you take me over to Brenda's house?"

Andre frowned. "Man, all of these bad bitches out here, and you want to go by Nukey's mama's house. What kinda sense do that make?" Andre didn't understand. "I mean she's fine. But she's no comparison to all these young hos out here."

Kevin wasn't trying to hear it. "Don't try and figure me out, nigga. Just take me where I need to go."

"Am I dropping you off?" Andre said.

"Yep."

"Good. 'Cause I gotta hurry up and get back down here."

Without saying another word, Andre whipped the truck around in the middle of the street and drove him to Brenda's. The house was dark when they pulled up. No lights were on in the house except for the little bit that was coming from the TV. Andre pulled into the driveway and honked his horn.

"Stop honking that loud ass horn," Kevin said.

"I want the bitch to come out the house," Andre said. "I want to see what she got on. To see if she called you over here to fuck or play games."

Kevin opened up the door. "It ain't like that, dog. Her son got killed last night and she just need to be with somebody right now." Kevin got out of the back seat.

The front door was open and Brenda was standing in the doorway when Kevin walked up on the porch.

"She is a fine old broad," Andre said, after seeing Brenda on the porch. "I know she can suck a good dick with them big lips."

While Andre backed out of the driveway, Keith watched Kevin and Brenda hugging in the doorway. All of a sudden a funny feeling came over him. He wanted to come in and find out just how bad she was taking Nukey's death.

"Keith, you alright man?" Andre broke his concentration.

"Yeah, I'm cool," Keith assured him. "I was just thinking 'bout something."

"Good!" Andre said. "'Cause we about to find us some pussy

for tonight."

* * *

Brenda's house had a sweet smell to it. The Temptations song, "I Wish It Would Rain", played softly while they sat and talked. When Brenda asked Kevin who he thought killed Nukey, Kevin quickly shifted the blame onto some Crips from another neighborhood.

There was silence for about ten minutes.

"Can I get your something to drink?" Brenda broke the silence.

"Yeah," Kevin said. "But don't put no ice in it."

Brenda fixed two glasses of E&J brandy. She looked back at the doorway to make sure that Kevin wasn't watching. Then she took a tube of eye drops from her pocket and added eight drops of it into Kevin's glass. She smiled as she stirred his drink. Making sure that she didn't get their drinks mixed up, Brenda picked his up with her right hand and rejoined him on the couch.

"Thank you." Kevin took the glass from her.

Brenda handed it to him carefully. This time she sat a little closer to him. "You're welcome."

Kevin downed the drink quickly. Brenda couldn't help but stare at him as she awaited the outcome. Kevin thought that she was staring at him out of lust. Suddenly, he began to feel dizzy. Then, his stomach started to feel queasy. He wanted to leave, but he felt like he couldn't move.

Kevin held his stomach with one hand and put his other on his forehead. "I think I'm 'bout to throw up," he grunted.

"You OK?" Brenda asked.

"I think I need to lie down for a minute."

"Come on," Brenda took him by the hand. "You can lay down in the bedroom."

Kevin threw his arm around Brenda and one step at a time they walked to her room. He lay flat across the bed when he felt her get into the bed next to him. Even though he was perspiring heavily, Kevin eased his hand over to Brenda's breast. He wasn't surprised when she didn't resist.

Before long, Brenda was on top of him, kissing him on his neck and face. Kevin's stomach was hurting so bad that he didn't even feel it when she pulled off his clothes.

Even though Kevin felt like he was dying, his hormones were still very much alive. His dick stood so hard that it felt bigger than normal. Brenda kissed him from his neck all the way down to his pubic hair.

Feeling her soft hand wrap around his dick, Kevin prepared himself for the warm feeling of her mouth on him. Instead, he felt something much worse. Something cold and sharp slashed through the vein in his dick.

"Ooooow! Ooooow!" Kevin screamed and grabbed his crotch.

Blood soaked his hands and the bed sheets. He rolled off the bed in a desperate attempt to get away. He was sick, in pain and screaming out of his mind when he heard the familiar voice of a man.

"Ya want to pay me now, huh mon?" Ben asked as he stood over Kevin.

Kevin opened his eyes but the Visine had his vision too blurry for him to see anything. Brenda tried to attack him, but Ben held her back.

"Did my son scream like that when you cut his dick, you cocksucker?" Brenda yelled.

Two huge dudes with dreadlocks walked into the room. Ben stepped back and watched his flunkies go to work. Even though Kevin couldn't see, he refused to go down without a fight. He got to his knees and attempted to swing at one of them. But the other dude kicked him in the head and knocked Kevin back down to the floor. Repeatedly, the flunkies punched and kicked him in the head and face. They stomped him until he remained still.

"He still breathin'," one of them said as he grabbed Kevin's legs.

Ben said, "Take him out to the car."

Brenda followed the two men while they dragged Kevin

through the house. She turned around after Ben called her back into the bedroom.

Brenda stepped into the room. "Wha—" She never heard the .38 slug that lodged into her brain and sent her body crashing to the floor.

Ben looked around to make sure that he wasn't leaving anything behind. Then he left.

* * *

Kevin woke up coughing. It was too dark to see where he was. He attempted to sit up, but hit his head on something hard and he fell back down. That's when he realized that he was in the trunk of a car. He coughed again from the smoke filling his lungs. He couldn't see the blaze, but he knew that the car was on fire. Steadily coughing, he beat and kicked at the insides of the trunk trying to get out. But it was no use. The metal had gotten too hot for him to touch.

"Helllp," Kevin screamed. "Heeeeeelp!" He knew that nobody could hear him.

The thought of never seeing his son again instantly brought tears to his face. Kevin's cough got worse. He prayed that the smoke would kill him before the fire got to him. *Your life really does flash before your eyes,* he thought, as visions of himself as a child went through his mind.

Kevin's eyes closed and the coughing stopped as his body slipped into everlasting sleep.

Chapter 13

It had been a long night. Keith stood over Selina's toilet, pissing out last night's alcohol. He had Andre drop him off at Selina's after they left the club. They spent the whole night role-playing and all kinds of kinky shit.

Keith got up early because he wanted to swing by Brenda's to pay his respects. It wouldn't look right if he didn't show his concerns about Nukey getting killed, but he knew that it would be hard to look his own victim's mother in the face.

He flushed the toilet. Selina lay naked on her back watching TV. She smiled when she saw him come through the door.

"You about to leave, *papi*?" Selina asked.

Keith slipped into his pants. "Yeah, I gotta run," he said. "You know one of my little partners got killed. I gotta run by his mom's house to pay my respects.

Selina spread her legs so that he could see her pussy. She opened and closed them slowly, teasing him.

Keith frowned and said, "I know you ain't still ready to fuck, after all that banging that we did last night." He pulled his shirt over his head. "And what possessed you to put that big ass mirror on the ceiling over your bed?"

Selina looked up at her own naked reflection in the mirror and smiled. "I like to see you while you eating my *chocha*, *papi*. Plus, I like to watch your ass muscles work when you're on top."

Keith looked up at the mirror. He smiled as a freaky thought came to him. "I didn't think of that when you were swallowing this dick last night. Next time I'ma see how yo' ass muscles work, when I'm hitting you doggy style."

"You didn't hit nothin! I won that gunfight last night," Selina bragged.

"I don't know how. I'm the one with the pistol."

Selina spread her legs open again, giving him a clear view of her pussy.

"Take a look at the size of my wound. I can take a .45 lug in there," she said proudly.

Keith's phone rang. "Hello," he answered.

It was his mama. "Have you seen the news this morning? They found Brenda dead in her house this morning."

"Nah, I didn't catch it," Keith said slowly. His stomach and head starting to hurt. He couldn't believe what his ears had heard.

"Keith," his mama shouted.

Keith cleared his throat and said, "You sure it was Brenda?"

"Yeah, I'm sure. They had her and Nukey's picture on the news this morning."

Keith was worried about Kevin, but tried to conceal it from his mother. "You heard from Kevin today?"

"No. Kim called here this morning looking for him."

"I'ma try to get in touch with him. I'll call you back, Mama," Keith tried to hurry his mother off the phone.

"You be careful, Keith," she said worriedly. "I don't want nothing to happen to y'all."

"OK, Mama."

"Talk to you later."

Keith hung up with his mother, then tried to hit Kevin on his cell phone, but the phone kept going immediately to his voice mail. *He got his phone off,* Keith thought. So he paged Kevin several times from Selina's house, putting 911 behind the number.

Selina got worried after she saw the worried look on Keith's face. She slipped into her night gown and came up behind him.

She wrapped her arms around him. "What's wrong, *papi?*" She said softly.

"Hopefully nothing." Keith removed her arms from around him and picked up his keys. "If my brother calls back, tell him I'm on my way home and to call me on my cell phone."

Keith switched on the TV in his Lexus and turned it to channel nine. He didn't want to miss anything that the news had to say about Brenda's murder. All sorts of crazy thoughts ran through his mind. Did Kevin kill her? Did Brenda's brothers kill Kevin because she knew that they were the cause of Nukey's death? Where the hell was Kevin? Keith was deeply worried abut what was next to come.

* * *

Tukey and Mi'kelle had moved all of the furniture out of their way. They needed more room to exercise, so that they could repeat everything that the aerobic instructor on TV did.

Tukey was upset and had to do something to relieve her stress. Once again, Keith left her to sleep alone last night. She knew that if she called him, he would have some bullshit excuse. So she decided to wait until he got home.

After the aerobics tape went off, she and Mi'kelle took baths, then fixed something to snack on. Tukey was on her knees, putting paper down on the floor so Mi'kelle wouldn't make a mess, when she heard the door come crashing in.

"FBI. Get down! Get down! On the ground, now!" several white men yelled as they came through the door, pointing guns. "Search warrant! Let me see your hands."

Two of the FBI agents contained Tukey and Mi'kelle, while the others searched the house.

A tall, graying white man had Tukey face down with his knee planted in her back. "Gimme yo' hands," he yelled at her.

Without resistance Tukey gave him her hands, then he roughly cuffed her. He turned her over and sat her against the wall.

The other agent said, "I'm going to take the baby outside."

"Put me down," Mi'kelle yelled as she was being carried away.

Tukey wanted to cry when she saw the huge white man taking her baby away. But she knew that this was not time to get weak. She had to prepare herself for the long interrogation that was ahead.

"Terry," one of the other agents yelled. "I need to see you in the dining room."

Agent Terry left Tukey alone for a moment. He headed into the other room where his partner was calling him. Agent Nowak was bent over a vacuum cleaner. He'd removed the cover and where the bag should have been, they found a bunch of cash packed tightly in large bills.

"There's another vacuum in the closet," Nowak said.

Agent Terry removed the other vacuum from the closet and removed the cover. Inside he found another batch of cash.

"Pack all of this shit up," Terry ordered. "Let's get her downtown, see if she'll talk."

Keith had just turned onto his block when one of the kids in the neighborhood flagged him down.

Keith rolled down his window. "What's up, li'l dog?"

The boy ran up to Keith's window, breathing hard. "The police is at yo' house," he said in between breaths.

Keith looked in every direction to make sure that he hadn't been seen. Then he quickly handed the boy a fifty and sped off in reverse. He drove backwards to the intersection, where he spun the car around. In a hurry, Keith put the car in drive, constantly watching his rearview mirror for signs of the police.

"What the fuck is goin on, now?" Keith asked himself. He tried Kevin's cell phone again. And again the voice mail came on. "Shit." He hung up to call Selina.

"Hello," Selina answered in a sleepy voice.

"Has Kevin called back yet?" Keith asked anxiously.

"Not yet baby. What's wrong? You sound funn—"

Keith hung up before Selina had a chance to finish talking.

"Damn it!" Keith cursed as he beat his fist on the steering wheel. He didn't know what was going on or what to do. Chilling at Selina's and waiting on Tukey or Kevin to call him was his only option at the moment. So he decided to do that.

Tukey's heart was racing while she nervously waited for the cops to book her. While she waited, she watched as all the cops and agents on the case high-fived and congratulated each other. They took all sorts of pictures with the cash that they confiscated from her house.

The bullpen downtown was packed with whores, junkies and women of all sorts. Tukey sat on the ground with her back against the wall and waited for her name to be called.

"Tukey Tosh, please step forward," a heavyset red-headed white woman said. She unlocked the cage door so Tukey could step out.

Tukey followed the woman to the booking counter. She was ordered to immediately strip down to her pants and shirt. She had to take off her shoes, socks, jewelry and belt, then put it on the counter to be checked in.

The turnkey didn't like Tukey's nonchalant attitude while she was being booked. Like she wasn't scared. She was used to girls crying or either making trouble after they came in.

They fingerprinted Tukey, then sat her in a small room. Three chairs, a desk and a tape recorder were the only furniture in there. Tukey waited for what seemed like an hour before the agents came through the door.

One sat while the other stood in front of her and looked down at the top of her head.

The one standing began by saying, "I'm Agent Nowak and this is my partner Agent Terry. Let me start off by saying that this is the worst day of your life. And you're only what, twenty?"

Agent Terry cut in, saying, "I know that you're scared, but trust me, things will go a whole lot better if you tell us what we need to know.

"Know about what," Tukey asked calmly.

"About the dope that your boyfriend's selling," Agent Nowak said. "Or more importantly, abut the five kilos that he was sup-posed to sell to Chris, but he never showed up. You do know his friend, Chris?"

"Yes," Tukey admitted. "But me know not'ing about no five kilos dat him was suppose to sell to Chris."

Terry stood up in anger. He sat on the desk in front of her and stared her hard in the eye. He leaned toward her and said, "We found over three hundred grand inside of y'all's house, Tukey. Three hundred grand. Now you're gonna sit here on your pretty little ass and tell me he don't sell dope?"

Tukey remained calm. "Dat's exactly what me telling ya." She stood up. "Besides, it not him house or him money."

"Tell us who's it is then, Tukey," Nowak said.

"Tell me how ya get a warrant to search me home?"

Terry cleared his throat. "Chris is a very reliable confidential informant of ours. He's made several outstanding narcotics busts for us in the past."

"And we completely trust his word," Nowak added. "That's more than I can say for you, Tukey."

Tukey looked from Agent Terry to Nowak. "Yu know what me t'ink? Me t'ink yu made a mistake. Evidently Chris gave ya the wrong information dis time, so ya kicked in me home for not'ing."

"For nothing?" Terry could not believe what he'd just heard. "We kicked in your door after receiving word from our confidential informant that there was dope in your house. We acted on it, and managed to confiscate over three hundred thousand in cash inside the home of a woman who don't even have a job. Now you tell me how we made a mistake?"

"Did ya check me background?" Tukey asked.

The two agents looked puzzled. What was she getting at? Nowak quickly opened her file that was on the table and scanned through it. When he finished, he looked up and said, "It says here that you were arrested three times for the sale of stolen merchandise and was sentenced to serve six months in juvenile. So?"

"So," Tukey began, "all you got is the money dat me made from selling stolen merchandise. Not drugs. Me been doin' it for years." She hoped that they were convinced.

Nowak looked at his partner, then back to her, and said, "You expect us to believe that you accumulated all of that money selling stolen goods?"

"Yes. And me would swear to it in open court," she warned them. "Me sure dat a jury would be convinced after the prosecutor brings up me background. Don't ya t'ink? And if dat ain't enough, me lawyer can add dat me don't have any receipts for me furniture or the t'ings dat me have locked away at me storage room." Tukey remembered that she thought someone was following her the day they went to the storage place. "Me sure ya already been to me storage place."

"How do you know that?" Terry asked curiously.

Tukey didn't speak, she only nodded her head toward the file on the desk. There was a picture of the storage room hanging out of it. Nowak saw the picture and quickly slid it back into the file.

"I bet you think you're pretty smart," Nowak said. "Let's say that the grand jury does buy your little stolen merchandise story. You'll still spend two years of your life in a federal institution."

"Think about your daughter's well being," Terry added. "Don't ruin her over trying to protect some scumbag from going to jail."

"Dat scumbag is her father," Tukey stated. "And me would rather spend two years in jail than see him spend twenty over some bullshit."

"It's your life," Terry said hotly. "I'll give you thirty days to think about what you're doing. And I bet that when you come back you'll tell us so much, we'll have to stick something big into your mouth for you to shut up."

"Me know one t'ing ya won't be able to use," Tukey pointed at Terry's crotch.

"Let's get out of here, Jeff," Terry said. He snatched the file off the desk.

Keith's head was hurting so bad that he fell asleep on Selina's couch. She was in the kitchen making tacos when she heard Keith's phone ringing. Trying to ignore it, she hummed a tune while preparing the homemade taco sauce. But it kept ringing.

Wiping sauce off her and onto the apron, she peeked into the living room. Still sleeping. She strolled over to the phone and answered it.

"Hello!"

"Who the fuck is dis?" Tukey yelled.

Selina knew that she had fucked up. So she hung up the phone and gently placed it on top of Keith's chest. Then crept back into the kitchen.

This time Keith woke when the phone rang. He answered it.

"Hello," he said sleepily.

"Me just know dat ya not sleep over ya bitch house, while me sitting in jail," Tukey said angrily. "Please, tell me ya not."

"Baby, what—"

"Me hate you!" Tukey yelled, cutting him off.

The line went dead in his ear. Keith jumped up from the couch and headed straight for Selina. She didn't bother to look back when she heard him come up from behind. He spun her around and pushed her up against the stove.

"What the fuck did you do?" Keith yelled in her face.

"Nothing. I didn't do nothing," Selina lied.

"Bitch, I'll slap the shit out of you if you lie to me again!"

Fear came across Selina's face after she realized how serious Kevin was.

"I answered it 'cause it wouldn't stop ringing *papi*," she pleaded. "I'm sorry. Please don't hit me."

Keith let her go. Before he left the kitchen, he knocked the pot of sauce off the stove. He hopped into his car and took off.

* * *

"Law Office of Brad W. Simon" is what the sign read where Keith turned into the parking lot. Inside the building, he took the elevator to the third floor. He marched right into Brad's office without saying a word to his secretary.

Brad was on the phone with a client when Keith barged into his office. Brad removed the phone from his ear and asked, "Who the hell are you?"

Before he answered, Keith shut the office door, then took a seat in one of the comfortable leather chairs. "My name is Keith Banks and I wish to retain your services," he said in a serious voice.

"Look here, Tony," Brad said to the person on the phone, "I'ma have to call you back." Then he hung up. "Now back to you. What is it that you want me to do for you, son?"

While Keith explained to him everything that he knew about what went on, Brad got on the phone and called around for the whole story. This was his field. He knew what was going to happen to his clients before it happened. No matter the outcome, he still charged a high fee.

Keith sat nervously while Brad found out what the feds had on him and Tukey. He scribbled a few notes and made a few faces while he listened. From what Keith could make out here and there, it didn't sound too bad. Except for the part about them finding the money and seizing the house.

Now Keith was broke. All he had left was his Lexus and he came there prepared to sign it over as payment to Brad. Even if Tukey left him after this, he wasn't about to turn his back on her. Not now anyway.

Keith sat up and gave Brad his full attention after he hung up the phone. "Well, I've got good news and bad. The bad news is that they've seized your house as well as over three hundred thousand in cash. And they're trying to build a case on you."

"Get to the good news," Keith said.

"The good news is, Tukey has somehow talked them into believing that she acquired the money selling stolen merchandise. They don't believe her, but as long as she sticks to her story, there's nothing that they can do to you."

"What about my daughter?"

"The grandmother's already picked her up." Brad sat back in his chair and shifted his bulk sideways. "You know that grandparents have the same rights as the actual parents in matters such as this."

Keith stood up and walked over to the big picture window that overlooked the whole downtown area. He sighed. "What reason did they have for kicking in my house?"

Brad took off his glasses and placed them inside his breast pocket. "Well they claim that they had an informant that told them about buying five kilos from you."

Keith shook his head. It had to have been Chris. You couldn't trust nobody these days.

"You have any idea who that could be?"

Keith shook his head. "A partner of mine."

Brad shrugged his huge shoulders, and said, "I see that all the time in my line of work. Now, my fee is gonna be roughly twenty grand. If she gets a bond, the hearing won't be until Monday, and it'll be a signature bond."

Keith took out his car keys and threw them on top of Brad's desk. "They took all of my money, but my car is worth more than that. The title is in the glove box. Since it's in her name, you'll have to get her out to sign it." Keith walked out of Brad's office.

Keith hopped on the bus. It was crowded and smelled of sweat and cigarettes. He found a seat near the back of the bus next to a bag lady. He was too stressed out to be complaining. All he wanted to do was hear from Kevin and that would ease half of his stress.

In all of his twenty years, Keith hadn't been through so much in one week. At the snap of a finger, he was back to square one. Only this time he didn't have a connection, his girl was in jail and his only brother could be laying somewhere dead, for all he knew.

He needed to do something. He couldn't go back to Selina's house 'cause he might end up beating her ass. Mama's house was out of the question. Keith knew that she was going to be on his nerves about Kevin. The only place left to go was over to his uncle Joe's house, so that he could sit and clear his head. Keith lay back and closed his eyes until he reached his destination.

Chapter 14

Seventy-two hours ago, Keith had it all. A new Lexus, his own home, a fine bitch and over three hundred grand stacked. All of which had vanished, just like that.

The weekend had come and gone. Keith sat on his uncle's couch chain-smoking blunts, like he'd been doing all weekend. He waited impatiently by the phone for Tukey's lawyer to call and let him know if she'd received a bond. He didn't want to be at the hearing. How could he face her? While Tukey was being taken to jail for him, he was laid up with Selina. Then to top it all off, the bitch answered his phone. Tukey still hadn't bothered to call back.

After countless phone calls and pages, he still hadn't heard from Kevin. All of their plans were shot. Keith had planned on flying down to California and taking care of Ben. Now it was too late. He had to worry about Ben coming to take care of him. Ben would come, that was for sure.

A special news broadcast came on the TV for the tenth time. Keith turned the volume up.

At around two a.m. Friday morning the fire department and police officials responded to a call from an elderly woman. She reported looking through her back window and seeing a large fire burning behind her house about a hundred yards away in a wooded area. Firefighters arrived shortly after receiving the call. The fire turned out to be a burning car. That's when they discovered a burned human body in the trunk of the car. They stated that the only way to get identification of the body was through dental records. The only teeth that remained were gold, one of them a very rare canine tooth that could possibly be identified by a family member.

When the broadcast went off, Keith closed his eyes and prayed that there was another person in Kansas City who had the same rare tooth that his baby brother had in his mouth.

* * *

Tukey was impatient and angry that the judge was taking so long to come out of his chambers. Members of her family filled the courtroom, along with the prosecutor and the two agents that busted her. But Keith wasn't in sight. Tukey was fed up with his shit, and this was the last straw. So many times she had overlooked his fucked-up ways, but this was too much. Here she was, putting her life on the line for him, and he couldn't even show up for the hearing. She had never attempted to fight him before, but if she got out on bond, there was gonna be hell to pay.

Tukey smiled and almost jumped out of her seat when she saw the double doors open. But it wasn't who she was looking for. Instead, a tall, heavy-set, graying old man came walking in with a briefcase. He went past her and stopped at the court clerk. After having a brief conversation, he came over and took the seat next to Tukey. He extended his hand to her for a handshake.

"How are you holding up, Miss Tosh?" he began. "I'm Brad W. Simon, your attorney."

"Me OK," Tukey said, relieved to see him. "Who hired yu?"

"Your boyfriend." Brad unlatched his briefcase.

Tukey got excited. "Is him outside?"

Brad smiled. He loved her Jamaican accent. He wondered to himself how these lovely young women ended up ruining their lives by messing around with guys like Keith. He'd seen this too many times in his lifetime.

Brad looked at her pretty face, and regretted that he had to let her down. He said, "No, he's not outside. He's over to his uncle's house, waiting on me to call him with the news."

Tukey's eyes dropped to the floor. She didn't want to make eye contact so that Brad wouldn't see the hurt in her eyes.

The door that led to the judge's chamber opened and the bailiff entered the courtroom. "All rise, for the Honorable Judge Albert J. Thomas, presiding."

The whole courtroom rose until the judge was seated.

Judge Thomas held the documents up and began reading from them. "Miss Tosh. You are hereby being charged with possession of over three hundred thousand dollars worth of U.S. currency, that you received from the sale of stolen property. A charge to which you've already admitted when you were arrested. Just for the record. How do you plead?"

"Your Honor." Brad stood up. "This is a bond hearing, not a—"

"I know what this is, Mr. Simon," Judge Thomas cut him off. "I'm merely asking her plea for the record. Is that alright with you?"

"Yes, Your Honor," Brad said, then sat back down.

"Once again, Miss Tosh. How do you plead?"

Tukey stood up. "Guilty, Your Honor."

"Thank you, Miss Tosh. You may have a seat." The judge cut his eyes at Brad. "You may speak, now Mr. Simon."

"Thank you, Your Honor," Brad stood again. "Your Honor, we request that Miss Tosh be released on bond into the custody of her mother, who is here in this courtroom, today. At least until this case is disposed of, that is. If the bond is granted, I'm sure my client will be more than willing to provide you with any information needed, as well as to turn over any passports that she may own. Since she has no co-defendant, we don't have to worry about any witnesses being harmed due to her release. Thank you." Brad sat back down again.

"Does the prosecution object to any of Mr. Simon's wishes?" The judge asked.

The prosecutor stood up. "Ah, no, Your Honor."

"Good! Miss Tosh, I'm gonna grant you bond," the judge said. "But you must obey all laws and report to your assigned pre-trial officer. I'm giving you a signature bond and I'm ordering you to remain in the custody of your mother. Do you have any questions?"

"No, sir." Tukey replied.

"Good! This court is adjourned."

Tukey turned to face Brad. "What now?"

"They're about to take you back to your cell, until your mother brings your clothing," Ben explained. "Then you'll sign some papers, and that's it. I'll be waiting out front when you get through."

The bailiffs uncuffed Tukey, then took her back to the holding cell. Brad had to explain to her family just what was going on. When he finished, he excused himself to make a call. Plus, he needed Tukey to sign the paper work to the Lexus.

* * *

Night had fallen. Keith, his uncle Joe and a few of his cousins played cards at the dining room table. Joe popped the top off their third bottle of Rémy Martin. Brad Simon had already called and informed Keith that Tukey had been released. Yet and still, Keith hadn't bothered to call her.

Keith wanted to stay drunk to forget about the burned body that the police had found. Earlier, his mother had called and told him that she had a bad dream and that she wanted to go look at the body. If the gold tooth belonged to his brother, then Keith would know it on sight.

Cousin Rick cut Joe's ace of hearts with a two of spades.

"Shit!" Joe yelled and jumped up. "Man, fuck this shit! I'm tired of playing cards. Let's call up some bitches, man."

Keith looked over at Joe with an irritated look. "Man, sit your ass down, bef—" The doorbell interrupted Keith.

Joe walked over to the door to look through the peephole.

"Who is it?"

"Anitra."

Joe smiled as he opened up the door. "That's what I'm talking 'bout. Let's get some women up in here."

"I need to talk to Keith," Anitra said, not trying to hide the anger in her voice.

"Keith. Somebody out here for you," Joe yelled over his shoulder.

Keith got up to see who it was. A stupefied look appeared on his face after he saw Anitra standing there.

"What's up?" he said as if he didn't know why she was there.

Anitra said, "Tukey wants to talk to you."

"Where she at?"

Anitra looked back toward the white Toyota. "In the car."

Keith looked over her shoulder at the Toyota filled with girls. Tukey was in the passenger seat.

"She gettin' out or what?" Keith was confused.

"No!" Anitra said harshly. "She wants you to ride with us over to my house, where y'all can talk in private."

Keith stared at her curiously. "She mad?"

"No. But she's scared."

He sighed. "Alright." He followed her out to the car.

"Get in the back,"Anitra ordered him.

Keith was too drunk to find the door handle. One of the girls in the back seat opened the door and stepped out. "Get in," she said, gesturing for him to sit in the middle. He got in between her and Tukey's Amazon cousin, Mendy.

Wait a minute. Something's not right about this scene, Keith thought. He was drunk, but not drunk enough to not notice the angry faces on every girl in the car.

"Why don't you pull over right her, Anitra," Keith suggested. "Me and Tukey can step out and talk."

"Me don't want to talk here," Tukey said without looking back at him. "If yu don't want to talk to me, us will take ya back to Joe's house."

"I want to talk."

Anitra drove for three blocks, made a right, drove another two blocks, then parked in front of someone's house.

Simultaneously, all four girls opened their doors and exited the car.

"I guess we're all goin' in," Keith said, then got out of the car as well.

He was nauseated and felt as if he would soon throw up. He bent over behind the car with his mouth open, waiting on something to come up. When nothing happened, Keith stood up straight. All four of the girls had made a circle around him. He blinked his eyes a few times, trying to focus.

"What the fuck are y'all—"

They all rushed Keith before he could get his words out. Tukey hit him with the first punch and knocked his drunk body back against the car. Keith covered his head as he slid to the ground, while they kicked and punched him.

"You bitches...I'm a...shit...y'all bet," Keith tried to say something intimidating, but he couldn't finish a sentence.

Somehow, he managed to get to his feet and swung his fist through the air. The girls backed off for a second. As soon as he stopped swinging, they were at him again. Anitra caught him good with a closed fist to his face.

"Ouch," Anitra screamed, holding her hurting hand.

Keith ducked Mendy's wild punches and ran to get some distance.

He laughed. "You bitches done snapped," he said, breathing hard. "Tukey, I can't believe you was in on this."

"Me can't believe yu done me dat way," Tukey yelled. "Me love yu and yu cyaah even understand dat. Me about to go to jail for yu, and yu can't even show up for court."

Mendy grabbed hold of Tukey. "Forget about him, girl. He's a loser. Look at him. He's drunk. You can do better than him."

"Listen to that shit if you want to," Keith warned. "Listening to them bitches will get you nowhere with me."

"She don't need you," Anitra hollered. "You ain't shit, pussy!"

"Fuck all you hos." Keith turned around and ran back to his

uncle's house.

* * *

The next morning, Keith, his mother and his stepfather walked out of the county morgue. Tears drenched their faces. They, along with their family dentist, had just positively identified Kevin's body. Several times his mother had almost collapsed. Together Keith and his stepfather had to carry her to the car.

"What did he do?" his mother cried loudly. "He didn't do nothing! Oh, God!"

Keith helped her into the backseat and climbed in next to her. He couldn't take seeing his mother break down like that.

At their mother's house, Keith sat alone in their old bedroom and stared at the walls. His eyes were puffy and couldn't squeeze out another tear. Visions of Kevin burning up inside of a trunk kept popping in and out of his head. His friend, partner, shoulder to lean on and only brother was gone, forever.

What happened over at Brenda's house that night? Some kind of way, Ben had his hand in this. Keith knew that for sure. But it wasn't about to go unsettled.

Chapter 15

Kevin's funeral was packed with friends, family and a bunch of nosy people hoping to get a view of his body. To their disappointment the body had already been cremated, so the casket remained closed. One by one, mourners walked by and viewed the pictures of Kevin alive that had been placed on and around the closed casket. Each gave condolences to his mother who sat weeping on the front row.

Off in the family room, next to the chapel, Keith sat alone and grieved by himself. His Armani suit became wrinkled from sitting on the hard wooden chair. Judging by the way he was dressed, in his Cartier rimless glasses and crocodile shoes, you would think that Keith was going to a club, not a funeral. His grief didn't alter his taste for fine clothes. If Kevin had not been cremated, Keith would have sent him off in the best suit that Armani had to offer.

There was a short knock on the door, then Tee stuck his head in. "Vedo wants to come in and talk to you," he said.

Keith cleared his throat and said, "Let him in."

Vedo was short and brown-skinned with a low faded hair cut. He walked in and left Tee outside the door. Keith stood and they exchanged a long hug.

"I'm sorry 'bout Kevin," Vedo said softly.

"Yeah, me too," Keith said and sat back down in the wooden chair.

Vedo walked over to the window and stared out at the cars passing by.

"I...I think I know who killed Kevin," he said without looking at Keith.

Keith slowly raised his head. "Who?"

"Jamaican Ben," Vedo said with conviction. "Matter of fact I know he killed him." Vedo turned away from the window and met Keith's gaze.

"Start talking," Keith demanded.

Vedo's head dropped. "The day before they found Brenda's body," he began slowly. "I saw Ben and a couple of big dudes pull up to Brenda's house. I was sitting in my driveway next door when they pulled up. I called him over to holler at me for a minute. Then I—"

"How do you know Ben?" Asked Keith, curiously.

Vedo looked up at Keith. "I get my weed from him."

"Since when?" Keith said surprised.

Vedo sighed. "I met him about a year ago at Brenda's house. I guess they were fucking around, or whatever. Brenda introduced us and things went from there."

"Go on," Keith said. "Tell me what you saw."

"Anyway, I asked him what he was doing in town, and he said that he had some business to handle. Later on that night, I saw him come running out of Brenda's house, pull his car up the street, then walk back down. A little while after that, I saw y'all drop Kevin off. I didn't suspect nothing at the time, 'cause I know Ben was the one who put y'all on. I thought that Kevin was taking care of some business or something." Vedo walked back over to look out the window. "Not too much later, I heard a gun shot. By the time I got up, Brenda's house was dark, and everything was quiet."

Keith jumped up and grabbed Vedo by the arm. "And you didn't think to call me, or better yet, go over there and make sure your boy was alright?" Keith said harshly. "You stupid or some-thin', nigga?"

Ashamed, Vedo shook his head.

"So you've known all along?" asked Keith suspiciously. "Why come out with it now?"

"It took me a minute to put it together," Vedo explained. "I didn't figure it out until Brenda and Kevin turned up dead."

Keith let go of his arm. "My brother's blood is on your hands. So you gon' help me set that bitch ass Ben nigga up."

"That's why I'm here," Vedo said.

* * *

That night, Keith, Vedo and Tee sat inside Vedo's Chevy Impala and discussed what to do. Keith didn't have to try hard to convince Tee to go out to LA with him to kill Ben. All he had to do was state the fact that there might be some money involved in it.

Vedo called Ben and placed an order for three hundred pounds of his Jamaican funk. He would drive down there and pick it up. As far as Keith could tell, the conversation went smoothly. Ben didn't suspect a thing.

The next day the three of them got into Vedo's mama's mini-van and hit Highway 70 going west, straight to LA. Vedo's mama wouldn't miss her car because Vedo always borrowed it for days at a time. She liked driving his Impala better than she did her van, anyway.

Thirty hours later, the three of them checked into the Mustang Motel. They unloaded their bags, which contained two AKs, a Tech Nine and a few handguns. Any other time, Keith wouldn't be caught dead on the highway with that kind of artillery. But his only brother had been killed and he didn't have time to worry about going to jail. At this point he didn't care, just as long as he got revenge for Kevin's murder. He thought about something Tupac had said in one of his rap songs: "I'll get them niggas back before you're buried."

Keith and Tee fell asleep. The long drive had taken it's toll on them. Keith's eyes slowly fluttered open after he heard Vedo's cell phone ring. Vedo's sudden whispering caused Keith to remain still and try to hear Vedo's conversation, but Vedo was talking too low to be heard. Keith yawned loudly and rolled over to alert Vedo that he was awake.

Like a man waiting in on his wife on the phone with another man, Vedo quickly hung up the phone.

"Who was that?" Keith asked suspiciously.

"Huh? Oh, that was my girl," Vedo said unconvincingly. "She's trippin' on me leaving town without her." Out of habit, he sat his phone on the table on his way into the bathroom. "I'ma take a shower real quick."

Keith got out of bed as soon as he heard the shower come on. Vedo's phone started to ring. Keith picked it up and winced when he saw Ben's number come up in the caller ID. He pressed the talk button on the phone.

"Yeah," Keith said, trying to imitate Vedo's voice.

"Vedo, dis is Ben again. Me change me mind. Me want ya to come up to the door by yaself. Leave them two suckers in the car. Me gonna take car of dem meself. Me got ya money wit' me."

"Cool." Keith tried to contain his anger. Then he hung up, furious.

A setup. Now he knew what took Vedo so long to come forth with what he knew about Kevin. That slick bastard Ben had been behind it all along.

Keith walked over to the bed to wake Tee up. He was a little groggy at first, but after Keith told him about Ben and Vedo, he woke right up. Now that they knew, they had to figure out the best way to handle the situation. And they had to figure out what to do about Vedo before he got out of the shower.

Vedo was surprised to see that Keith and Tee were up and fully dressed when he got out of the bathroom. They were sitting at the table loading clips. Vedo saw his phone sitting on the table and rushed over to get it. He checked to see if Ben had called back, but Keith had already erased the number. Vedo couldn't believe that he'd left his phone out there the whole time that he was in the shower. He was glad that Ben hadn't called back and that one of them didn't answer the phone.

"What's up, nigga?" Tee said to Vedo. "You act like you spooked or something."

"Nah. I thought that Moms had called, and I missed it," Vedo lied. "You know how she be trippin'."

"No, I don't," Tee said, smartly.

Keith gave Tee the "shut the fuck up" look. "Yo' mama know that we wit' you?" Keith asked.

"Nah. She don't even know that I went out of town. You ain't got to worry," Vedo assured him.

Tee stared hard at Vedo. "What do we have to worry about?"

"Wha? What the fuck you trying to say?" Vedo asked.

This time Keith didn't stop Tee.

Tee stood up with the loaded nine Double M in his hand. "You know what the fuck I'm saying, bitch." Tee hollered. "Nigga stop—"

"Fuck you, nigga," Vedo snapped back. "No, I don't know what the fuck you saying."

Tee pretended to turn away. Then he swung the gun and hit Vedo upside the head. Vedo fell onto the bed bleeding. He jumped up and tried to rush Tee, only to get hit again repeatedly.

"Get up, ole pussy ass nigga," Tee yelled. Tee grabbed Vedo by the shirt and slung him into a corner. Then he cocked the gun and pointed it at Vedo's head. "What you really bring us here for?"

"You know why we here, nigga," Vedo said as he held his bloody head. "Keith, what the fuck is goin' on, man?"

Keith stood up and walked in his direction. "What's goin' on is we know you was trying to set us up. I always knew you was a bitch. I just thought you was my bitch, nigga," Keith said harshly. "Now you was just gon' sell me out for some other nigga 'cause he got the dope." Keith kneeled down and grabbed Vedo by his head. "Tell me somethin', bitch. How much money did he plan on paying you?"

Vedo's breathing was heavy. "Man, I swear I ain't—"

"Lie to me," Keith interrupted, "an' that's yo' ass."

Vedo could see the seriousness in Keith's eyes. "A hundred

thousand."

"A hundred thousand," Keith repeated. "We grew up and threw up together, and you'd sell me out just like that?"

"Man, it wasn't like t—"

"Shut the fuck up," Tee said. He kicked Vedo in the stomach. "I ain't never liked yo' soft ass, anyway."

"What's his plan for me?" Keith said.

Head throbbing, Vedo spat out all the details to Ben's plan. As far as he knew, all he was suppose to do was to bring them to Ben's ranch house. Then Ben would take it from there. Vedo's money would be given to him upon delivery. Little did Vedo know that he never would've lived to spend it.

Keith had figured out the plan already from the phone conversation. Ben wanted Vedo to come up to the door by himself. So that meant that Ben planned on taking him and Tee out in the car. Which didn't make sense. If Ben was coming to kill him, why would he stay behind in the car?

"So he's at the ranch house?" asked Keith. "Cool, I know just where he at. Me and Tukey spent a weekend up there." Keith sat back down. "Call him and tell him that we're on our way."

Vedo got up slowly. He limped over to his cell phone, took a seat at the table, then dialed Ben's number. He saw Tee's fist draw back out of the corner of his eye, but he was too slow to react. Vedo felt something hard hit him on the side of his head, then blackness.

Keith looked down at the pathetic figure sprawled out over the floor. "Tie his hands behind his back. Use his shoe strings. I'll be right back," Keith said on his way out the door.

A moment later Keith came back carrying a small trash bag that he stole from a housekeeping cart two doors down. Vedo was tied up next to the bed. Tee had packed all of their bags and was wiping the place down.

Keith kneeled down beside Vedo, lifted his head, then slid the bag over his face. He tied a knot in the bag to ensure that no air could get in or out.

"Where you get that bag from?" Tee asked curiously.

"Off a cart two doors down."

Tee frowned. "You stupid or something? How you know the—"

"Relax, nigga. That cart's been sitting there since we got here," Keith assured him. "Get everything together so we can get the fuck outta here."

Just as they were leaving, Vedo woke up, kicking. Lack of oxygen had his limbs jerking out of control. He'd awakened just in time to know that he was dying.

* * *

Ben's ranch house was surrounded by a long white picket-style fence. A lengthy bumpy dirt road led up to the large four-bedroom house. From what Keith could remember, there were no cameras there.

Keith stopped the van at the beginning of Ben's long driveway. They cocked and loaded the two AKs.

"So what's the plan?" Tee asked, preparing himself for what lay ahead.

"Ain't no plan. We gon' do it like we would if we was in the hood," Keith said. "We gon' kick up in that muthafucka blasting. It won't be no more than three people here, including him. Ben don't like nobody around but his two flunkies, especially if he planned on killing us. Another thing: Vedo didn't get to make the call, so he don't know that we're here yet."

With a red handkerchief Keith wiped the rifles down, then slipped on black batting gloves. Burners are what they called them in KC.

Keith put the van into drive. "Ready?"

"Let's do this," Tee said, anxiously.

The tires kicked up dust as Keith sped up the driveway. They reached the front of the house and made an abrupt stop; both of them hopped out of the car like they were a federal task force.

Tee reached the porch first and fired rounds into the door before Keith kicked it open. A long dreadlock-wearing Jamaican hopped up and attempted to draw his gun. Tee fired several rounds into his chest and knocked him into the fireplace. Three shots were fired from the kitchen, hitting a wall next to Keith's head. Keith ducked behind the couch. In between fire, he peeked his head around the couch and saw that the man firing the gun, was hiding behind the kitchen wall. Keith sprayed the wall until he could see through it. He heard the man's body fall to the floor. Keith got up and headed for the back, signaling Tee to follow.

They both jumped over the dead man's body, which was now filled with holes. The back door was wide open, as if someone had made a fast escape through it. Keith and Tee rushed out the door when they heard the engine of a car roar to life.

"He's in the car," Keith hollered to Tee.

Tee turned around and ran to the front to try and cut Ben off if he escaped Keith. Keith had just leaped off the porch when Ben took off in his car toward the ranch entrance. Keith immediately shot at his tires. The car swerved and sent Ben crashing into a tree.

Tee ran up on the car, ready to fire if Ben made a move. "Don't move, muthafucka," he yelled as he pointed the AK at the closed window.

Keith came running up and snatched the door open. Blood ran down Ben's head from the crash. He was dazed a little, but still able to understand what was going on. He knew there was no chance that they weren't gonna kill him. So he decided to go for it.

"Jamaican funk, muthafucka," Ben yelled as he came alive. He kicked Keith in his chest. Before Tee could react, Ben grabbed Tee's AK by the barrel and kicked Tee in his stomach. Tee instantly let go of his gun.

Ben cocked it to be sure that it was ready to fire. He never heard the slugs that entered his face and sent him back into the car. While on his back, Keith had taken out his nine and fired three shots into Ben's face. Ben's body crumpled to the ground like old clothes.

Keith looked over at Tee, who was holding his stomach. "You

alright?"

Tee nodded his head.

"Good. Now help me drag his ass into the house."

They dragged Ben into the house and left his body on the living room floor. Tee found a bag full of money on the coffee table. It must have been the money that they were gonna fool Vedo into thinking that he was getting. Now it belonged to Keith and Tee.

Keith doused the curtains with cognac that he had found behind the bar. Then he set them on fire. When he was satisfied with the blaze, he gently closed the door and left.

Two miles down the road they came upon a pond, where Keith hopped out with the bag of guns and their gloves. Tee stayed inside the car. It didn't take two of them to get rid of the evidence. When Keith got out of Tee's sight, he opened the bag and removed the nine that he'd shot Ben with, and put it into his pocket. Then he threw the bag, along with the rest of the stuff, into the pond.

"You get rid of that shit?" Tee asked after Keith got back into the van.

"Yeah," Keith said. "Now hit the highway so we can get the fuck away from here."

* * *

Back in Kansas City, they pulled the van into the lot of a closed junkyard. Keith used a screwdriver to pop the VIN number off the dashboard while Tee scraped the numbers off the doors. A crowbar that they found on the ground was what they used to smash the hood in and break the windows. It only took a minute to make the van look as if it had already been there.

"You get the bag?" Keith asked.

"Right here," Tee held up the bag full of money.

"Good! We can walk over to my aunt's house to split it up," Keith said as they walked away. "Remember, if anybody ask you where you been, you wasn't with me. So you tell 'em what you want. Just keep my name out of it."

Chapter 16

Four months later

Mi'kelle woke up on the living room floor in front of the TV. After wiping her eyes with her small hands, she looked around and didn't see anyone else.

"Mama," she cried out as she headed for the bedroom. Anitra's bedroom door was closed, but Mi'kelle walked in anyway. She saw what appeared to be two bodies under the covers. "Mama," she said again, but got no answer.

Fed up, Mi'kelle turned around and went back into the living room. Quietly, she slipped on her clothes and shoes, unlocked the front door and went outside to play. Her pink bike with white training wheels was waiting for her on the grass, by the sidewalk. She looked back toward the door to make sure no one was watching, then she rode off.

Since no one was around to stop her, Mi'kelle rode all the way down to the corner of the block. She fell once, dusted herself off, picked the bike back up and started riding again.

Keith happened to be riding past when he saw Mi'kelle riding her bike in circles in the middle of the street. Mi'kelle looked up in time to see a small green car pulling over to the side. Her eyes got big and her mouth dropped after Keith got out of the car and ran toward her. She hopped off her bike and ran for the house. Mi'kelle knew that she wasn't supposed to be playing in the street. Being in trouble wasn't even a question. An ass whipping was the only way to discipline a child, to let Keith tell it.

Keith caught up with Mi'kelle right before she made it back to Anitra's yard.

"Why you running from me," Keith yelled as he snatched Mi'kelle by the arm. "You know damn well you ain't suppose to be playin' out in the street. Don't you?"

Mi'kelle answered with a nod of her head.

Keith looked up at Anitra's doorway. "Where yo' mama at?"

Mi'kelle pointed at the house.

Keith picked up Mi'kelle and carried her inside. "Hello," he called out when they entered the front door. There was no one in the living room. "Where she at, Mi'kelle?"

Mi'kelle pointed down the hallway.

Keith left Mi'kelle in the living room and walked down the hallway toward Anitra's bedroom. The bedroom door was cracked. He peeked in and saw someone moving around, so he opened the door.

What Keith saw made his stomach tighten and his temperature rise. Anitra was standing by the dresser, trying desperately to hurry into a pair of panties, while Tukey gathered all of the sex toys they had used the night before. They'd woken up after hearing Keith talking to Mi'kelle in the living room, and rushed to hide all evidence of them being sexually involved with each other.

"What the fuck y'all doing?" Keith asked harshly.

Tukey froze. She was holding a long green dildo in one hand and sex oil in the other. "Me...we...it's not what ya t'inking," she said nervously. "Me...oww!"

Keith hit Tukey with a closed fist across her face. The toys fell out of her hand as she fell back onto the bed.

"Get out of my house," Anitra yelled.

Keith wasn't trying to hear her. He picked Tukey up and punched her again. This time blood ran out of her nose. Tukey wanted to fight back, but couldn't get past the pain. Her head was spinning and she barely knew where she was. Never before had Keith hit her so hard.

Out of pure fear, Anitra picked up the lamp and threw it at Keith's head. He was too busy choking Tukey to see it coming. The lamp hit him in the side of his face and staggered him sideways. Anitra zipped by him to reach for the phone.

Blood ran down Keith's head into his eye, causing it to burn. He bent over, and felt around in a pile of clothes for something to stop the bleeding. He picked up what he thought was a towel. He didn't notice until he was finished that he had cleaned the blood out of his eye with Anitra's dirty panties.

Keith glanced over at Tukey on the bed, who was rocking back and forth. He shook his head as he left the room. Anitra had Mi'kelle in her arms and had just hung up the phone when Keith walked into the living room.

"I called the police on yo' crazy ass," Anitra yelled, backing away from him. "Now get the hell out of my house."

Keith stared at her coldly. It wasn't a nigga, but a girl that fucked his bitch. "You trifling ass bitches," he said, hotly. "In there sucking on each other's pussies while my daughter's outside playing in the street." He made his way to the front door. "I should've known yo' dyke ass was sniffing around her for something. You want to be me? Huh, bitch?"

"Just get out of my house, Keith," Anitra yelled.

"I hope y'all be happy together." Keith slammed the door on his way out.

* * *

Tukey stood in her mother's doorway and hugged Mi'kelle tightly. The day had finally come for her to check herself into a women's federal prison camp in Bryan, Texas.

She wore dark sunglasses to hide the black eye that Keith had given her the day before. She hadn't cried. The time wasn't what bothered her. The only thing that upset her was the fact that she was leaving her daughter.

Tukey said her goodbyes then got into the car with Anitra.

Anitra put her hand on Tukey's shoulder and massaged it gently. "You OK?"

"Umm hmm," Tukey said, staring out of the front window. She was trying to avoid looking back at the face of her crying daughter. "Let's just get out of here."

When they arrived at Bryan Federal Prison Camp, it didn't look nearly as bad as Tukey had expected. In fact, it looked kind of like a motel or something. It was made out of clean gray block, trimmed in red, with a red roof. There were a few buildings, but she didn't bother to count them. She would find out soon enough. The lawn looked well maintained, by inmates she was sure, and there were plenty of shade trees and flowers scattered about.

Tukey turned to Anitra and gave her a long hug and a kiss on the lips. Then she looked at the joint one more time, sighed, and went inside. In the clothing room she was stripped, measured and weighed. She was issued three khaki uniforms, towels, underwear, sheets and a pair of prison-issue boots. They made Tukey carry it all by herself as they walked her to the dorm where she would be staying.

The guard led Tukey to a bunk off in a corner by a window. A tall, heavyset woman with a pretty face lay on the bottom bunk reading the book, *True To The Game.*

"This here is your bunky," the guard said. "Her name is Niecy. And she should be able to fill you in on how things work around here." The fat guard glanced around the room and checked it for cleanliness. Satisfied with the way the dorm looked, she focused her attention back on Tukey. "Like I was saying, anything else you need to know, check the manual that they gave you in R and D." Then she left.

There were two wooden desks by the bed. Both were cluttered with books and things that belonged to Niecy. Tukey was just about to sit her stuff on top of one, when she heard Niecy speak up.

"That's my desk," Niecy said without taking her eyes away from the book.

"What about the other one?" Tukey asked politely.

"That's mine too."

Tukey dropped her stuff on the floor. "Well, what the fuck am me suppose to do? Keep me stuff on the floor?"

Niecy looked over at Tukey for the first time after hearing that Jamaican accent. That's when she noticed how tall and powerful Tukey looked. She would have been automatically intimidated if she hadn't seen Tukey's black eye.

Niecy stood and stared Tukey dead in the face. "Bitch, I don't give a damn where you put yo' shit. Keep on disturbing my reading time and you gonna get yo' other eye blacked too."

Tukey responded by smacking Niecy across her plump face. The she smacked her a second time before Niecy had a chance to recover. "Let's get somet'ing straight, bitch," Tukey said. "First of all, me not ya bitch, ya mine." All the other girls in the room stopped what they were doing so they wouldn't miss anything. "Second of all, if me want all dis space, me'll take it. And t'ird, move ya shit to the top bunk; the bottom is mine."

Niecy held her sore cheek and looked at Tukey in astonishment. Tukey threw Niecy's stuff off the desk and onto the floor. Tukey turned to meet Niecy's gaze. "If yu t'ink yu ca'an take me, get up and try it."

The other girls looked on, hoping to see more.

"Damn, I was just talking shit," Niecy said, backing down.

"Me wasn't," Tukey said, seriously. She began to put away her things. "Me here for some nigga. Dere's not'ing funny about dat."

"The same nigga that blacked your eye?" Niecy said, trying to be friendly.

Tukey slowly nodded her head.

* * *

A month later Tukey had settled in, met friends and was going on doing what she had to do to adapt to jail life. She was standing in line for mail call, hoping to receive a letter from Keith. After all that she had done for him, she was sure that she'd hear from him any day now. Once again, mail call ended without a single letter from Keith. Tukey left mail call reading the card that Anitra sent her, and a scribbled letter from Mi'kelle. It was scribbling, but she loved to read it anyway.

Niecy was braiding Shantí's hair, who sat on a pillow on the floor between Niecy's legs. Tukey came in smelling the sweet scent on Anitra's card.

"Hey hey," Shantí said excitedly. "Somebody got some sweet mail. Is it from Keith?"

"No," Tukey said, rolling her eyes. She sat down at her desk. "It's from me girlfriend, Anitra."

"Girlfriend?" Shantí and Niecy said simultaneously.

"Oooooh," Niecy said. "Somebody's a carpet muncher." She gave Shantí a high five.

Tukey looked puzzled. "A carpet muncher? What ist dat?"

"A hairy pussy eater," Niecy said. "You know what I'm talking about. Don't try to front."

Over the weeks Niecy and Tukey had become good friends. They shared everything and looked out for each other. Whatever one had, the other had also. Niecy even tried to lock her hair up in dreadlocks like Tukey. Niecy was from Minnesota and had already done six months when Tukey got there.

Shantí and Tukey had also become good friends. Shantí was short, about 5'4". A "redbone" is what the boys on the streets called her. Her freckled face and pigtails made her look younger than her twenty-two years. Like Niecy, she was serving a sentence for check fraud.

"Me don't eat pussy, so me not a carpet muncher," Tukey checked them. "Me get me pussy ate." Tukey laughed on her way out of the dorm.

* * *

Tukey woke up that morning from a nightmare. She dreamed that some man had taken Mi'kelle and had done strange things to her. Suddenly she heard a soft moan coming from the top bunk. "Ummm....ummm." A slight vibration rocked the bed gently. Quietly as she could, Tukey slid out of bed and jumped up. She caught Niecy with her legs open and her hands under the covers.

"What yu doin'?" Tukey asked, though she already knew the

answer.

Niecy's eyes popped open at the sound of Tukey's voice. She blushed; she was too embarrassed to answer so she just lay there, unable to respond.

"Dat's OK, girl," Tukey said. "Not not'ing wrong wit' touching yaself. Me do it all the time." Tukey got back into her bed.

Niecy breathed a sigh of relief. The last thing that she wanted to do was get sexual with another woman, and she was glad that Tukey didn't approach her like that. If Tukey was a dyke, that was her business, but Niecy wasn't trying to head in that direction.

* * *

The next day, Tukey was folding clothes in the laundry room. That was her job while she was at the camp. After four weeks she still hadn't gotten good at folding clothes and Shantí had grown tired of showing her how. Over and over, Shantí took Tukey through the process of folding sheets, but Tukey was too busy trying to hold on to the manicure that she got before she came to jail.

A girl that they called Butch got fed up with Tukey holding up progress. So she stepped to Shantí about her problem. "Why can't yo' African friend here get it right, Shantí?" Butch said.

Tukey looked over at Butch, who worked out and outweighed her by at least twenty-five pounds. She had a deep voice and wore a box-style hair cut. That was one of the reasons whey they called her Butch, among other things.

"She gon' get it right," Shantí said, trying to keep the peace.

Tukey stepped in front of Shantí and stared Butch dead in her eyes. "Me don't need ya to take up for me, Shantí," Tukey said. "If bitch, me mean Butch, got a problem, let her take it up wit' me."

Butch looked up at Tukey, who towered over her by two inches. "Bitch, I been having a problem with yo' fake accent-talking ass. You walk around here all day like yo' man gon' come see you." Butch put her hand over her own mouth. "Oops, my bad. You ain't even got a man. You got a wo-man."

Everybody in the room started to laugh.

Tukey found it amusing herself. "Ya want to eat this pussy,

don't ya, Butch?" Tukey said with a half smile on her face.

Butch looked at her and pretended to be disgusted. Deep down she wanted to say yes, but her ego kept her from saying so. She was jealous of all of the attention that Tukey got from the other girls.

With her hand on her hips Tukey walked around Butch and looked her up and down. "Umm hmm. Me bet yu would love to get a taste of me fat, chocolate, creamy Jamaican pussy." Tukey leaned close enough to her ear so Butch could hear her whisper, "Here, kitty kitty kitty."

Butch pushed Tukey away. She drew back her fist, ready to swing, but the guard walked in, hollering, "Tukey Tosh! You got a visit." Tukey stepped up. "The rest of you skanks get back to work." The guard waited until everyone started working again before she and Tukey left.

Back at the unit, Tukey showered and got dressed. She made herself look as good as possible in the government-issue uniform. She was nervous, hoping that Keith was waiting in the visiting room to surprise her. She hadn't seen her man in so long and she couldn't wait to get her hands on him.

To her surprise, when Tukey got into the visiting room, Anitra was sitting in a chair by the vending machines waiting on Tukey to come out. Tukey was upset at first, but the fact that Anitra had come all this way to see her brought joy to her heart.

Tukey ran over to Anitra with her arms out. "Hey, baby," Tukey said. Anitra got up to embrace her.

"I've missed you so much." Anitra held Tukey at arm's length, trying to get a look at her. "You pickin' up some weight, girl."

"Me hope in all the right places." Tukey spun around for her. Anitra stared at her like she wanted to kiss Tukey. Tukey read the look on Anitra's face and became nervous. She glanced around at all the nosy visitors in the room who were watching them. *Fuck it,* Tukey thought. *Ain't nobody in that room ever did nothing for me.*

They hugged and kissed each other like it was their first time. The other visitors became immediately disturbed that they'd done such a thing while kids were around. The guard in the visiting room went over and spoke with them to satisfy the angry looks on the rest of the visitors' faces.

For hours Tukey and Anitra sat and talked about the streets, what was going on out there, had she seen Keith and etc. At times Anitra even snuck in a few feels, which Tukey stopped because she feared that one more incident would get her written up. A write-up meant a shot in prison terms, which could lead to a loss of good time.

Anitra bought a sandwich and a bag of chips for Tukey out of the vending machine. "Here you go," she said sitting it on the table.

Tukey took a few bites of the sandwich then set it down. "Keith got a new bitch out dere now, huh?"

Anitra frowned. "Girl, why are you so concerned about Keith's trifling ass? Shit, look how he treated you," Anitra tried to explain. "If I was you, I—"

"Just tell me, Anitra," Tukey cut her off.

Anitra sighed. "Look, I don't know for sure, but the word is that he's done moved in with some Puerto Rican bitch."

"Him what?" Tukey said a bit too loudly.

Anitra looked around at everyone staring at them.

Tukey said, "Ya mean to tell me him still messin' wit' dat tramp bitch?"

Anitra nodded.

Tukey shook her head. "Me can't believe dis," she said in a weak voice. "Me in jail for him. Me go get drugs for him. Me give me life for him and him leave me for a not'ing-ass bitch." Tears formed in her eyes.

Anitra threw her arms around her. "Girl, you got to put Keith behind you. Whatever y'all once had is over and done with. Now you're experiencing the real Keith. You can't do nothin' for him, so he don't need you."

"How's Mi'kelle?" Tukey asked as she wiped tears from her eyes.

Anitra smiled. She was happy to be done with the Keith conversation. "She's doing real good. Lately, she's been spending more time at the swimming pool than anything," Anitra informed her. "Her and Arie been kickin' it. She's suppose to send you some pictures sometime this week."

"God, me miss her," Tukey complained.

Anitra held Tukey's hand, smiling. "She misses you too. I'm a try to bring her up with me, next time that I come."

They said their goodbyes, then the guard escorted Tukey back to the unit.

* * *

After sitting for two hours watching the institution movie, the girls sat around playing Spades, eating nachos that Niecy made, and telling stories about their street lives. Shantí gave Niecy the finger and said, "Girl, I couldn't see myself fuckin' one of those niggas you fuck with, anyway."

"Why not?" Niecy asked, defensively.

"I can just look at them broke-dick-lookin'-ass niggas in your picture book and tell that they ain't got nothin' going on," Shantí said. "And yo' boyfriend, Bugga Bear. What kinda name is that? He look more like a booty bandit."

Everybody in the room fell out laughing.

Niecy stood her ground. "He might be. 'Cause every time he gets through fuckin' me in my ass, I need a booty bandage."

"I said booty bandit."

"Whatever."

Another girl who was sitting at the table with them, named Kelly, joined in the conversation. "Tukey, why don't you tell us about you? What were you doing on the street?"

"Yeah, tell us Miss Keisha off *New Jack City*," Niecy joked.

"Keisha off of *New Jack City*?" Tukey said, confused.

Niecy said, "You know the girl that said, 'Rock-a-bye baby'."

Tukey laughed. "Girl, yu need to stop." Tukey tried to continue playing cards, but the girls just stared at her. "What?"

Kelly said, "Girl, we know all of you Jamaicans be into the

shoot'-em-up, drug dealer, gangbang type of shit. Stop all that fakin'."

"Did Keith have a monster or what?" Niecy asked.

"What is a monster?" asked Tukey.

Niecy sucked nacho cheese off her fingers. "A big dick," she said plainly. "I heard them Jamaicans got dicks big as dildos."

Tukey sat down her cards. "For ya information, Keith ain't Jamaican."

"Oh, well, that explains it," Niecy said. "Niggas hate to visit a bitch in jail."

"You sho' right about that," Kelly agreed.

"Really, Tukey, tell us about yo' life," Shantí begged.

"OK, OK," Tukey gave in. "But no questions until me finished."

"Me finished," Kelly mocked her. "God, I love your accent."

"Hush, now," Niecy said. "Let her talk."

Kelly, Niecy and Shantí sat quietly like children being read a book, while Tukey took them through her life. Tukey started from the first time that she saw Keith. How sexy he looked in his football uniform, and how she bled after he popped her cherry in the back seat of his mama's car. She also told them about her uncle Ben and how he put Keith on in the dope game. The trips she took on the planes back and forth to LA, with hundreds of thousands of dollars taped to her body. They all almost cried after Tukey told them about what happened to Kevin. The part about her getting turned out by Anitra, though, really got their attention. They laughed and clapped after Tukey told them about the time she and her girls jumped on Keith while he was drunk. Then they almost cried again after she told them what happened to her when Nukey and his uncle robbed her. She ended the story with the part about the feds kicking in her door, taking everything. The reason why she was there today. Eventually she took the case, Keith left her hanging and that was it.

Tukey didn't even think about telling them the whole story about Nukey, even though it would've gotten her much respect.

The fact remains that ninety percent of federal inmates are snitches. So she kept her mouth closed on that subject.

When Tukey finished, her audience sat there, speechless.

Kelly broke the silence. "So you are Keisha off *New Jack City*. Girl, I'd kill to have lived yo' life. All that money."

"What?" Niecy said. "Fuck that. She need to be plotting on killing Keith's scandalous ass." Niecy was upset. "Sorry muthafucka."

Tukey put her arm around Niecy's back. "Calm down, baby," Tukey said.

"I'm serious, Tukey. He owes you a lot. If he ever gets his money right again, you ought to get his ass for everything. You deserve it."

"Amen to dat," Tukey said under her breath.

Chapter 17

Keith stashed his half of the hundred grand that they took out of Ben's house in a storage room, several months ago. Since that time, he had been staying with Selina in Kansas, working as a construction laborer for her uncle Pablo. Selina was happy with Keith working and the fact that he came home every night made it all good. But little did she know, Keith was anything but happy with the situation.

The only reason for him going to work in the first place was so he could lay low for a while so he could get his head together. Plus, Keith didn't want to catch no heat about Ben's murder. If the cops did figure out that his killers were from Kansas City, they'd be looking for a drug dealer, not a man who went to work everyday.

As expected, it didn't take Tee long to run through his half of the money that they took from Ben. Now he was back to depending on Andre to help him out here and there.

By now, Keith had fallen in love with Selina. Surprisingly, he never even brought up Tukey's name. Ben's murder had a lot to do with it. Then again, Keith felt guilty for leaving her in jail like he did. Or maybe it was because Selina was a wild beast in the bedroom and did everything that Keith told her to do. He only had to put his hands on her one time since they'd been together. When he asked about her baby's daddy, Selina quickly snapped on him and said things that she had no business saying. To make sure that it would never happen again, Keith slapped her and knocked her clean across the room. Like women do every time they get mad at a nigga, Selina put him out of her house. Keith returned a week later and apologized for hitting her. Then, after a good fucking, everything went back to normal.

The job of a construction laborer was becoming to be too much for Keith to cope with. Getting up every morning at six o'clock and not getting off until two in the afternoon. Even when it was cold outside they had him out there building scaffolds and hauling bricks back and forth. It was hard work for a man who was used to selling dope for a living. The eight hundred dollars a week that he was making would have been something to the average man. But Keith was bigger than that. Every day that he woke up, he worked on a plan to get back in the game and get rich or die trying.

There were a bunch of young dudes Keith's age and younger who lived in the same apartment complex as he and Selina. They were low-income, run-down apartments on the edge of poverty. There was a lot of drug dealing around, but nothing major was going on around there. Nothing that any real nigga with a few kilos of that white lighting couldn't take over. The complex had Keith's name written all over it, and it was just a matter of time before he would be back in business.

Keith wasn't sure yet, but he had an idea that Selina's uncle Pablo was into more than construction. Pablo had a big semi truck that stayed parked on the construction site at all times. A couple times a week, Keith would see Pablo or one of his boys open the back and haul out big wooden crates. Then the truck would disappear for days. Then it would return and they'd be hauling crates out again. Funny thing was, Keith never saw them use whatever was inside of those crates at the construction site. They would always take the crates somewhere else to open them.

Every day after work, Keith would stop and chat with the corner hustlers who lived in the neighborhood. He was baiting them to be future workers in the new drug ring that he was going to form. He kept a small red notebook in his dresser where he wrote all of his notes for what he was about to do. Keith really felt that this time his dream of being rich would come true.

A self-made millionaire.

The next day, the manager was in Pablo's trailer, passing out checks. Keith opened his up and let out an intentional sigh.

Pablo looked up from his desk. "What's wrong, my friend?" Pablo asked with a gold-toothed smile. He was a tall Puerto Rican, standing just over six feet. He had naturally red hair and freckles scattered underneath his cold eyes. To Keith, he looked to be about forty or so.

"Peanuts," Keith complained. "Ain't worth my hard work. I've got a family to feed."

Pablo eyed him carefully. He sat back down at his desk and leaned back in his soft leather chair. "You know my friend," Pablo began. "These days money ain't hard to get. I think you know what I'm saying." Keith nodded his head in agreement. "Some people work hard for it, and some don't."

"How'd you start your own company?" Keith proceeded with the conversation.

Pablo smiled. "I'm sure you already have your own assumption, *amigo*. So why don't you tell me what you think?" He removed a cigar from his breast pocket.

"Drug money," Keith said in a low voice.

Pablo smirked. "I knew this day would come, my friend. I can tell by that hungry look in your eye, man." Pablo stood up and faced a window. Through it, he could see the rest of his workers going home for the day. "I saw you," Pablo said. He turned around to face Keith. "You were watching my trailer out there real close one day. And I said to myself, either this guy wants in on what I'm doing, or he's a cop with a death wish."

"I hate cops," Keith assured him.

Pablo sat down again. "My niece told me all about you. And from what I hear, you got ambition. Ambition goes a long way in my line of work."

"I ain't a stranger to having money, Mr. Zaragoza."

"Then tell me what it is that you're looking for."

"A connection, a plug; you know, somebody to back me up. It's gonna take a man with dope as long as Prospect to assist me with what I'm about to put down. Word on the street is that it's dry right now. With the right connection, I could take advantage of this situation and go straight to the top."

Keith knew that he was being given the opportunity to sell himself, and that this would be his only chance at getting next to the man.

Pedro took out a pen and started writing something on a small piece of paper, then handed it to Keith. "Come up with all of the cash that you can. Then give me a call."

Keith smiled as he took the number from Pablo. "*Grácias, amigo.*" Keith was headed for the door when Pablo called out his name.

"Keith," Pablo said. Keith turned to look at him. "I don't believe in droughts, *amigo.*"

"That's good to hear," Keith replied. Then he left.

He stopped by the store on his way home to pick up a bottle of Rémy to celebrate. Some of the young corner hustlers that he spoke with the other day were standing at the counter, buying the same thing. Keith could tell by the brown Carhart jumpsuit that one of them was wearing that he was about to post up on the corner for the night. The jumpsuit and the drink would keep him warm while he stood out there waiting for customers to drive up. Keith knew 'cause he'd been there himself.

After he shelled out $42.00 for the fifth of Rémy and a cup of ice, he ran out to his old truck to try and catch up with Mann, the dude in the jumpsuit. Mann was walking about a half a block from the apartment complex when Keith saw him. He honked his horn. Mann turned around immediately recognized the old pickup. Keith lived just next door to him.

Keith rolled down his window. "Get in, nigga."

Mann had to lift the truck's old passenger door just to get it open.

"Slam it hard," Keith told him after he saw that Mann was having trouble closing it. Mann kept slamming the door, but it still wouldn't close. "Hold on." Keith got out of the truck, walked around to the passenger side, he jiggled something on the inside of the door, then slammed it shut.

"You need to fix that shit, man," Mann complained after Keith got back in. He was emptying the tobacco out of a cigar that he was about to roll. Mann was a slick-looking dude. Brown-skinned, tight face, not very tall, but his frame was what a woman would call sexy. He stayed in the townhouse next door to Keith, with a fine-ass girl named Nia. Nia was fine as hell, about five-six, long hair, honey-colored skin and a big ass. She reminded Keith of Faith Evans: kind of funny-looking, but fine.

"I'm incognito in this truck." Keith pulled away from the curb.

"So when you gonna start getting down?"

Keith turned the heat down. "I just got through hollering at my plug a minute ago," Keith said. "So it's gonna be real soon."

"Ah yeah?"

"Yeah! I've been tryin' to get that fat ass manager at the front office to rent me them two vacant townhouses across from us. If she comes through with that, then we gon' sew this bitch up."

"Shit, man, I'm down for whatever," Mann said. He took a lighter out of his pocket, fired the blunt up, took a hit, then passed it to Keith. "I'm ready to make some real money. Fuck this corner shit."

Keith pulled into the parking lot of the complex. He took out his bottle of Rémy, poured a shot into his cup, downed it, then poured another one. "This is what I want you to do," Keith said. "Gather up all of the guys around here corner hustling. Then bring them by my pad when I get home from work tomorrow."

"Alright," Mann said. "It's a done deal."

The house was clean from top to bottom. From the kitchen

Keith smelled chicken frying on the stove. As soon as she heard him come in, Selina flew from the kitchen with her arms out. She helped him out of his work clothes, then led him to the bathroom, where a tub full of hot water and bubbles awaited him. After Selina helped Keith into the tub, she ran back to the kitchen to tend to her chicken. Keith soaked for about an hour thinking about Kevin. How he wished that there was some way to bring him back. What Keith was about to put down was something from the old school. Some late eighties shit that he used to see on TV. He only wished that Kevin was here to be a part of it. Without him, nothing seemed right anymore. Keith finally got out of the tub after he heard Selina call his name for dinner.

"Time to eat, *papi*," she yelled from downstairs.

Their three-bedroom, two-bathroom townhouse was nice. It was the surrounding area that made it look fucked up. The neighborhood used to be flooded with dope and ballers back in the day. But the spot got too hot and the police ran everybody off. Some went to jail and some just relocated. Naturally, the young kids grew up and now they were selling drugs on the same corner. Only now there was no leadership around; no one to show them how to do things right. That's where Keith came in.

Keith came down the steps in his green terry cloth Polo robe that Selina bought him for his twenty-first birthday. Chicken, green beans, macaroni and cheese and a glass of Rémy Martin sat on a TV tray in front of the TV.

"Sit down, baby," Selina said. "I wanna rub your feet while you eat."

After he finished his dinner, Keith called Mi'kelle to let her know that he'd pick her up when the week ended. He loved his daughter and wished that he could spend more time with her. But right now he was on a mission and he didn't have the time.

"What's on your mind, *papi*?" Selina asked. She knew that Keith was only quiet when something was on his mind.

"I'm quitting my job tomorrow," Keith said plainly.

A frown appeared on Selina's face. She squeezed a tender spot on his foot.

"Ow!" Keith yelled, snatching his foot out of her hand. "What the fuck you do that for?"

"'Cause you promised," Selina said hotly. She got up and stomped into the kitchen.

Keith followed. Selina had already started washing the dishes when he came into the kitchen. He came up behind her and wrapped his arms around her waist.

"What's wrong, baby?" he asked, already knowing her answer.

"You know what's wrong," Selina said. She poked him in his stomach with her elbow, then let go of the dish that was in her hand and turned to face him. "You promised me, *papi.*"

"I know I did, but—"

"But what, huh?" Selina's voice was angry. "You ain't satisfied with going to work and coming back home to me everyday?"

"Stop hollering! Terry might hear us."

"He's over to his daddy's house," Selina said in a low voice.

Keith stared at her with suspicion for a moment. "His daddy's house? I thought you said you didn't fuck with his daddy?"

"Yeah, well," Selina looked down at the floor. "He called and said that he wanted to see his son. What was I supposed to do?"

"I wonder why I've never met this cat," Keith turned to walk away. "You know what? I don't even give a fuck."

Selina followed Keith into the living room. "My baby daddy ain't the subject. The subject is you and your lies."

Keith was sitting on the couch with his feet up now. "You know what? You got a bad fuckin' mouth."

"Fuck you!" Selina stuck up her middle finger.

Keith sighed. "Look, baby. Either you wit' it or you ain't. It's simple as that."

Deep down, Selina didn't mind him getting back into the dope game. She missed Keith the baller. The one she fell in love with. Wanting a regular kind of guy was the lie she'd convinced herself that she wanted. But Selina really knew otherwise. Still, she had to pretend that she wasn't with it.

"Just be careful," Selina gave in. "I don't want you to end up like Kevin did."

Keith got up from the couch and hugged her.

"Kevin was something different." Keith held Selina tight. "That's not gonna happen again." He pulled back so that he could see her face. "I'm gonna make everything right. You'll see."

* * *

They had made love for about an hour. Keith lay knocked out with his feet hanging off of the bed. Selina's eyes popped open. She reached over and touched his chest to make sure that he was asleep. Keith didn't move. Easing out of the bed, she slipped on Keith's robe and house shoes. Then she quietly tiptoed down the steps. Careful not to make a sound, Selina picked up the phone and started dialing numbers.

"Hello," some man's voice answered the phone.

"This is Selina. How's my baby?"

"Girl you ain't got to call here," he snapped. "This my son too."

Selina went quiet for a moment. "I'm gonna tell Keith about us," she said, finally.

"What you gon' do some shit like that for?"

"Because," Selina explained, "I think I'm in love with him."

"Look, Selina," the man began to explain. "The only reason that I let you fuck around with that nigga in the first place was so you could rob his ass for me. Now you—"

"Well, he ain't got no more money," Selina reminded him. "So ain't no reason for—"

"Believe me," he pleaded, "he'll bounce back, it's just a matter of time. You think he's happy staying there with—"

Selina heard footsteps and hung up the phone. She turned around to find Keith standing behind her with an accusing look on his face. Not sure of how much of the conversation he heard, she didn't know what else to say but, "What are you doing sneaking up on me?"

"Why did you sneak out of bed and come all the way downstairs, just to use the phone?" Keith said with a serious look on his face. "Somethin' you trying to hide?"

His calmness scared Selina.

"No. I just didn't want to wake you up." She kissed him on the cheek, hoping that would calm him down. "Come on baby, let's go back to bed." She took his hand. "I'll do that thing you like."

* * *

When Keith showed up for work the next morning, he saw Pablo sitting in his Navigator, talking on his cell phone. Pablo honked his horn when he saw Keith standing there. Keith got into the front seat and without so much as a hello, Pablo drove off.

They drove to a popular Mexican restaurant on the west side. The Westside was the part of town where mostly Mexicans and Puerto Ricans lived. Occasionally you'd see a few blacks scattered about. The neighborhood wasn't run down, but it wasn't what you would call nice either.

Most of the big-time black drug dealers who didn't have an out-of-town plug either got their dope from the Westside or the Mexicans over in Kansas. The people on the Westside may have looked poor, but there was probably more money on the Westside than any other side in the city.

The restaurant was half-empty when Pablo and Keith stepped inside. They stashed themselves in a quiet booth off in a corner and waited patiently until a small Mexican waitress came over to take their orders.

"*¿Qué gustaría comer?*" she asked as she placed two menus on the table.

"I'll have the *picadillo con huevos. Grácias*," Pablo said before closing up his menu.

"*¿En qué puedo servirle?*" She gave her attention to Keith.

"What do you want to eat?" Pablo helped him out.

"Aw, OK," Keith said, finally understanding. "Let's see. I'll have some eggs, coffee and a couple slices of toast."

Pablo translated what Keith said in Spanish for her.

The waitress smiled. "*Grácias, señor.*" She took the menus on her way to the grill.

"They only speak Spanish here?" Keith asked.

Pablo shook his head. "She's probably new. Or she don't like you," he joked.

Keith shifted in his seat to get comfortable. "So why are we here?"

"To discuss business in a nice environment," Pablo said. He offered Keith the chips and salsa that were already sitting on the table as an appetizer.

Keith declined. "I'm listening."

"You can make a lot of money fuckin' wit' me, my friend. I got connections from California to New York." Pablo fired up a cigarette. He held the smoke in for a minute, then slowly let it out. "Have you ever seen a ton of cocaine?"

Keith whistled. "No, sir I don't believe I have," Keith said. "But I'd like to believe that I was on my way to seeing one, before all of that bullshit started happening to me."

"You could be sitting on millions and you couldn't buy a ton of cocaine if you didn't have the right connections." Pablo shook his head. "Money ain't worth nothing if you can't make it grow."

"What do you have in store for me?"

Pablo put out his cigarette. "You start out buying from me. Then when the time is right, I'll take it from there. Think you can come up with, say...fifty grand?"

"For what?" Keith asked curiously.

"Show of good faith," Pablo said. "To let me know that I'm dealing with somebody. Not just some punk looking for a handout."

"I'll get the money," Keith assured him.

"Good!"

* * *

Keith stuck key number 136 into the lock to the storage room and turned it. He opened the door and stepped inside. From the pillow of an old couch he pulled out a green plastic bag. He stuck his hand inside and removed one of five stacks of cash that was in there.

Fifty thousand was Keith's split from the money that they took from Ben. Instead of ducking it off, he saved it until he was ready to really get back into the game. He felt like luck was on his side for sure this time. He lost Ben only to gain Pablo. Who could complain?

Mann and four other dudes were sitting on Selina's steps when Keith pulled up in his old truck. Keith smiled at the sight of them sitting there, waiting on him like loyal soldiers. Their being on time for the first meeting was already a sign of good faith.

The five of them followed Keith inside and took seats on the couch. Keith waited until Selina passed out cups of Rémy before he took the floor. Standing in front of the fireplace, he asked Mann to introduce him to everyone. There was Twain, a short stocky dude with braids; Rock was tall and muscular and would also be the one that Keith would choose to be the muscle; Blue, with whom Keith was already acquainted; and last, there was Capone, who was also short and stocky. In the past, Keith personally witnessed several ass whippings that Capone had given to other dudes in the neighborhood. Mann would be Keith's right hand man.

"First off, how much cash are we working with?" Keith said.

The only one of them able to come up with more than a grand was Mann. Their money came up to about twenty eight hundred total, which they were instructed to hand over to Selina.

"Now," Keith went on, "before I announce what my plan is, is there anybody here that don't want to be a part of it?" He looked around, but no one spoke up. "'Cause once you're in, you're in. I don't want to hear no bullshit, 'cause I won't tolerate it." He waited for his words to sink in. "Right now I'm working on getting the two townhouses across the street from my place for us to work out of. That way, I can keep an eye on you. The money that y'all turned in today will go toward getting those townhouses. Weight will be sold out of one, and twenties and fifties will be sold out of the other. I expect all of you to direct every one of your customers to the piece house, and anybody you know that buys weight, to the weight house." Keith's voice rang with authority. He knew what it took to run such an operation: it took leadership. A leader couldn't show any signs of weakness 'cause the followers would just take advantage of it.

Keith went on. "Cooking the bread. Does any one of you know what that means?" They all looked at each other, but nobody seemed to know. "That means stacking dollars. Bread is money and you don't take the bread out of the oven until it's finished. For the first two months the only payment that you'll receive from me is nothing."

They all looked crazily at each other, hoping that one of them would say something. "I'll feed you," Keith continued, "pay the rent and bills. But no one, and that includes me, will spend a dime until the first batch of bread is through cooking."

Keith took his red notebook from atop of the fireplace. After he referred to his notes, he went on speaking. "I know y'all tired of standing on that corner, hustling day and night. And after all that hard work, only coming home with a few hundred dollars. Meanwhile, cats from other 'hoods roll through here on Daytons and shit, flossin' on y'all. I promise you, if you stick with me, that day is over. After the first two months, I'll give each of you $1,500 bonuses to take care of your business with. Then, we're gonna continue to cook the bread some more, at least until mid-summer. Then I will personally buy you the car of your choice, put it on rims, plus a beat package from Loud and Clear."

Selina smiled while they clapped and cheered Keith on. Keith raised his hand signaled them to be quiet. "I know right now it don't seem like much. Yo' friends gon' say stuff like, 'man they stupid for working for that nigga.' They'll laugh at you. But wait until the summertime. You'll be riding through their hood on Daytons, making a grand a week. That's more than you ever made petty hustling on that corner out there. That's more than your mama, daddy and your grandmas ever made." Keith put his hand on Mann's shoulder.

"Of course Mann here will be making twelve hundred a week, since he's my second in command." Keith smiled. "I know that there will be times when y'all will try and question how much money I'm making, and that's cool. Just remember, it's what, five of y'all? At a thousand dollars a week apiece, that over a quarter of a million dollars a year out of my pocket. Not to mention bills, bonds, cars and clothes for y'all."

Keith looked around the room and saw the seriousness in their faces. They had already taken the bait. The rest was up to Keith. "It's simple," Keith went on. "You can roll with me, or you can stay stuck in the same position, like you've been doing. Probably for years."

Not one of them disagreed with Keith. In fact, they were already picturing the new lives they were about to have.

Keith looked over his notes one last time to make sure that he wasn't forgetting anything. "Just a few more things, then I'll be through," he said to regain their attention. "Some kind of way, and I don't know how yet, we're gonna get the other two town-houses next to the two that we're gonna be getting. That way, we can expand without worrying about nosy-ass neighbors."

"You mean, like maybe having a weed spot too?" Mann asked.

"Whatever's poppin'," Keith said. "Weed, meth, I don't give a fuck. Getting paid is our objective."

"When do we get started?" Twain said.

"Mann and I will get in touch with y'all within the next few days. Until then, put out the word."

Selina had to add her two cents. "One last thing," she said. "I'll do my part and make sure y'all have plenty of bitches to keep y'all company."

"Bet," Twain said on their way out the door.

Keith snatched his car keys up from the table. "I'll be back."

"Baby," Selina called.

Keith turned around. "What's up?"

She smiled. "You a cold piece of work. You see how they was eating that shit up?" She wrapped her arms around him. "I love you."

"I just bet you do." Keith broke away from her. He patted her on the ass. "Be right back."

He drove up to the front office and parked behind Dawn's car. Dawn was the manager of the apartment complex. She was cute, but a little too overweight for Keith's taste. She was determined to get a piece of Keith despite Selina. Usually he wouldn't give her the time of day. But he knew he had to do what he had to do, if he wanted those two townhouses.

Keith checked his waves before he walked into her office. Dawn was sitting at her desk smiling from ear to ear when she saw Keith's sexy ass walk through the door. She loved how lean and muscular he looked in his work clothes. She preferred him to be dirty when he fucked her.

"Hey, boyfriend!" Dawn stood up and straightened her clothes. They hugged and for the first time, Keith kissed her on the mouth.

"Ummm," Dawn moaned softly. "What was that for?" She was surprised that he'd actually kissed her like that.

"Just for being you," Keith said coolly.

"Yeah, right," Dawn let go of him. She picked up a stack of papers from her desk. "It wouldn't have nothing to do with these, would it?"

"What's that?" Keith looked at the papers, even though he knew.

"The paperwork for those two townhouses." Dawn waved the stack through the air. Keith reached for them, but she quickly snatched them back. "Not until I get what I want."

"What's that?"

"You, in my bed, tonight," Dawn said slowly. "I've got something special planned for you."

Keith forced a smile. "Ah, yeah? Is eight o'clock too late?"
"Perfect."

Keith pulled up at Dawn's house a little after eight. It wasn't easy for him to explain to Selina that he had to fuck the manager of their apartment complex. She was upset, but understood that the sacrifice had to be made in order to get the townhouse.

Scented candles were burning, the lights were out and Maxwell was playing when Dawn opened the door. "Come in," she said in a sexy voice. Keith peeped her short, sexy nightgown as he followed her into the living room.

Sadly, it revealed her huge gut and a few stretch marks. Dawn thought that she was looking sexy, and she was, in a Nell Carter sort of way.

After countless glasses of Rémy Martin that she served him, Keith finally worked up the nerve to take Dawn up to the bedroom. Unfortunately for Keith, she wanted to ride him. Dawn didn't take off her gown. Instead she took off the huge panties that she had on underneath, then climbed into the bed. It creaked as it slowly sank in the middle.

When Dawn pulled back the covers, she noticed that Keith's dick wasn't hard yet. She eased her face down between his legs. Her warm saliva made his dick stand instantly. At one point Keith looked down and saw that she had his whole dick in her mouth. Like a professional, Dawn sucked every inch inside her fat jaws. Then she stopped. Keith didn't open his eyes when he felt her climb on top of him. Dawn lifted her belly as she eased her warm pussy onto his dick.

"Ooh, shit," Keith moaned. Her pussy felt like a tight glove.

Swaying her hips back and forth, Dawn worked him until she felt his dick throbbing inside her. She smiled to herself and hoped that she had pleased him, so that he would return for more.

The next morning, Dawn handed Keith the keys to the two townhouses. He left there pleased with the outcome of the situation. He picked up the fifty grand from his place, then went to meet Pablo at the construction site.

Pablo was on the phone with someone when Keith walked into his office trailer. "I won't forget," Pablo was saying in to the phone. "Gracias." Then he hung up. He looked at Keith. "What's up, my friend?" Pablo sipped his coffee. "You got the money?"

"You got the stuff?" Keith shot back. He was a very serious person when it came down to doing business.

Pablo laughed to himself. "'*Mi hijo*, I give shit like this away." he reached for a bag beside his desk and placed it on top of his desk. "Check it out."

Three unwrapped kilos were sitting neatly in the bag. Keith nodded his head with approval.

"It gets much greater, later," Pablo assured him.

Keith picked up his tool bag, pulled another bag out of it, then threw it onto Pablo's desk. "Fifty G's. Want to count it?"

Pablo tossed the bag onto the floor near his desk as if it were nothing.

"I'll be in touch," Keith said on his way out.

Pablo nodded.

* * *

Keith used the old furniture that he had in the storage room to furnish the townhouses for the time being. A couple of TVs, two run-down couches, a couple of tables and a PlayStation. He cooked up two of the keys into sixty-five zones of straight raw, instead of the usual seventy-two zones that it was supposed to be. Together, they cut and bagged up $120,000 worth of dime pieces. With Selina's help it took them three days.

Everybody got on the phone and called everyone that they knew who bought weight or rock and told them what was going down. Twain posted up on the corner, directing every corner customer around to the townhouse. Two-for-one would be sold for the first two months, which was a sure way to get the spot dumping.

The last kilo Keith cooked up to thirty-six ounces for the weight house, which Mann would be running. Keith gave them two nines and a AK for protection. He dropped nine ounces in the weight house and $2,000 worth of pieces in the crack house. Then he told them that he didn't want to see any one of them, unless they needed more dope.

Chapter 18

The summer had hit. The extremely hot Texas weather reminded Tukey of the time that she visited Jamaica. If you didn't know any better you would have thought that the camp yard was a training ground. Women were outside jogging, jumping rope and exercising all over.

Tukey and Shantí were busy doing calisthenics when Niecy walked up to them, carrying mail. Tukey and Shantí wore matching gray jogging shorts and gray t-shirts. They stopped for a water break.

"Anyt'ing in dere for me?" Tukey asked before drinking from her jug.

Niecy sorted through the mail. "Let's see. Oh, here you go, Miss Tosh."

Tukey got excited. "Gimmie dat!" She snatched the letter out of Niecy's hand. The letter was from Keith. Her heart felt like it skipped a beat, after seeing his name on the letter.

Shantí could tell who it was from by the expression on Tukey's face. "Somebody got a letter from Keith."

"How ya know?" Tukey asked with a huge grin on her face.

"'Cause, it's written all over your face," Shantí said.

Tukey blushed. "Hush, now. Let read my letter in peace." She walked over to sit on a nearby bench. There was a money order inside, but she paid it no mind.

The letter read:

Dear Tukey,

I'm sorry I ain't had the chance to write or even come up to see you. Shit, it's been what, nine months since I saw you last. I haven't been doing too good out here, so I couldn't send you much.

Your daughter's getting big. We spend every weekend together. I've been working a lot, so I won't be writing you much. I hope you understand.

Love, Keith

Tukey turned the page over, hoping to read some more, but the letter was over. It was short and sweet. Curious about how much he sent, she took the money order out and read the amount. It was twenty dollars. Tukey jumped up mad and ran toward her unit.

Niecy wondered what was in the letter that made Tukey take off so fast. "Where you going, girl?" Niecy yelled at her. "I wonder what was in that letter," she said to Shantí after being ignored by Tukey.

Shantí shrugged.

Tukey hopped on the phone to check her bank account. She had a feeling that Keith needed some help. If he needed some money, she was gonna send him all she had on her books. Tonight, she would write him back and apologize to him for what she'd done with Anitra. This was it, her chance to make amends with the man she loved.

Tukey had a little over five grand in her account. After Ben was killed, her uncle Dave took over for him. When Dave found out that Tukey had gotten locked up, he sent her six grand for her personal needs.

Next, Tukey placed a phone call to her mother, Arie. After she told he mother about her plan to send Keith all of her money, she got cussed out.

"Girl, are ya crazy or somet'ing?" Arie said. "Dat man done moved to Kansas and is over there making more money than him ever have. Mi'kelle's got so much new stuff, me don't know where to put it all. Me can't believe him write ya wit' dat sad story. And ya say him only sent ya twenty dollars?"

"Yep," Tukey said softly. Her excitement left almost as quickly as it came. She was hurt. Out of all the shit he had done to her, this took the cake. To please Keith was all she used to live for. But for niggas like him, that wasn't enough. Tukey's hurt turned into rage. She felt betrayed, bamboozled, led astray, hoodwinked. "Me call ya later, Mama," Tukey said.

"OK. Ya take care of yaself," Arie told her.

"Bye." Tukey hung up the phone and went straight to her room. She stomped over to her bunk, kicking over trash cans as she went. She was in a rage. Suddenly, she started tearing the sheets off of her bed, knocking things off her desk and Niecy's. When she ran out of shit to mess up, Tukey lay on her bunk and cried her eyes out.

Shantí snuck over to Tukey's bunk. "Tukey, what's wrong?" She heard her sobs.

"Get outta here," Tukey yelled, embarrassed that Shantí had seen her soft side.

"But I—"

"Out...now!" Tukey didn't care to hear her explanation. She got up and stared coldly at Shantí, like she would hit her if she didn't leave.

"OK," Shantí said, defeated, then walked out without saying another word until she got out into the hallway. "It ain't my fault you keep letting that nigga trick you."

Tukey hopped back on her bed and buried her face in her pillow. Her tears began to flow again.

* * *

The last six months had gone well for Keith's operation. Both townhouses were furnished lavishly. Leather sofas, big screen TVs, new bedroom sets and they had every game system that was out. From sun up to sundown, the boys remained posted up in the townhouses. Keith didn't want to miss a dime. Selina did as she promised by providing them with different females to keep them company while they worked, even though they were a bunch of young, gold-digging bitches who wanted to smoke weed and drink at their expense. Plenty of pussy and alcohol kept the boys content while they raked in piles of money.

Sometimes, on weekends, they'd knock off ten kilos by selling only ounces. Their combined clientele gave them almost as much business as a Wal-Mart. Two-for-one kept the smokers coming from miles away, just to get that extra piece of dope. As long as Keith was breaking whole kilos down, two-for-one would never hurt his pockets. That made it hard for any other dealer in the area to make any money around there.

Keith kept all of the promises that he made to the boys. After the first two months of cooking the bread was over, he gave them fifteen hundred apiece, plus took all of them shopping. That was peanuts compared to what they had made for him.

When the summer hit, Keith went to the auto auction and paid cash for each one of their cars, using one of his white client's names. He bought Twain a 1995 STS Cadillac; Capone a 1994 Suburban; Rock a 1995 Impala; and Mann a 1996 GMC Yukon, four-door. Any engine trouble Keith had fixed right away. A week later, he bought dubs for his whole crew to floss on. Six months of around-the-clock hustling had paid off for them, and not one was complaining. This time last year, they were copping eight balls, selling dope on the corner. Of course, for the time being, they only got to show their cars off on Sundays, their only day off.

The only problem that they had was from the neighbors next to the townhouses. There was a family on each side, and they were constantly complaining about the traffic. For a while, money seemed to silence them, but then the traffic started getting out of hand. It became too much for them to bare. So they on more than one occasion asked Keith to cut it out.

Pablo had grown to love Keith like a brother. They'd even started hanging out together. Barber shops, restaurants, clubs, you name it, they were together. It was like they'd grown up together.

Pablo even helped Keith get a hundred-thousand dollar loan for a house in Shawnee Mission, Kansas, for which Pablo's company co-signed. It was like Pablo's connections had no limitations. Running out of dope was the least of his worries. The drought had ended and everybody had dope. But it hadn't put a dent in Keith's pocket. It was too late; his low prices had spoiled his customers. Keith was the man. There wasn't anything that anybody in the city was buying that he couldn't afford. He'd be a multimillionaire by the end of the year; that was a promise from Pablo.

The hand on Keith's platinum diamond-studded watch read two o'clock. He finished his last game of pool, then he and Tee hurried out of Pete's Lounge. They hopped into Keith's brand new Escalade, which sat on twenty-three-inch rims. Tee was driving while Keith made some calls on his cell phone.

Keith hesitated for a moment. "What's the area code for St. Louis?" he asked.

Tee thought about it. "Three one four," Tee said. "Who you calling?"

Keith finished dialing the number before he answered. "You remember Big Leon and Kees?"

"Yeah!"

"I got some work for 'em to do."

Someone answered Big Leon's phone. "Yeah."

Keith said, "Let me speak to Big L."

"Who dis dirty?"

"KB."

"Hold on."

Keith could hear the guy yelling in the background for Leon. "Leon, telephone nigga."

A second later Big Leon got on the phone. "Hello."

"This Kansas City Keith, nigga," Keith said.

"KB?"

"Yeah, nigga."

"What's up, dirty," Leon said, finally figuring out who he was talking to. Then he yelled to somebody in the background. "Hey,

Kees! KB on the phone."

Keith could hear Kees talking shit in the background. "On my mama, I was about to call that nigga," Kees said loudly.

"What's up wit' ya, playboy?" Leon said.

"What's up is I've been back on for the last six months and you ain't called me," Keith complained.

"Shit, if the price is right, I'll come down," Leon said. "How's the weather down there?"

"Little birdies are flying everywhere, baby," Keith said, in code.

"I'll tell you what, man," Big Leon said. "I'ma shoot up there this weekend so I can check you out."

"Cool," Keith said. "Let me holla at Kees for a minute."

"Hold on. Kees, come get the phone, nigga," Big Leon yelled.

Kees came on the line. "On me, nigga, I was just about to call yo' ass. What's up wit' ya, dirty?"

"I need some work put in," Keith said it like it was nothing.

"Aw, yeah? Look here, dirty. I don't speak Chinese. Let's talk about the green."

"You know I gotcha," Keith said. "See you this weekend."

"On me, dirty," Kees said before he hung up.

Tee pulled into the complex parking lot and parked beside Rock's Impala. They went inside the weight house where Rock sat at a table counting stacks of cash.

"What's up, nigga?" Rock said to Tee.

"Shit," Tee looked at all the money that was on the table. "Y'all got all the money." He took a seat at the table.

Keith glanced around the room and noticed that Mann was missing. "Where's Mann at?"

"Upstairs with that bitch, Marcy," Rock said. "Tricking off."

"That figures," Keith said. He cut the TV on and put a game in the PlayStation. "Let's go, nigga." He threw a controller in Tee's direction.

Tee sat down in the leather recliner in front of the big screen TV. "You know you can't win. I don't know why you trying."

"Shut up and play, muthafucka," Keith taunted. "Twist up a blunt, Rock."

Rock picked up a large zippered bag from the table in front of him. Two days ago, it held a pound of weed. Now there was less than an ounce left in the bag.

"Damn niggas got them vacuum lungs around here." Rock shook his head at the little bit left in the sack.

"Y'all smoking the weed up wit' all them funky ass hos," Keith said.

"Sheeit, that's that nigga Blue," Rock said, splitting the blunt in half. "Man, Little Capone walked in on him eating Shunda's pussy last night."

They all laughed.

From where Keith was sitting he could see Selina pull into the parking lot in her new Kompressor. She got out wearing a pair of tight Capri pants and a blue tank top. Her erect nipples shone through her shirt. She had a new tattoo around her ankle that read, "KB". A huge smiled appeared on her face after seeing Keith's truck parked there.

The door was already halfway open when Selina walked into the weight house. Her smile disappeared when she saw Tee sitting there.

"What's up, Boo?" Keith said with a blunt hanging from his mouth.

Selina smiled again. "Hey, *papi*," she said lightly. She sat down on Keith's lap. They gave each other two soft kisses while looking into each other's eyes.

"This is my partner, Tee," Keith said. "You already know Rock."

Selina gave them a quick wave, showing them the huge platinum-set rock on her left ring finger.

Tee noticed the finger that her ring was on and spoke up immediately. "Damn, Keith, I didn't know you got married, nigga."

"Engaged," Keith corrected him.

"Engaged," Rock repeated, being funny. "I told him not to do that shit, man."

"Fuck you, Rock," Selina yelled. "You just mad that Jackie don't fuck with you like that."

"Mannn, fuck Jackie. I put her dumb ass outta here last night," Rock said in his defense.

"Whatever," Selina said. "Can I talk to you outside, Keith?"

Keith let Rock take over his game while he stepped outside to holler at his girl.

"What about the blunt?" Rock asked as Keith walked away with it.

"Roll another one, nigga."

Selina lead Keith all the way outside to her car. She sat on her trunk with her legs spread and signaled him to come.

"What's up, Boo?" Keith slid between her legs. She looked like a young J-Lo sitting on the trunk of her little Benz.

"I need some money," she said shyly.

"How much?"

"Like a G."

"A grand, huh?"

"Yeah, a grand."

Keith looked at her while sucking on his teeth. "What for?"

"I saw these cute pair of gator boots I just know you'll look good wearing. You'd look like Puff Daddy," Selina baited him.

"Like Puffy, huh? You love you some Puff Daddy, don't you?"

"Hell yeah," Selina agreed. "Why you think I buy you so many Sean Jean outfits? That's my nigga."

"Umm hmm. Where Terry at?"

"Grandma's," she said. "Nah, but seriously baby, I can't believe how far we've come so fast. It seems like all this happened overnight. Like all of a sudden we got all this money and stuff."

Keith looked at her suspiciously. "What the hell you getting at?"

Selina toyed with the platinum emblem on his chain. "I think it's time for you to quit while you're ahead, *papi*."

Keith laughed at her. "What? Them little niggas in there put in work for me to get where I am. Now that you got what you want, you expect me to just walk out on them?"

Selina didn't say anything.

While they stood outside talking, Tee sat inside the house and watched as the money kept on rolling in. Somehow, he had to get Keith to let him in on some of the action. Keith hadn't really done nothing for him since he got back started. And his brother Andre was so busy spending money on his new wife, that he didn't find much time to hustle anymore.

Tee watched as Rock counted stacks of big-faced hundreds and tried to contain his envy. Even though Keith had always looked out for him, he couldn't help but be jealous of Keith's success. Keith was too lucky for Tee. Sooner or later, he was bound to fall off again. Tee felt bad for thinking bad about his partner like that, but he couldn't help it. He hoped that Keith would fall off. This time for good.

Keith got a call from Pablo, who asked him to come by his house, alone. On his way to drop Tee off at home, Tee finally asked Keith to cut him in on the money. Keith didn't answer him for a minute. He didn't want to let Tee down, but he had to on this one.

Keith promised Mann and the rest of the group that they were a self-contained unit. Meaning no outsiders. And that rule went for everybody, including the boss. After Keith told him no, Tee sat there and pretended not to be mad about it. But Keith knew better. Hell they grew up together, and he knew Tee like he knew his own daughter. Keith hated to shut Tee out like that, but Tee was a grown man, capable of handling his own. Shit, Tee had just as many chances as anybody to come up. But he chose to spend his money foolishly; that was on him. That's what Keith tried to tell himself. But Tee was his dog, so Keith had to try and make something happen for him. He decided to front Tee a couple of keys as soon as he got some more dope. This was gonna be his last chance. If Tee fucked that up trying to be flamboyant, he'd be left out in the cold.

After he took Tee home, Keith drove over to Pablo's. He pulled into the driveway behind Pablo's mistress' Land Rover. Her house was the biggest on the block. Her grass was so green that you could tell that it was cared for by professionals. It had its own glow.

Keith had never met the woman, but he'd heard that she was a bad bitch. He checked his reflection in her glass screen doors before he rang the bell. She answered the door with an expensive towel wrapped around her naked body.

"You must be Keith," she smiled, showing off a set of perfect white teeth. "Come in, please. I'm Jessica."

Keith's eyes were stuck on her. He guessed her to be about 5'1, petite, with a firm set of titties on her. She had long blond hair that almost matched her bright skin color. Keith loved blonde Mexican chicks; it made them look naughty. He begged Selina to dye her hair, he even offered to send her to New York to have it done by some real professionals. But she wouldn't do it. He would have to accept her as is.

Keith wondered why Jessica answered the door wearing nothing but a towel. Didn't she know he was coming? She looked to be about half Pablo's age, which really didn't matter to her considering Pablo's status. He was a rich man and money always attracted young hos.

Jessica grabbed Keith's arm and led him toward the back of the house. She made a stop in the kitchen to grab a bottle of tequila and an extra glass for Keith. For the first time he noticed that her body was wet. At first, he assumed that she had just gotten out of the shower but after she grabbed the tequila, Keith knew there must have been a pool or something out back. Jessica slid open the patio door and they stepped out onto a large wooden deck. Pablo and a replica of Jessica were hugged up in a huge hot tub, kissing on each other's bodies. The other girl had to be Jessica's twin.

Pablo looked up with a huge grin on his face. "Keith," he said excitedly. He let go of the girl, then got out of the tub, butt naked.

Keith stood there in shock.

"What's wrong, my friend?" Pablo placed his hand on Keith's shoulder. "We're all human here. Take your clothes off, hop in." Pablo took the bottle of tequila from Jessica on his way back in the tub.

"Come on," Jessica said. She took off her towel and let it drop to the floor. She had a Playboy centerfold's body with tan lines around her breasts and waist. Her ass cheeks jiggled as she stepped into the hot tub.

Pablo playfully dipped his head under water then resurfaced. "Come on, chicken," he called to Keith as he wiped water from his face. "Show the girls you're a Mandingo warrior. Break out that big black anaconda."

Jessica and her twin Jessy shook their heads. "Yeah, *papi.* Show us," Jessy said, getting even more excited.

Keith could imagine what they wanted to get into. *Fuck it,* Keith said to himself. He removed his clothes then stood there proudly, letting them admire his manhood.

Jessica's eyes got big. "*qué grandé es,*" she said under her breath, but loud enough to be heard.

"Umm hmm," Jessy agreed.

Keith finally joined them in the tub. He and Pablo took turns going from sister to sister. At times they both teamed up on one, and sometimes the twins teamed up on one of them.

They had finished off their second bottle of tequila when Jessica excused herself. A minute later she returned with a small, moon-shaped mirror. As she got closer, Keith noticed the huge pile of white powder on top of it.

"Who wants the white girl?" Jessica asked with the prettiest smile on her face.

"Ooh, I do, I do!" Jessy raised her hand and jumped up and down like a child.

Keith watched while they all took turns snorting lines off the mirror. After they got through, all of them turned toward Keith and stared at him with devilish looks on their faces.

Pablo held the straw out toward him. "Your turn, amigo."

Keith put his hand up. "I don't fuck around," Keith said in a serious voice.

Pablo sniffed. "Sure you do. Try a little with your friend," he pressed.

Jessy slid her hand between Keith's legs and massaged his dick. "Come on, *papi.* Try it for me. I promise you'll like it."

"I can't," Keith shook his head. "Maybe some other time."

Jessica moved beside Keith. "I'll tell you what. I'll go down and suck your dick while you snort a line," she said, trying to persuade him. "Would you like that?"

"Come on, *papi,*" Jessy pleaded. "We'll take turns. After she get through, then I'll go down on you."

Keith glanced at Pablo, who shrugged then took another shot of Tequila.

"Fuck it. I'll try a little," Keith agreed. He poured himself a shot of Tequila, then downed it. "Bring it on."

Jessy scooped up a small amount with her fingernail, then held it up to Keith's nose. Jessica positioned herself between his legs, preparing to go down. "Ready?" Jessica said. Keith nodded his head, then she went under.

He snorted Jessy's fingernail clean. Keith could almost taste the cocaine as it traveled up his nose. It was a cool, yet strange type of feeling. He was tense at first, but as the cocaine settled in, he started to relax. His dick had become ten times more sensitive, feeling it being sucked underwater.

"Shittt," Keith hollered. Jessica had her jaws full of his dick. Then she came back up for air.

"How does it feel, *papi*?" she said before she'd caught her breath.

But Keith was too stuck in the zone to talk abut it. All he could say was, "Next."

Jessy and Jessica switched. This time, Keith took a bigger dose of cocaine, while Jessy went to work underwater. He felt his nuts burst, the he passed out.

* * *

Keith woke up with a pounding headache. He looked around the dark room but didn't recognize his surroundings. He knew that he was in someone's bedroom. By the way the sheets felt against his naked skin, he could tell that they were expensive. Then he remembered being at Jessica's house.

He felt someone's small foot brush up against his leg. Keith pulled back the covers and flinched when he saw the twins, Jessica and Jessy, sleeping next to him. He rubbed his hands across his face. "Shit," he said softly. He saw an antique-looking phone sitting on the stand next to the bed. He picked it up, fingers shaking as he dialed the number to Tee's cell phone.

"Hello," Tee answered. In the background, music and what sounded like a crowd of people mingling could be heard through the phone.

"Where you at?"

"I'm at Pete's Lounge. Where you at?"

"Man, you ain't gon' believe this shit," Keith said, then went on to explain what had happened to him.

"Damn, nigga you kickin' it like that? Just give me the address and I'm on my way."

"Nah, man I can't," Keith said, hating to disappoint his friend again. "Pablo's kinda funny about shit like that. Shit, I'm lucky to be here."

"Aw, yeah?" Tee sounded disappointed. "I'll holla at you tomorrow, then."

"Do that. I've got a deal for—"

Tee hung up in Keith's face before he'd finished talking.

Keith put the phone back on the hook. He stumbled over something as he got to his feet and tried to find his clothes. He could hear a TV while he walked through the house, looking for the bathroom. Clearly he took a wrong turn because he ended up in the living room. He saw the back of Pablo's head resting on the couch, staring at the TV screen. He had on a blue silk robe and his feet were propped up on the coffee table. Pablo turned his head toward Keith after he heard footsteps. He picked up his glass of tequila from the table, then gestured for Keith to come over and sit.

"What's wrong, my friend?" Pablo said. "Can't sleep?"

Keith sniffled and wiped his nose with the back of his hand. "My nose keeps on running."

"You're draining," Pablo said calmly. "Shit's bad for you."

Keith looked confused. "Why do you do it?"

Pablo smiled. "Gives you one helluva orgasm." He turned his attention back to the TV. He was watching an old Mexican fuck flick. There was a scene where some short, uncircumcised Mexican was fucking a black woman guard, inside his prison cell. "I love it when the ho comes out of a bitch. Don't you?"

Keith grunted and lay his head back against the oversized sofa. His head was pounding and his heart was beating a little faster than normal.

Pablo saw the sweat beads all over Keith's face. He got up, went over to the bar and fixed Keith a shot of whiskey. "Here, drink this," he handed Keith the drink. "It'll make you feel better."

Keith took it. He frowned as the sour liquid went down his throat. When he opened his eyes again, Pablo was dangling a set of keys in his face. He saw the word U-Haul on the key chain. The he remembered seeing one parked on the street when he pulled up. "What am I suppose to do with these?"

Pablo sat back down and made himself comfortable before he answered Keith. "I packed a hundred keys inside that U-Haul that is parked in front of the house." He took a quick sip of his drink. "I brought eight hundred of 'em in from Arizona, yesterday. Priced way too high."

Keith sneezed. "Ah, shit," he said as he wiped his nose with the back of his hand. "What's my price?"

"A million two," Pablo replied as if it were chump change.

Keith looked upset.

Pablo noticed the grim look on his face. "What's wrong, my

friend?" he inquired. "You said that you were ready for the big time. Well, here it is."

"I'm ready, but a million two seems kinda high. Don't you think?"

Pablo smiled. "It is if you were the one who drove to Arizona and picked it up yourself. But here in the city, it goes for one point two all day long. You pay twelve a kilo and sell for twenty one or twenty two. Either way, you're gonna make a fortune." Pablo thought for a moment. "Come to think of it, you got a crack spot. Shit, you gon' make a killing."

So that was the reason for the extra two hundred thousand, Keith thought. Pablo knew that Keith had a jumping-ass crack house, and would probably triple the profit. Why wouldn't Pablo try and benefit from it?

It really didn't make a difference to Keith what price he paid. He just wanted Pablo to know that he knew he was trying to get over. Keith got up and stumbled back into the bedroom to get his keys and shirt. He was ready to go. Business had to be handled. He would have Mann come by and pick up his Cadillac, later on.

* * *

It wasn't even six o'clock in the morning when Keith pulled into the parking lot. All of the lights in Selina's townhouse were on. He parked the U-Haul where it wouldn't be in anybody's way. He had already stashed the dope in a safe house that he'd bought over a month ago. Only Selina knew where it was located, because she was the one who ran the dope back and forth to the spots. In the basement of the safe house he installed a huge steel safe embedded in concrete, to which Selina didn't have the combination. She had access to all of the dope, but his money status was his business. Keith could care less about her seeing all the dope because she couldn't count the money value of it.

When Keith opened the door, Selina was slouched down on the couch, drunk and still drinking. He shook his head in disgust at the sight of her. She looked real pathetic, sitting there with her face all frowned up, like a wino.

Selina pointed her finger at him. "I know where you were at, t-t...tonight," she said in a drunken slur. "My uncle, he...he not right."

"What the fuck you talking—"

"Why did we get engaged, anyway, huh?" Selina sat her bottle down next to her. Then she took off her engagement ring and threw it at him. "Two whores are more important than what you got at home?" She nodded off and almost passed out, but caught her head before it fell.

How in the hell did she find out what Keith had been into tonight? Only Pablo could've told her about that. Keith had left the twins in bed, still asleep. He didn't feel well and wasn't ready to deal with Selina's bullshit at the moment. Sleep was what he needed.

Keith reached down and scooped Selina from the couch and into his arms. She was what he needed also. She rested her pretty head on his shoulder while he carried her up to their bedroom.

"I'm still mad at you, *papi*," Selina muttered.

"I know," Keith said, putting her into the bed.

Chapter 19

It was the weekend. Big Leon had already called to let Keith know that he was on his way from St. Louis. It wasn't likely that the task force would kick in over the weekend, so he loaded the houses up with dope. Keith put ten keys in the weight house and over fifty thousand dollars worth of pieces in the crack house.

It had been a good week. Instead of the usual grand, Keith paid them all twenty-five hundred for the week, which they were more than grateful to get. They felt like they were a part of something now: a family. They were no longer known as Twain, Rock, Mann, Blue, and Capone. They were known as the ballers who had the Silver City Projects sewed up.

Selina was grooving to Mary J. Blige while she counted last night's profits for Keith. Plus, she had to skim her cut off the top to go shopping with. Keith was chilling at the spot across the street with the crew. Selina was happy because Keith had stayed at home for the last few nights, making love to her until the sun rose. Yesterday they went out as a family, taking Mi'kelle and Terry to Worlds of Fun, then to the toy store this morning. Both of the kids were fast asleep upstairs.

Selina's cell phone rang five times before she realized that it was ringing. She answered, "Hello."

"What did he say?" It was her baby's daddy.

"Look, boy, you just can't call me like that," Selina whispered for no reason. It wasn't like Keith could hear her from across the street. "What if he was here?"

"He ain't there, though. Look, let's cut the bullshit. I love you and you love me. Find out how we can get this nigga and get outta town. I told you that he would come back up. Lucky muthafucka. It was just a matter of time."

"Was he really snorting cocaine with two bitches last night, or did you make that shit up?"

"Did you ask him?"

"Yes," Selina said, cautiously.

"What did he say? Did he deny it?"

"He didn't say." Selina became irritated. "Look, I'ma have to call you back." She hung up and sighed. "Shit!"

Keith was standing in the parking lot, trying to talk civilly with the two neighbors who lived next door to the crack house. There were eight townhouses on their court, four on each side. The occupants of the other three townhouses on Selina's side were all young black girls, so they weren't a problem. It was the occupants of the two townhouses next to both of the spots who were a pain in the ass.

"There's just too much traffic day in and day out," Larry, one of the neighbors said. He pointed to his wife. "She is upset and so is Mr. Woods." Mr. Woods stayed in the townhouse next to the weight spot.

"Where is Mr. Woods?" Keith asked him.

"My guess is, he's at work," Larry said angrily.

"So my money ain't enough for you?"

"No," Larry shook his head. "Not anymore, it's not."

"OK," Keith said. "You won't have no more problems out of us, after today. Satisfied?"

"We'll see," Larry said, turning away. "Come on, baby." His wife followed him.

Keith called a meeting at the weight house. He stood in front of the huge sixty-inch screen and waited for everyone to be seated.

"Quiet please," he ordered. "Now, tonight we gon' shut down shop. That means both houses."

"What kinda shit you on?" Capone said loudly.

Keith raised his hand and signaled him to be quiet. "Don't panic. It won't be for long. Maybe a week, at most. Consider it a paid vacation, 'cause your weekly earnings will still be paid to you. All of y'all know abut the problems we're having with the neighbors. Well, tonight I plan on fixing that problem."

Rocky understood just what he was saying. "Let me handle it."

"Not this time, Rock. So this is what I want. All of you go out tonight and be seen. You being seen tonight is very important. I don't think that I have to explain why. This place is our meal ticket, fellas, and I ain't trying to lose it. Not if I can help it. Now let's pack all of the dope up and take it to Selina's. She'll take it from there. Let's move."

Keith touched Mann on the shoulder. "You got the keys to my Cadillac?"

"Yeah," Mann said, reaching into his pocket. "Here you go."

Keith took them, then handed Mann the keys to the U-Haul truck. "Drop it off at the same place that you picked my truck up at. Have Capone follow you over there."

"Alright," Mann said.

After the houses were cleaned and all the dope was moved, Keith told Selina to take everything to the safe house. He'd meet her and the kids out at his mama's house.

* * *

His mama was unlocking the door to her car when Keith pulled up. She stopped what she was doing and waited for Keith to get out of his car. She had a bone to pick with him. She knew that he had proposed to Selina, faking like he was gonna be faithful. Now she had Selina calling her late at night, drunk and crying about Keith not coming home.

Keith got out of his truck. "Hey, baby. Where you going?"

"Why you didn't take yo' ass home last night?" his mama said, hotly.

Keith frowned. "Mama, don't start with that." He took a seat on the steps next to the driveway. "I get enough of that at home. Where you headed?"

"I'm about to go get your nephew. As a matter of fact, I need some money. I got to get him some clothes for the summer."

Keith pulled a bankroll out of his pocket, counted out five hundred, then handed it to her. "Tell Kim I'll drop her off some more money later, so she can take care of all the bills and shit." Keith stretched. "Tell her to write me out a list of everything she needs."

They heard tires screeching down the street. Keith looked that way and saw a lime green 1963 drop Impala bending the corner on three wheels. He could hear the pipes getting louder as the car accelerated.

"That crazy ass nigga, Kees," Keith said, smiling. He could see the red bandana on Kees' head, blowing in the wind.

Kees pulled over and parked in front of Keith's mama's house. He threw the car in park but left it cocked up on three wheels. Big Leon wasn't with him. In the passenger seat was his cousin Tone. Kees hopped out the car without opening the door. His dark skinned lanky frame was about six feet, three inches long. His hair was long and freshly braided.

"What's up, nigga," Kees said, flashing eight gold teeth when he smiled. The shook hands. "Got my nigga Tone wit' me."

Tone walked up to Keith and they shook hands also.

Keith's mama shook her head. "Don't be hangin out in front of my house with no bunch of niggas Keith. I ain't playing," she hollered as she got into her car.

Kees waited until Keith's mama's car disappeared over the hill, before he said, "Damn, nigga, she think you a child or something?" He shook his head. "So what's up? What you need done, nigga?"

Before Keith had a chance to answer an old tow truck pulled up and parked behind Kees' car. It was Big Leon. He had to hit the gas a few times before shutting it off. He hopped his short frame out and wobbled his way to the back of the tow truck. From a locked compartment he removed a purple Nike gym bag, then relocked it.

"KB, what's up, dirty?" Big Leon said. He spoke with a Mississippi accent.

"Waiting on yo' fat ass." Keith shook his hand. "That bag for me?"

"Sho' is, nigga, if the price is right. But tonight, I'm trying to kick it wit' yo' ass. We can take care of bidness in the morning, before I leave." He handed the bag to Keith. "My clothes in Kees' back seat. We stayin' at the Relax Inn, across the street from Niecy's."

Keith threw his arm around him. "Let's go in the house, nigga."

Right away Kees made himself at home. Without asking, he opened up Keith's daddy's liquor cabinet and opened a bottle of Rémy Martin. Keith came upstairs after stowing the bag that Big Leon had given him. Kees was pouring himself a drink. That's when Keith noticed that Kees had been in his daddy's cabinet.

"I see you've made yourself at home," Keith said to Kees, who was sitting on the couch with his feet up. Tone sat next to Big Leon on the other couch.

"On my mama, nigga I do this everywhere I go," Kees said in a loud voice. He had a bad habit of always putting things on his mama. He sipped his drink. "So what we need to do?"

Keith sat down next to him. "I got a problem with the neighbors that live next door to my place of business. They ain't trying to cooperate with what I got going over there. So I need you and Tone to go over there and straighten shit out. I need them complaining muthafuckas outta there, tonight."

Kees took another sip of his drink. He looked like he was thinking. He finally said, "You know if I do this dirty, everybody in the house is gon' get done. I hate leaving witnesses and shit."

"I'm saying," Tone agreed.

"Look, Kees," Keith said. "It's two townhouses. One dude

lives on one side and one lives on the other. My houses are in the middle. Spare their wives, if you can."

Kees smiled wickedly, showing off his gold teeth. "I'll see what I can do. We gon' need a fifty sack of dosha, nigga, and two throwaways. I'll steal the car myself." He swallowed the rest of his drink. "Aw, yeah. You gon' have to show us where they live, dirty."

"Cool!"

Kees slammed the empty glass down on the table next to the bottle, then stood up. "We gon' chill at the room until later, dirty. Come on, Tone." Kees headed toward the door.

"You niggas be careful, man," Big Leon got up. "Let me get my shit out yo' car before I end up with a case, fuckin around with y'all."

Kees grabbed Big Leon's bag out of his car and handed it to him. He hit the switch and sat the fourth wheel back down on the street.

Tone took a half-smoked blunt out of the ashtray and fired it up. "Fuck Keith's soft-hearted ass, talking 'bout spare them bitches for?"

"Sheeit," Kees said, putting the car in drive. "On my mama, nigga, I'm killing everybody in there. Straight up." He hit another switch to stand the car up high, then pulled off.

* * *

Kees was dressed in a black Dickies outfit, black Chuck Taylors and had on a pair of black batting gloves. Tone wore the same. They were parked behind McCall's gas station in a stolen old Ford Fairlane. Kees waited until the blunt was finished before he pulled off.

A couple of hours ago, Keith drove them by Larry's and Mr. Wood's homes so they would know exactly which two townhouses to hit. Kees had been to Kansas City so many times that he knew most of the streets by heart. But since the townhouses were in Kansas, Keith had to show him an escape route. To assist them with their mission, he gave them two brand new nines that he got from Pablo. Then Keith and Big Leon left for the club. They didn't want to be anywhere around when people started getting killed.

Slowly, Kees eased to a stop on the back street next to the townhouses. They hopped out and left the doors open just a little, so that they could hop back in with no trouble if something went wrong. They made sure no one was around, then pulled black ski masks over their faces. Mr. Woods' house was the first one that they came upon. They could see or hear no movement inside the house when they peeped in the back window.

"They sleeping," Kees whispered. "Get us in there."

On cue, Tone pulled out a small crowbar that was attached to his belt. Trying to be as quiet as possible, he popped the screen door open. They waited to see if the noise had woken anyone up. No lights came on inside the house, so they proceeded with caution. Out of his back pocket Kees pulled out a small thing shaped like a gun with a something key-like sticking out of the barrel of it. He slid the key-like part into the lock, then pulled the trigger. It opened right up. Kees and Tone did this kind of shit for a living, so getting into the house wasn't a problem.

They pulled out their guns and went in, Kees first, followed by Tone. They came upon the living room, walking slow and ready to fire at the sight of anybody. The stairs that led to the bedroom creaked when Kees stepped on them. So instead of tiptoeing, they ran up the stairs and stormed into the bedroom.

After Mr. Woods' door flew open from Kees' kick he immediately got up and tried to reach his dresser, where he kept a loaded .357 Magnum. With his long legs, Kees kicked Mr. Woods into the wall before he could make it to the dresser. Woods fell and hit his head hard on the wall. Blood ran down the side of his chubby face.

"Where the fuck you think you going?" Kees yelled harshly. The wicked smirk on his face let Mr. Woods know that he was enjoying himself.

"My money's in my wallet on the dresser. Take it," Mr. Woods pleaded.

His wife remained in the bed terrified to make a move in any direction. She stared up at Kees and hoped that he would take the wallet and go away. Her husband was on the floor bleeding to death and she wanted to get to him.

Kees turned his head and met her stare. "Bitch, don't look at me," he yelled at her. But she couldn't take her eyes off him. "Can you hear?"

"Come on, Kees, let's get this shit over with," Tone said.

Mr. Woods heard Tone say Kees name and would remember it if they let him live. "What's this all about?" Mr. Woods said.

Kees stepped closer to him and aimed his gun at Mr. Woods' face. "Yo' mouth," he said, then pulled the trigger three times.

When Mrs. Woods saw half of her husband's brains splattered against the wall, she screamed as loud as she could. But only for a second. Tone stepped forward and shot her repeatedly.

Larry jumped up off the couch and ran upstairs to get his gun after hearing the gunshots nearby. When he came downstairs, he had a loaded .38 revolver in his hand. Cautiously, he approached his front door with his gun drawn. His hand was shaking so much, you could hear the bullets rattling inside the chambers. He attempted to look out of the peephole, but his door flew open and hit him in the chest. He fell backwards, firing the six-shot revolver wildly.

Kees had kicked in the door. He knew that there was a good chance that Larry had heard the gunshots at Mr. Woods' house, so it didn't make sense wasting time trying to sneak in. They had to hurry up and finish the job before the police showed up.

The bullets flying past them made Kees and Tone fall to the ground for cover. After Larry fired all six shots, they heard the gun click. It was empty.

Kees looked over at Tone. "Let's go get this muthafucka."

Tone got up and rushed through the open door. Larry took off running toward the kitchen. Tone aimed and fired, hitting Larry twice in his back. His wife heard the shots and came running down the stairs. One look at Kees standing in her living room with that gun in his hand, and she turned and tried to run back up the steps. Kees heard her footsteps, then took off after her. From the bathroom doorway, Kees could see her shadow through the plastic shower curtain. He hit the switch and turned the light off.

"Nooo!" She screamed in terror.

Kees smiled as he fired repeatedly into the shower. The body hit the tub hard. He turned the light back on to catch a glimpse of his work. The curtain was ripped to pieces. Her body was curled up in the tub, full of holes.

Tone heard police sirens. "Come the fuck on, Kees," he yelled up the stairs.

Without hesitation, Kees turned and ran for the stairs. It took only three jumps for his long legs to reach the bottom of the staircase. Tone had the car started by the time Kees got there. Before Kees could get both feet into the car, Tone was already pulling off.

The first officer to arrive at the scene was alone. He saw the old Ford swerving and pulled in front of it, trying to stop them with his car. Tone hit the gas and ran dead into him.

The impact made Kees slam his head into the dashboard. "Damn!" he hollered.

If Tone was hurt, he didn't show it. Quickly, he slammed the Ford into reverse, pulling his front end out of the police car, and backed away. With blood running down the side of his head, the policeman got out and fired through their windshield, grazing Kees' neck. Tone, still driving backwards, drove for four blocks until they reached Kees' car. Kees was bleeding but that didn't stop his legs from moving. The top to the Impala was already down. They hopped in and smashed out right before the police helicopter arrived.

Before Kees and Tone had left to do the job, Keith stopped at a pay phone and called Dawn, who had given him the number to Larry's house. He called but no one answered. He left a message.

He said, "Larry, I bet you and Mr. Woods thought y'all were slick, beating me out of all that money. You never planned on opening up a gas station, did you? You're gonna be dead before sunrise." He'd left the message for the police to listen to when they started investigating the murders. That way, they'd have a bogus motive for the killings.

* * *

Tee, Big Leon and Keith were all out on the dance floor getting down when Kees called Big Leon on his cell phone. It took a minute for Leon to dig his phone out of his pocket.

"Yeah," he answered it loudly.

"Leon, this Kees, dirty. We had to head back to the Lou. Me and Tone already on 70 as we speak. Tell Keith it's done. And, he better send my fifty grand to me by you, or his ass is done, too. On my mama, nigga, I'm out." With that, he hung up the phone.

Big Leon hung up, then put the phone back into his pocket. There was no need to discuss that with Keith, tonight. Pussy was the only thing on his mind at the moment. After the song went off, Big Leon followed the girl that he was dancing with over to her table.

"Bring us two shots of XO," he said to the waitress, then took a seat next to the girl. "So, Kesha. You goin' home wit' me tonight, or what?"

Kesha tried to play the shy role. "I don't even know you."

"Ain't nothing to know. I'm Leon and you Kesha. Pleased to meet you," Big Leon pressed.

The waitress brought their drinks.

"I don't want you to think that I'm easy or nothing like that," Kesha said. She had a pretty brown childlike face and a squeaky little voice. But looking at her body, no one would dispute that she was a grown woman.

"Stop faking with my man, girl," Keith said, appearing out of nowhere. "He came all the way down here from St. Louis to kick it. Now, show my man a good time."

"Why don't you mind yo' own business," Kesha said with sass. "If I do leave with him, it ain't got nothin' to do with you, Keith."

"You can't talk to my dirty like that, girl," Leon jumped in.

"Yo' dirty ain't the one tryin' to fuck tonight. Now is he?"

Kesha asked.

Leon looked over at Keith. "Get lost, Keith. I can't fuck you."

Keith whispered in Big Leon's ear. "Let me know before you leave, if you leave with her."

"Come on, baby." Kesha grabbed Leon's hand.

"I'll call you in the morning, Keith," Leon said. "Aw, yeah. Kees called and said everything's all good."

Keith looked at Big Leon for a moment, letting his words sink in. Then he smiled. "Cool," he said. "I'll catch up with you in the A.M." Keith stopped at the bar letting Tee know that he was about to leave with Jessica, one of the Mexican twins that he invited to the club.

The next morning, Big Leon met up with Keith at his mama's house. Selina was waiting on the steps when Keith pulled up. Somehow, she had gotten word that Keith was out with some bitch last night, instead of being at home with her and the kids. She confronted him as soon as he stepped out of the car.

There was a hundred and eighty grand in the bag that Big Leon gave Keith the day before, for ten kilos. Fifty grand of it he gave back to Big Leon to take to Kees and Tone.

Satisfied, Big Leon packed the dope inside of three old tires and rims, using a machine on the back of the tow truck. That was his reason for driving it in the first place. He was especially happy to only be paying eighteen thousand a kilo. In St. Louis, the price of one kilo could go for as high as thirty grand. He told Keith that he had to leave so that he could stop and pick up Kesha. She wanted to kick it in the Lou for a few days.

Keith called him a "trick," but that didn't stop Leon. Kesha must've had some fire-ass pussy.

Chapter 20

To Tukey's surprise, she received a second letter from Keith, with a fifty-dollar money order inside. In his letter, he said that things had been looking up for him and he hoped to be back on his feet by the time she got out. The return address was from his mama's house. Tukey shook her head, threw the letter away, then walked to her room. She decided to play the game with Keith, since he wanted to play with her mind.

Tukey sat down and prepared to write her letter. She started off by telling Keith how much she loved him and couldn't wait to come home to him. Everything in the past was forgotten and that they needed to move forward with their lives. She ended the letter saying that he was her everything. Sealed with a kiss.

Tukey put the letter in an envelope, then took it to drop it in the mail box. On her way back to her room, she saw Shantí walk by her, looking as if she'd been crying. She was sniffling and wiping her eyes with the back of her hand.

Tukey stopped her. "What's wrong wit' ya, girl?" Tukey asked, concerned about her friend. "Yu look like yu mad about sum't-ing."

"I'm OK," Shantí said unconvincingly.

Tukey took her by the hand and led her back to her room. Niecy was laying on the top bunk, reading a magazine and paying them no mind. Tukey and Shantí sat on her bunk next to each other.

"Now, be honest wit' me, Shantí," Tukey said. "Why yu cryin'?"

Shantí's cute little yellow nose had turned red from her blowing it so hard. Her legs shook nervously. Tukey noticed that she kept avoiding eye contact with her. Niecy stopped reading and tuned in after she heard Tukey ask Shantí why she was crying.

Shantí attempted to speak, but the words wouldn't come out.

Tukey put her hand on Shantí's shoulder. "It's OK, girl. Tell me what's wrong."

Shantí's fingers fidgeted. "I really don't know how to tell you. I'm so embarrassed about it."

"Embarrassed?" Tukey was confused now.

"When I came to this place, last year." Shantí paused. "They did a blood test on me. And...and they said that I was HIV positive." She started crying again. Tukey got her a paper towel from her desk, then handed it to Shantí. Her face was too wet for one paper towel, so Tukey grabbed the whole stack.

"Does ya mum know?" Tukey asked. She really didn't know what to say to a person in her situation.

Shantí shook her head. "That ain't the worst part."

Niecy's heart was pounding so fast that she could've sworn that they felt it shaking the bed.

Shantí went on, saying, "Last month they tested me again, and...and they found out." She paused. "I got full-blown AIDS."

Tukey gave her a big hug, unafraid of catching the disease from her. They both sat there, holding each other and crying. The summer of 2001 was coming and Tukey and Shantí had been friends for seventeen months now. Tukey waived her rights to the halfway house and would be back on the streets in three more months. So would Shantí.

Niecy couldn't hold back any longer. She hopped down from the top bunk and joined her two friends. Together they cried and hugged each other like they were sisters.

After chow, Tukey and Shantí walked a few laps around the

track. Just by looking at her you couldn't tell that Shantí had AIDS. Her body was still firm and she was very pretty. But twenty years old was too young to be dying.

"Why don't ya come home wit' me," Tukey suggested. "Us can get you the best medicine. Me ain't got the money yet, but me will, real soon." Tukey stopped and turned to face her. "Yu like a sister to me. Us can have a lot of fun before yu get too sick to do anyt'ing."

Shantí smiled weakly.

"All yu got to do is change ya home plan wit' the counselor lady." Tukey pressed. "What ya say?"

"OK," Shantí agreed. They hugged again, then continued around the track. Tukey wanted to get as many laps in as she could before it got dark.

Friday night the girls hung out in Kyla's room, gossiping, telling stories and talking about what they'd be doing if they were out. Kyla was a shit-talking, jazzy girl that everybody liked. She wasn't what you would call attractive, nor would you call her ugly. She was just a simple girl who didn't tell lies to kick it. That's why Tukey liked her so much.

Tukey started tripping because Kyla had never shown her any pictures of her family, boyfriends or anything else. Kyla was also from Kansas City and Tukey wanted to see if they knew any of the same people. Kyla dug into her junky locker, searching until she found her picture book. She pulled it out and pretended to blow dust from it. Tukey took a seat at her desk, then Kyla sat the album down in front of her.

They were about halfway through the album when Tukey saw something that caught her eye. "Is dis Tee?" Tukey asked, pointing to a picture of someone who looked like Tee, but a few years younger. Also in the picture was Selina and a little boy. Tukey recognized the unmistakable face of Selina right away.

"You know my cousin, Tee?" Kyla asked, surprised. "Ain't he fine?"

"Who dis girl in the picture?" Tukey asked, like she didn't

already know.

"He don't mess with that whore no more," Kyla said with pride. "He told me that she used to set niggas up for him. She'd fuck 'em and everything. But they broke up 'cause she didn't like the fact that they couldn't be seen together."

"Why not?" Tukey inquired.

"Because he didn't want none of the dudes she set up to link him to her."

Tukey wanted to be mad at Tee for doing Keith like that, but she couldn't. In fact, she was kind of happy that Keith was being tricked all along. But she didn't like the fact that Selina was the bitch who was playing with her man's head. And it cost them their relationship.

* * *

The day had finally come for Tukey and Shantí to be released. Shantí was excited to get out and to be going to Kansas City to live with Tukey. Tukey couldn't wait to get out so that she could get her life in order. And get her fuck on. After a tearful goodbye to their friend Niecy, Shantí and Tukey walked to R&D to change into the clothes that Anitra sent them a week ago. They walked out of the front door with nothing but a check for the money they had on their books and a copy of their medical records.

Anitra was waiting in front of her car, wearing a sexy red mini-sundress, sandles and Cartier shades. Tukey smiled at the sight of her. She reached out and ran for her. Shantí watched in fascination as the two women hugged and kissed each other passionately. Anitra's nipples stiffened and poked through her dress. Tukey backed her against the car and stuck her hand under Anitra's dress. She felt around until she felt Anitra's warm juice on her fingers.

"What about me?" Shantí said, breaking them up.

"Sorry," Tukey said, letting go of Anitra. "Dis is me friend, Shantí dat me told ya about. Her gon' be staying wit' us."

Anitra gave her an approving look. "Hi, Shantí! You're as fine as Tukey said you was." Anitra complimented her on her looks because she knew that Shantí had the AIDS virus, and she wanted to make her feel good about herself.

"Thank you!" Shantí said shyly.

On the ride back to Kansas City, Shantí slept in the backseat, dreaming that she was being made love to for the last time. The dream was so intense that she felt herself explode inside her pants. Too shy to speak up, she stayed wet until they stopped for gas.

When they got home that night, Anitra showed Shantí to the guest bedroom, then helped her get settled in. At that moment Anitra and Tukey were too exhausted from the ride to fuck, so they lay in the bed and held each other until they fell asleep.

Tukey felt a tingling sensation between her legs and woke up panting. She was naked with her legs spread while Anitra was sucking on her soft pussy lips. Anitra gently eased two fingers in and out of her snatch, while she nibbled away on Tukey's clit. Tukey moaned softly while she squirmed from side to side. Anitra raised Tukey's butt up high off the bed, and let her tongue travel down to her ass. Tukey's body jerked slightly after she felt Anitra's tongue enter her ass.

"Ummmm," Tukey moaned.

With a steady motion, Anitra worked her tongue in and out of Tukey's ass like a dick. Tukey needed something to suck on. First she licked her fingers, then rubbed them around her hard nipples. Then she put her own titty into her mouth, gently biting and sucking on it. They went on that way for a while, until Tukey's body craved more. Her mouth released her titty and she muttered the words, "Put that dick in me, now. Please! Me want it, now."

Anitra got up. She lubricated her eight-inch dildo then strapped it on, making sure that the tickler touched her clitoris. By the time she got back to the bed, Tukey was on all fours, ready to get fucked. Her pussy lips were spread and her big firm chocolate ass was tooted up in the air.

"Take me pussy," Tukey said in a low voice. Anitra grabbed her ass cheeks and spread them apart. Tukey grabbed hold of the sheets and arched her back as Anitra entered her. "Ahhhh! Ahhh!

Shittt," she hollered as the dildo dug deep into her.

Tukey's pussy got dripping wet as she loosened up. Anitra grabbed her by her waist and worked her like a dog. Tukey started humping back, but when the dildo went too deep, she tried to get away. Anitra held onto her, banging her, making her head ram into the headboard.

Shantí lay in her bed, listening to Tukey beg Anitra for mercy. She could hear them panting like two dogs. Shantí had never had sex with a woman, but she wished that she was in there getting fucked like that.

Anitra switched positions. Now she had Tukey's feet on her shoulders. Tukey had her legs gaped wide and with her hands on Anitra's ass, guided her to her G spot. Her pussy was so wet that it made sucking noises every time Anitra pulled out.

"Ooh, Ooh, ooh, oooooh." Tukey's mouth fell open as she felt herself explode all over the dildo for the fifth time. Her come was so thick, it looked like her pussy had been lathered with Ivory soap. Tukey turned to face Anitra and looked at her like she was a god. Almost two years of backed-up come had finally been released. Tukey sat there unable to move because her legs were shaking out of control.

Anitra slid up under Tukey and threw her arm around her. "Did you miss me?"

Tukey was still in a daze. She had to catch her breath before she could speak. "Yes, me missed ya, a lot," Tukey said.

"Did you miss Keith?" Anitra asked, not really wanting to know.

Tukey frowned. "Fuck Keith!" she said, harshly. She suddenly got quiet. Her sudden silence let Anitra know that she did. "Yes, me miss him. But me can't help it. It's like....me don't know. Me can't explain it."

"Whatever," Anitra said hotly. She was beginning to believe that there was nothing she could do to make Tukey stop loving Keith. It didn't matter that she was there for her while she was in jail. Nor did it matter how many times she made her come during sex. "Why don't you just be with Keith, then?"

Tukey sighed. "Dat's not fair, Anitra."

Anitra got under the covers. "Good night." She ignored Tukey.

Tukey shook her head as she stared at the ceiling. She was caught up between two different types of love. One whom she wanted, but he didn't want her. And the other, she just didn't really know how she felt about.

* * *

Meanwhile, Keith was living it up like he had a license to sell dope. The police investigated the murders for about two weeks. During that time it was so hot around there that Keith couldn't even come home. But after the heat died down, business went on as usual. He had to spend a weekend with Dawn in an expensive hotel to get the townhouses that Larry and Mr. Woods lived in. After Keith did that with her, it was on for real. He assigned each one his own townhouse. Rock had the weight house. Capone had the crack house. Twain ran the new weed house, and Blue ran the new meth house. He gave Selina's old townhouse to Mann so that he could oversee all of the houses, since he was Keith's right hand man. His job was to supply the houses and keep a record of everything coming in and goin' out. Keith didn't want any of the guys trying to get slick and start selling their own dope as well as his out of the houses.

Keith and Selina had a huge wedding in the backyard of their new house. His friends didn't approve of him marrying so young, but he did it anyway. Keith believed that a man of his status should be married to keep him away from the gold-digging sack chasers out there.

Keith kept all of his new toys in his five-car garage. The Escalade, the Benz, a Lexus, a newly restored '69 Camaro and two BMW motorcycles. The house had a Jacuzzi room with marble floors, where he threw small get-togethers on the weekends. Keith's coke habit was getting out of control. There was never a time when he was with Pablo that they wouldn't shovel coke up their noses. Selina woke up in the middle of the night a while back, and caught Keith in the bathroom with his face bent over a mirror, snorting. When she ran away in tears he was too fucked up to go after her.

His crew upgraded their dope house bitches to call girls, which caused his crew to be turned on to the powder, too. Weed was no longer their drug of choice; coke and cognac were the only things that you'd catch them using to get high. The call girls got so freaky when they were coked up that it took very little persuasion for the crew to shell out cash for pussy.

Keith even talked Selina into getting high one night. He tricked her into thinking that he would rather do it with her at home than with some bitches out in the street. That night, Selina woke up to find herself naked in the bed with Keith, Jessica and Jessica's twin sister, Jessy. She was so pissed off that she packed her shit and moved out. All it took was a new diamond bracelet and a new Jeep and she moved her stuff back in.

Keith gave Tee two keys hoping that he would come to his senses and do something good with the money he made off them. Instead of investing it, Tee remodeled his house and bought a new pair of rims for his Benz. Tee was jealous of the life that Keith had and his jealously grew stronger every day. Tee even reported everything that Keith did behind Selina's back, to her. At first, Keith thought that Pablo was the leak. He confronted Pablo about it, because Pablo was the only one who could've been telling her such things. Pablo denied the charges and was pissed that Keith would think of him like that. Keith apologized to him before he left. He didn't want to leave there with hard feelings from the man who helped pay his bills.

Keith didn't figure out that Tee was the leak until he walked in on Selina and Tee having a suspicious conversation in their kitchen. This was a night when Keith and Selina threw a party at the house. Keith didn't approach Tee with the accusations. He decided to let it ride until another day, when he wasn't so high. If a fight broke out between them, Tee would probably whip his ass.

Their house was packed with white, Puerto Rican and

Mexican bitches. Occasionally you'd see a black girl's face here and there. The only men invited were Keith's crew, Pablo, Tee and Andre. Keith had a body-shaped cake made and laid on top of Selina's naked body. She lay face up across a long table in the dining room, while the guests sliced cake off her body. Each piece of cake that was removed left a piece of Selina's body showing. She was high when Keith talked her into doing such a thing.

Keith walked around in a silk robe with a pair of black thong drawers on underneath. He carried a bottle of Moët in one hand and grabbed girls' asses with the other. The twins, Jessica and Jessy, both followed Keith around like two lost puppies. He couldn't get enough of them, just like they couldn't get enough of him.

When the last slice of cake was gone, Selina got up and walked around naked to find Keith. Icing was still stuck between her titties and her inner thighs. Nobody stared because they were too high and busy doing their own things. Selina found Keith in the bedroom. Jessy was sucking on his dick, while Jessica licked coke off the tattoo on his chest. It was a portrait of his grandma, with her death date, 1-14-91.

"Get the fuck outta my bed," Selina yelled, angrily. She grabbed the lamp off the dresser and threw it at Jessica. Luckily, she forgot to unplug it, so it didn't go too far. The twins grabbed their clothes and hurried out.

Keith looked at Selina like she was the one that was tripping. "Why you do that?" His whole upper body was covered in coke.

Selina rushed over to her closet, slipped on a dress and a pair of low heels. She looked at him and shook her head in disgust. Tears rolled down her pretty face. "I do everything that you ask me to," she cried. "But it's never enough. Is it?" Keith just stared at her through red, glassy eyes. "Look at you! You don't even know what's going on. Damn junkie,"

Selina walked out of the room. She stopped in the kitchen to fix herself a drink. She took a bottle of tequila out of the cabinet, opened it, then took a long swig. Her face frowned up as the warm liquid ran down her throat. From the bedroom next to the kitchen, she could hear some girl hollering out Twain's name. Selina shook her head. Just like that, her life went from shit to sugar, now it was shit all over again. And to add to all that, she'd developed a cocaine habit as well, thanks to Keith.

Selina had the bottle turned up to her face when Tee walked into the kitchen. "See what I mean, now?" he said, walking toward her. "Just like Tukey, he don't got no respect for you no more. Look how he did you in front of his friends. He used your body as a fuckin' cake holder."

Selina put the bottle down long enough to swallow. She cut her eyes toward Tee, then tilted it back up to her face again. This time, Tee snatched it away.

"Gimme it," Selina yelled as she reached for it.

Tee held it up in the air, out of her reach. He finally gave it back to her. "You belong with me, and you know it. We got a son together." He ran his fingers through her hair. "Let's finish what we started."

Selina sighed. "OK, you win," she said in a low voice. She couldn't believe that she was gonna go along with it. "What do you want me to do?"

"Get the combination to his safe. I'll take care of the rest."

"What are you gonna do?" she asked, curious. "You ain't gon' kill him, are you?"

Tee looked around to make sure that no one was around to hear what he was about to say. He could hear voices and laughter coming from the living room, but no one was close enough to hear him speak. He told Selina the story about what they did to Ben when they went to LA. He told her all of the details, only Tee left out the things that he did. Instead, he added Vedo as one of the killers. Then he told her that Keith killed Vedo so he wouldn't be able to talk about it. He didn't kill Tee because he trusted him. That's what Tee planned on telling the police as soon as Selina got the combination to his safe. They knew where the safe was; getting Keith to trust Selina with the combination was their only problem. In order for her to do that, she was gonna have to keep him high and do a lot of dick sucking.

Tee moved close to Selina and kissed her once on the lips. Then again. When she didn't resist, he did it again, this time sticking his tongue into her mouth. Slowly Selina put her arms around him, enjoying the familiar taste of his tongue. They stopped kissing just as Keith walked into the kitchen. Guilt was written all over Selina's face. She was so nervous that she let the bottle slip from her hand. It hit the floor and splashed tequila on top of Keith's house shoes.

"What y'all doing?" Keith asked curiously.

Tee put on a fake smile. "Nothin', nigga. We just talking, mostly about yo' ass," Tee lied with a straight face. He couldn't afford for Keith to become suspicious of he and Selina. Then, his plans would be ruined for good this time.

At that moment, Keith figured out where Selina was getting her information. It had to be Tee. There were only two people who could've told her about what happened that first night he did cocaine at Pablo's: that was Tee and Pablo. Now it all made sense. Tee had become jealous of his new success. Keith would've expected that from anybody else, but not from his lifetime friend, Tee, whom he always tried to look after. But that's how the game goes; you can't trust nobody.

Keith knew that there was a chance that being high could be the reason why he was so paranoid and suspicious. He wouldn't confront Tee about it now. But from now on he was gonna keep a close eye on he and Selina. Being careful and aware was the only way that Keith was going to survive in this business because at his level of the game, there where no such thing as friends.

"Y'all was talking about me, huh?" Keith smiled to try and ease some of the tension in the air. "Keep on talking, then. Don't stop 'cause I'm here."

Tee wasn't stupid and could see right through Keith; he was onto them. But Tee wasn't about to let up that easy. If his plan was going to work, he had to convince Keith, right now, that nothing was going on between them.

"Man, I hope you don't think nothin' is goin' on between me and yo' wife, nigga," Tee said, attempting to regain Keith's trust. "We been hangin' too long for me to try some sneaky shit like that, bro."

"I did at first," Keith said honestly. "But then I told myself that this coke has got me trippin'. My fault, dog."

They shook hands.

"I'm not you, Keith," Selina said, almost convincingly. She walked over to the closet to get the mop.

"Sorry about that, man," Keith said. "I'll tell you what. Go ahead and take Jessy home with you tonight. My treat to you, OK?" He patted Tee on his back, then left him standing there.

On his way up to his bedroom, Keith saw Mann over by the Jacuzzi freaking with Jessica. He started to say something, but decided to just blow it off. There was no use trying to stop a whore from whoring. He'd had enough for one night. In his room Keith sprawled out on his bed, but couldn't go to sleep. He did love Selina no matter how badly he treated her. The fact that she might be creeping with Tee was heavy on his mind. He hoped to God that they weren't. He'd hate to have to put Tee down over a bitch. After all, Selina was his wife.

Keith lay in his bed for over an hour, thinking nasty thoughts. He'd expected Selina to come up by now, but she hadn't showed. What if Selina and Tee were trying to set him up? What if Selina had been a setup all along? Keith smelled deceit. But why would she marry him if she and Tee were....*the money,* Keith answered himself. But she was there for him while he was broke.

"Fuck it," Keith said to himself. "Time will tell everything." He dismissed all of his thoughts and finally fell asleep.

* * *

Keith got up early that morning. He took a shower, threw on a red Roc-a-Wear jogging suit and a white pair of Nikes. Selina was still sleeping, her body sprawled out over the bed. The covers had slid to the floor. He stood over the bed and looked down at her. She was fine as hell. He prayed that what he thought last night wasn't the truth. After all, Selina had helped him during his climb to the top. She carried the dope back and forth to the spots and ran all of the errands.

Keith looked on the dresser at all of the pictures they had taken on trips together to Jamaica, Mexico and cruises to Hawaii. They had seen the world in a very short time. He thought that Selina was the happiest woman he knew. He made a promise to himself that if she turned out to be innocent, he would start treating her right again. Maybe even give up the narcotic.

Keith backed his Escalade out of the garage, being careful not to get a scratch on it. After snorting up a gram of coke, he cautiously pulled out of his driveway onto the street. He pushed a button and a TV popped out of the dash. His music automatically came on sounding crystal clear. *That was ten grand well spent,* Keith thought. The sunroof was open and the sun beamed in. Keith sat back comfortably in his leather seat as he bobbed his head to Jay-Z's "Hard Knock Life". After he hopped onto the freeway, he set the cruise control. The rollers weren't gonna pull him over for any bullshit today.

Keith exited the freeway in the city, headed for Swope Park. When he entered the gates, he followed the concrete path all the way around to the American Band Stand. There was a sandbox across from it where he once played as a child. He parked his truck next to it and got out. With the button on his keychain, he popped the hatch. A small shovel was laying beside his speaker box. Keith picked it up and took it over to the sandbox, where he stopped in the middle and began to dig. *Clink. Clink.* Keith stopped when he felt the shovel hit the top of the metal box. He'd found what he was looking for. He reached into the hole and pulled out a small gray metal box. On his keychain was the key that opened it up. He glanced around before he opened it up, but no one was in sight. It was a little too early in the morning for kids to be out playing. In the box was the gun that he used to shoot Ben. It was tucked and wrapped inside three zippered plastic bags. Before he buried it, he scratched off the serial numbers and wiped off all the fingerprints. Keith left the box but carried the gun with him to the truck. From the console he removed a pair of rubber gloves and slipped them on. Then he took the gun out of the bags. It still looked like new. He stashed the gun under his passenger seat and threw the bags out of the window. Tee's house was his destination. He wanted to take him to breakfast to apologize for what happened last night.

* * *

They ate at Niecy's on Prospect. Keith picked up the tab for the pork chops and eggs that they'd eaten. They were riding down Troost when Keith said that he needed to stop and get some gas. He pulled into the Amoco on 63rd street. Before he got out of the car Keith told Tee to check out the new gun that he had bought. It was under the passenger seat.

After Keith finished pumping the gas he got back into the truck. Tee was still holding the gun in his hand, examining it. "Where you get this?" Tee asked.

"I picked it up this morning," Keith said, opening up his console. He took out a Crown Royal bag then handed it to Tee. "Here. Put it in here."

Keith watched Tee carefully, making sure that he got his fingerprints all over the gun. Just in case something went down about Ben's murder, like Tee running his mouth, Keith would have a little insurance.

Tee put the Crown Royal bag with the gun in it back under the seat. Now that Keith was riding with the murder weapon, he had to drive with extreme caution. When he dropped Tee off, he hid it again until he needed it.

Chapter 21

Ever since Tukey got out of jail, she did nothing but kick it. Shopping, clubbing, freaking – you name it. She did everything that she could to help Shantí keep her mind off of her problems. She hadn't even called Keith to let him know that she was out. A month had passed, now it was time for her to get down to business.

Mi'kelle hadn't even seen her daddy. Tukey made a phone call to Keith's mama. For the first few minutes of the conversation, Tukey made small talk, telling the older woman how she was doing and so on. Then in a sneaky way, she slid in and asked for Keith's phone number. His mama couldn't be tricked easily though. She told Tukey that Keith was married and had moved on with his life, and that she couldn't give her the number. But Tukey insisted that she only wanted it for Mi'kelle, so she could get in touch with her daddy. Eventually Keith's mama gave in.

Keith was out bending corners in his '69 Camaro. Sitting on the passenger side was a bad-ass bitch with whom he'd been out shopping all morning long. He was so fucked up when he met her a week ago, that he could barely remember her name. It was Toni, or Tanya, or something like that. He really didn't care. All he knew was that she had some fire-ass head and loved to swallow his come.

Keith came to a stop at a red light. Two young dudes in a two-door Chevy Caprice on Daytons were gunning the engine on the right side of him. They gave him a nod, signaling him that they wanted to race. Keith revved his engine back at them to indicate that he was ready.

The girl sitting next to Keith got excited and braced herself for the takeoff. After the light turned green, Keith took off, burning little rubber. Every few feet, his tires would make a *Errk*, sound as the car sped up. Two blocks down the road, Keith began to slow down. He'd left the Chevy so far behind, it was hardly in sight.

"You kicked they ass, baby," the girl said excitedly.

"Little niggas can't fu—" His phone rang, cutting him off. "Hello."

"Ya t'ink ya can spend some time wit' me?"

Keith could tell by the broken English who it was. He wanted to speak, but didn't know what to say. After all, he did leave her while she sat in jail for him.

"Kitty cat got ya tongue?" Tukey asked jokingly.

Keith relaxed. "Nah, I'm alright. Just surprised to hear from you, that's all."

His sudden change in tone made the girl next to him look at him crazy. Keith saw the look out of the corner of his eye, but he ignored her. He was on the line with somebody more important.

"Surprised, huh?" Tukey said in a low voice. "Why don't yu come up to Pete's and have a drink wit' me?"

"Cool. When did you get out?"

"Me'll be waiting," Tukey replied, ignoring the question. She hung up.

Keith pulled over at a bus stop. He picked up a pop can out of his cup holder and handed it to the girl.

"What you want me to do with this?" the girl asked curiously.

"Throw it away in that trash can over there," Keith pointed to the can next to the bus stop.

"Why come I just can't throw it out?"

"Just do it," Keith said with frustration.

The girl sighed deeply and mumbled something under her breath as she got out. When she got to the trash can, Keith pulled off and let the wind close the door that she left open. Down the street he stopped, throwing out the bags of clothes that he had just bought her. The last thing the girl saw of Keith was the smoke that came out of his tailpipes as he took off down the road.

Since it was still daylight outside, the lights in Pete's were off. Only a few people were at the bar, and few couples were sitting at tables. Keith spotted Tukey, who was bent over the pool table, attempting a cross-corner shot. She was wearing a tight black leather skirt that stopped just under her butt cheeks. From where he was standing Keith could see her thong showing underneath. Like she had eyes in the back of her head, Tukey stood up straight and turned in his direction. She smiled and Keith found himself in love all over again. She wore that skirt like no other woman could. Her dreads were pinned up in the back and even with the lights out, her skin was still glowing. She put her finger up and signaled him to come over.

Keith strolled over to her, looking crisp in his Phat Pharm outfit. As he walked her way, his platinum chain and diamond bezel were having a shine-off with the disco light. Tukey almost lost her breath seeing how good he looked. Her pussy started to leak as she remembered how Keith used to fuck her brains out. She'd almost forgotten how badly he dogged her while she was locked up. For a moment they stood there and eyed each other. It had almost been two years since they'd laid eyes on one another. Over Keith's shoulder, Tukey signaled for the waiter to bring over two more of what she was already drinking. Keith stepped to her and gave her a long hug.

"Ya lookin' good, mon," Tukey smiled from ear to ear. She toyed with his diamond emblem. "Doing well?"

Keith shrugged. "I'm managing."

The waiter came with the drinks and sat them on the table.

"Dat's not what me hear," Tukey said. "Me hear yu worth a lot of money dese days." She took a sip of her drink. "Me guess dat's why ya sent me all dat money while me was doin' time for ya."

Keith looked wounded. He attempted to speak but Tukey put

her hand up and cut him off. "Me know yu meant well," she answered for him. She took another sip of her drink. "How's....Selina? Dat her name?"

Keith got serious with Tukey. He could tell that she was up to something by the way the conversation was going; he just didn't know what it was that she was up to. "What's your angle, Tukey," he asked taking control of the conversation. He snatched his emblem out of her hand. "If you got something to say, go ahead and get it off your chest. I ain't got time to be playin' fuckin' kids' games wit' you."

Tukey stepped close to him. In heels, she towered over Keith a little bit. Her hard gaze met his. "Yu right, muthafucka, me do got somet'ing to say." Her voice began to crack, but she contained it. "Yu a bitch ass muthafucka, for doin' me like ya did. Me did almost two years of me life in jail for ya. Now ya talkin' about yu ain't got time for games, like ya all dat now." She put her finger up in his face. "If yu wasn't Mi'kelle's father, yu would be dead for fuckin' over me." Her breathing was hard.

Keith knew that Tukey was right, so he didn't try and defend himself. He took a seat and started on the drink in front of him. Tukey joined him. After exchanging long, heated stares, they both started laughing.

"No," Tukey protested. "Me suppose to me mad at yu. Don't make me laugh."

"Why not?" Keith asked, giving her his sympathy look. She seemed to have gotten prettier with age. A little thicker in the hips, too.

Tukey folded her arms across her chest. "For some crazy reason, me still in love wit' ya fine ass, bwai." She moved her seat next to his. Their lips met and they kissed each other softly, for a long time.

"Ummm," Tukey moaned as Keith worked his lips down to her neck. "Stop it," she laughed. "Me need to tell yu sum'ting."

She took a minute to get herself back together. She picked up his hand and began to rub it gently. "Me don't know any other way to tell yu this. Selina is Tee's baby mama."

Keith's eyes shot daggers at her. His heart was hammering and a vein began to throb in his temple. It was worse than he thought. Not only were Selina and Tee fucking around, but she had a baby by him. Now he knew why he'd never met her son's father. Not only was Keith hurt, his ego was crushed. How could a shrewd nigga like him get suckered in so easily? The bitch put that pussy on him and slid right in. He'd been hoodwinked.

"Fuck you talking about?" Keith played as if he never suspected it.

Tukey finished the rest of her drink. "Me girl Kyla had a picture of them together, wit' dere son. She say Tee used to have Selina set niggas up all the time. Come to t'ink about it, yu remember when Tee mentioned sum'ting—"

Tukey's voice faded as Keith slipped into another world. *That bitch made a damn fool out of me,* he thought. Tee made a damn fool out of me. After all the losses that I took, trying to make sure that he was alright; look how he chose to repay me. It's my turn to start playing games, now. I can't lose.

Keith snapped out of his trance. "What's it gonna take to get you back on my team?"

Tukey stared at him through her sexy eyes. Slowly she caressed his neck and face. "Me never stopped bein' on ya team." She paused. "Yu stopped being on mine." With that, they started kissing again.

Keith broke their embrace. "I'm gonna need you to do me a favor, baby," Keith said smoothly.

"Anyt'ing, baby," Tukey said softly, letting him know that the ball was back in his court.

Keith took a cigarette out of its pack and fired it up. He inhaled the smoke while he thought for a minute. He glanced at Tukey's face for signs of trust. To him, she looked as trustworthy as she ever had, but looks can be deceiving. He put out his cigarette. Then he ran down exactly what he needed her to do.

* * *

The last girl left the women's restroom at the club. Selina was stalling by the face bowl, pretending to fix her make up. When she was alone, she dashed into the stall and closed the door behind her. She pulled out a small bag of white powder. Selina smiled to herself, anxious to get some up her nose. She dumped a little onto the back of her hand; one long snort and it was all gone. Her eyes closed while she waited for it to take effect.

Ten minutes later, Selina exited the restroom on cloud nine. It was just after midnight and the club was jumping. Somehow she made it to the bar, where she sat and drank a few Tom Collins. The tight-fitting reptile pants, high heels, cowgirl hat and strapless top she wore kept the niggas trying to get at her.

Keith hadn't fucked her in a good month. Cocaine and tequila was all it took for a lonely wife's pussy to get hot and led astray. Selina checked out the people on the dance floor through narrow red eyes. Shaggy's "It Wasn't Me", was bumping out of the club's system.

Selina saw something that made her heart skip a beat.

Tukey was on the dance floor. She had on a pair of black leather boots that came up to her thighs and a zebra patterned one-piece outfit with the back cut out. One dude was dancing in front of her and another was on her back, trying to keep up with the black stallion. She was so tall and her ass was so fat that it jiggled all up on the guy's stomach instead of his crotch.

Tukey turned Selina on. There was something about her that made Selina's pussy moist. Tukey's black ass cheeks clapped as she shook her thang from side to side, to the beat of the song. Ever since Selina saw a picture of her, she wondered what it would feel like to lay up with her. Tukey's body was so firm and muscular, yet so soft looking. It really wasn't the coke that had gotten Selina into the bed with Keith and the twins; that was just what she made herself believe.

Now Tukey was facing in Selina's direction, watching her with seductive eyes, as she swayed her hips back and forth. Tukey took a dip and raised her arms, as she pretended to hump the floor.

Selina licked her lips. She wanted so badly to touch herself while she watched Tukey out there, twerking her thang. She bit her bottom lip and gave Tukey the same seductive look in return. Subconsciously, her hand slid down between her legs. Tukey smiled, then disappeared into the crowd.

After the song went off, Tukey headed in Selina's direction. Selina could imagine what she looked like naked. Suddenly Tukey was standing right in front of her.

"Buy me a drink?" Tukey said.

Selina played it cool. "Sure, why not." She signaled for the waitress. "Two double shots of tequila, please."

"Drinking hard tonight, huh?"

"Yep."

The waitress brought them their drinks. Tukey picked hers up and damn near poured it down her throat. When she finished, she picked up the salt shaker and dumped some onto Selina's hand. Then she licked it off, slowly. Tukey noticed how erect Selina's nipples had become.

"Ya see sum'ting yu like?" Tukey said, coming on to Selina.

Selina nodded her head. "Yep. How about you?"

"Me don't go by looks." Tukey stuck her finger into her mouth. "Me like to taste t'ings first." Tukey nodded toward the bartender. "Buy a bottle and meet me out front. Me have a motor-cycle outside. Yu can come back for ya car in the mornin'."

Selina got excited. "Where we goin'?"

"Me got a room for tonight. Ya comin'?"

"*Cueste lo que cueste.*" Selina smiled. "Be there in a minute."

"Me be out front waiting." Tukey kissed her on the lips before she walked away.

* * *

When Tukey opened the door to the hotel room, she invited Selina in first. The lights were dim, but you could still see. Selina sat the bottle of tequila down on the table before she made her way to the bed. There was a small CD player on the table as well, sitting next to a large Coach bag. Tukey appeared in the bathroom doorway, naked. The sight of her took Selina's breath away.

Tukey saw Selina admiring her body and smiled. "Me was gonna take a shower. Want to come?" Her voice was heavy with sarcasm.

Tukey had lathered her body with strawberry perfumed soap. Selina could smell it when she came into the bathroom naked. Tukey was the one doing the admiring this time. Selina had a small, firm, honey-colored body without a blemish or bruise anywhere on it. Her full brown nipples and natural curly pussy hairs had Tukey's mouth watering. Selina threw her arms up in the air and spun around, giving Tukey a chance to really check out what she was about to get.

Selina stepped into the shower with her. She made the first move and wrapped her arms around Tukey, squeezing her ass. Tukey bent over and kissed Selina roughly on the lips. While they kissed, she could feel Selina's finger slide into her booty. Tukey's ass tightened up, then she began kissing her harder. Selina worked her tongue down to Tukey's breast, licking and sucking on her nipples.

"Shiit," Tukey moaned, while holding onto the back of Selina's head.

Sliding down to her knees, Selina slowly parted Tukey's legs. A quick tongue lashing in her navel, then she worked her way down to Tukey slightly kinky bush. With one hand on Tukey's thigh for support, Selina slid three of her small fingers into Tukey's pussy while she nibbled away at her clit.

"Ahh! Ooh! Oh, shiiit," Tukey moaned loudly. Selina knew all of the right spots to hit. She was a freak by nature, not by choice. Gently, Selina bit down on her clit with her teeth, causing Tukey's first orgasm for the night.

After they left the shower, Selina sprawled out naked across the bed with her legs gapped wide open. Tukey took a can of whipped cream from the bag that was on the table and she shook it well before she sprayed some around Selina's nipples, pussy and between her toes. Tukey was enjoying this.

Selina started to squirm after she felt Tukey's warm mouth on her toes. Tukey had her entire foot in her mouth, sucking on it like it was a dick. It felt so good that Selina thought it was one for a minute. Tukey nibbled and bit her way up to Selina's inner thigh. Selina bit her lip as she felt Tukey's lips sucking on her warm pussy. She threw both feet over Tukey's shoulders and let her go to work while she caressed the back of her head.

Selina let out a loud howl as she exploded into Tukey's mouth. Tukey could tell that she was coming by how violently her legs were shaking. Selina tasted so good that Tukey licked her all the way down to her ass.

"Ooh! Ooh! Ooh," Selina moaned feeling that tongue stab her ass like a soft dagger. After a while, Selina flipped over and got in the doggy style position so Tukey could have better access. "Fuck me, *mami*," Selina panted. "Get this *chocha*, baby."

She reached back and fingered herself while Tukey lubricated and strapped on her dildo. She bit down on her bottom lip when she felt the huge dick penetrate her walls. Her pussy was so wet that Tukey had no trouble getting all nine inches inside her. In and out she worked her. Selina's ass jiggled and clapped while Tukey fucked her in a steady motion.

Six positions and four orgasms knocked them both right out.

Tukey's eyes fluttered open. The hot sun was beaming in through the window. Selina was standing over her holding a white Styrofoam container in her hand. She had gotten up early to catch a cab so that she could pick up her car from the club. Then she stopped by Denny's and picked up breakfast for them. She extended the room reservation for another night before returning. Tukey took the container from her and sat up, not bothering to cover her exposed titties. She nibbled on a piece of bacon. "What's ya new husband gonna say about yu being out all night?"

Selina took off her clothes and got back into bed. "Fuck him. I'm tired of his shit, anyway. He turned out to be like every other dog-ass nigga out there." Selina looked at Tukey. "Besides, I think I want to be your woman after last night."

Tukey shrugged and continued to eat her food. When she finished she sat the empty box down next to the bed. The women cuddled up and talked to each other. Or rather, Selina did the talking while Tukey listened.

She told her everything that Tukey didn't know about Keith. Like how he hooked up with Pablo. Their new house. Where Keith's safe house was and a lot of other shit that they should not have been discussing. Tukey sat there and sucked it all in as if it meant nothing to her. But actually she was hurt. Keith had done and shared so much with a woman who didn't even have a kid by him. She listened to the story, but the whole time her blood was boiling over.

"Do you still love Keith?" Selina asked softly.

Tukey looked at her like she was crazy. "Fuck nah! Me wish dat bitch was dead in him grave. Yu know how him did me," she said, angrily.

Selina stared up at the ceiling deep in thought. "You know he has a lot of money stashed in his safe house." Selina looked at Tukey.

"Like how much?"

Selina shrugged. "Three million or so. He thinks I don't be keeping track of things, but I do."

"Three million," Tukey repeated loudly. "Me Keith's been workin' hard since me been gone. Damn." Tukey shook her head. "The t'ings we could do wit' dat kind of money." She threw that out there, knowing that Selina would take the bait. In one night, she had stolen Keith's wife and found out all of his personal business.

Selina looked at Tukey after hearing her say, "We." Selina sat up. A plan had been formulating in her mind. "You know what I've been thinking about?"

"What?"

"Taking all of his money and leaving town," Selina said in a serious voice.

Tukey almost laughed. She didn't expect Selina to be this easy, after she had been up under Keith. "Running off wit' him money,"

Tukey repeated. "Him would kill ya if him ever caught up wit' yu."

"No, he won't," Selina said confidently. Then she told her the story that Tee told her, about that guy named Ben that they killed in LA. Selina also told Tukey that Tee planned on dropping an anonymous tip on Keith about the murders. Tee knew that if they got Keith, he wouldn't tell on him, he'd just take the time all by himself. But they couldn't do it until Selina got the combination to his safe.

Tukey always knew in the back of her mind that Keith had killed her uncle. She just never spoke on it. Now it was confirmed.

Selina went on, saying, "Now, I don't want to be with Tee. I never really have. Now I want me and you to take the money and run."

"What about Tee?"

"I don't care about Tee," Selina said in a low voice. "We could kill him."

Tukey looked at her like she was crazy. "Who, me or yu?"

Selina stared into space. "Me, I guess." She looked at Tukey with her young doll face. That's when Tukey decided to do it herself. She believed that Selina would do it. But she didn't think that she could get away with it. Selina wasn't slick enough for something like that. Tukey couldn't afford to let Selina fuck everything up.

Chapter 22

Her eyes rolled into the back of her head. Sweat ran from her forehead all the way down to her nipples. With her hands planted on his sweaty chest, she rode his hard dick like it was the last one she'd ever ride.

His veins popped out of his forehead while he gasped for air. The swooshing sound that her pussy made only added to the sensation. "Yesss! Yessss," she moaned while she worked his come right out of him.

She heard him holler, "I'm 'bout to come!" She hopped off his dick and tried to catch his hot load into her mouth. Even she couldn't believe the freak that she had become. "Ummm," she moaned as she jacked his load into her mouth. His warm come was soothing going down her throat.

It had been a while since she'd had some real dick and she wanted more of it. Pulling his dick out of her mouth, she lay on her side and gapped her legs so that he could hit it sideways. Her inner thighs and pubic hairs were smeared with her thick white come. With her left leg over his shoulder, she got a grip on his ass and guided him inside her. Her warm pussy made his half-limp dick stand to attention again. She held onto his waist while he stroked her, making sure that he hit the right spot. She grunted, moaned, groaned and begged him to go deeper. That real meat felt so good to her. She reached up and grabbed her ankle, spreading her legs wider so her pussy could stretch out.

Sweat dripped off his face into her open mouth, but she was too far in the zone to notice. Her eyes remained closed while she imagined that it was Keith on top of her, doing this thang. Her soft thighs began to tremble. She squeezed her eyes tight with her mouth open as she waited to erupt. When Tee pulled out of her, come was still dripping off the head of his dick.

"Come here," she said, reaching for his dick. She put it into her mouth. When she pulled it out, it was clean, except for a little saliva on the head of it.

She fired up a blunt, took a few puffs, then passed it to him. Tukey relaxed in his arms and inhaled their sex smell until he finished smoking. She knew that it was a matter of time before he started filling her in about Selina. She could feel it. Some fire-ass head and a little weed was all it took to loosen tight lips. That's why she gave him her A+ performance. Tee was really a trick and Tukey was about to prove it.

They had mysteriously bumped into each other at the mall yesterday, while he was out shopping for shoes. Tee came on to Tukey. At first she offered a little resistance, but quickly gave in before he had a chance to give up. They agreed to meet up at a bar, where they had countless glasses of gin and juice. She played on his intelligence, using the information that she'd gotten out of Selina. She told him how much she really hated Keith and that she wished that he would end up in jail or dead somewhere. That brought a smile to Tee's face. He'd been wanting Tukey for years now. He wasn't gonna blow his chance this time.

"Has Keith ever fucked you as good as I just did?" Tee asked, rubbing Tukey's back.

"No!" Tukey answered. "Yu have some good dick." She reached under the covers and grabbed it. "And big one, too."

"I've been wanting some of that for a long time," Tee admitted. "You just wasn't trying to fuck with me."

"Yes me did," Tukey lied. "Keith was just in the way. Him cyaah fuck me like yu did tonight. Yu make me pussy tingle inside, mon. Ya know?" She stroked his male ego.

"Yes," Tee said. He soaked up everything that she was saying.

"If me had the money, us could just pack up and leave dis place." Tukey looked into his eyes. "Wouldn't yu like to see me naked on a beach somewhere?"

"Umm hmm," Tee agreed. "What if we could go sometime soon?"

"Cut it out, Tee. Us don't even fuck around like dat. Besides, where would us get the money?"

Tee hesitated for a minute. He wondered how much could he trust her. If he was to go by the way she sucked his dick, he would say that he could one hundred percent. He was tired of Selina anyway. Tee hadn't forgot that she fell in love with Keith and turned her back on him. If Keith weren't such a baller, Selina would still be with Tee. She turned her back on him. Now he would do the same to her, after she did what she had to do.

"What if I said that I was gonna rob Keith?" Tee finally said.

Tukey's plan was working. "Me would say, not'ing." She sat up in the bed. "Listen. Dere is no one in dis world who would love to see Keith fall more than me."

"Why is that?"

Tears began to form in her eyes. Tukey looked away from him.

"What's wrong?" Tee said. He put his hand on her shoulder.

"Me t'ink him killed me uncle in LA." She began to cry. This time she was serious.

"He did kill your uncle." Tee waited for his words to settle in. Then he explained what had happened, only he used Vedo's name where his should've been. If he'd told her that he took part in killing her uncle, they'd be finished just as soon as they started.

Tukey was crying in his arms. "Me want him to pay for what him done."

Tee held her tight. "He will. I promise you that." After she calmed down a little, he filled her in on his and Selina's plans. "But I don't want Selina anymore. After she does this, we're finished.

It'll just be me and you, baby."

The only problem was, it had been over a month since Selina started trying to get the combination. She kept coming up empty-handed. As far as Keith was concerned, there was no reason for her to know the combination to his safe. If he ever got kidnapped and needed some money, his mama already knew what to do. A bitch would rather see him dead before they would turn over the money. So Tee decided that they would have a better chance breaking into it. With Keith locked up for murder, he would have plenty of time to figure out how.

"Don't make me promises yu can't keep," Tukey said in a serious voice.

"What if I told you that I made the call to the police this morning?"

"Did yu?"

Tee nodded his head.

"What did yu tell them?" Tukey listened very carefully.

"I told them what Keith told me that he did, and where they could find him. As long as they don't know who tipped them off, I ain't got nothing to worry about. He'll have a hard time trying to explain where he was that night."

"Ya t'ink they'll arrest him?"

"Right now, for questioning. But I think they'll hold him for a while. I told them enough for them to be able to scare him into snatching the first deal they offered."

"Cool, mon." Tukey wrapped her arms around his neck and gave him a kiss for doing such a good job. "Listen, baby. Go in the bathroom and take a shower. Me got somet'ing me want to do to ya."

"Like what?" Tee said eagerly.

Tukey ran her finger down the middle of his back. "Yu ever had ya ass licked before? Trust me, it feels good, mon."

Tee hadn't had it done before, but it sounded good to him anyway. He would do anything to get her under his wing. He jumped up out the bed and ran for the shower.

Tukey got up and hurried into her clothes. "Baby," she hollered through the bathroom door.

"What?" Tee yelled back over the noise of the shower running.

"Me about to go get some ice. Be right back." She walked out the door and went to the front office. She put two quarters into the pay phone and called Keith.

"What's up, baby?" Keith said, answering the phone.

Tukey quickly gave him the run down on everything that Tee had just told her. Keith told her to keep with the plan and he would be in touch. "OK. Me love yu, baby."

"You too." Keith hung up.

Tukey reached into her purse, pulling out her knife, and stuck it into her back pocket. She glanced around the office to make sure that there were no cameras and that she wasn't seen by anyone.

Back at the room, Tee was laying on his stomach across the bed. Tukey walked over and smacked him on the ass cheek. "Ya ready for me, daddy?"

Tee closed his eyes and relaxed while Tukey took her clothes off again. She strapped on a two-inch anal dildo without him seeing her and she eased onto the bed behind him. She bent over and gave him a good kiss on his ass cheek to get him aroused. Tee squirmed a little. Tukey propped his ass up in the air and spread his cheeks apart. Then she jammed the dildo in him.

"Ahhhhh....ahhh," Tee screamed. He hopped off the dildo, holding his ass. "What the fuck y....what the fuck you do to me, bitch?"

Tee was curled up on the floor, almost in tears from the pain. He swore that he was gonna kill Tukey as soon as he got up. She'd crossed the line with that one. Tukey pulled out her knife and knelt down beside him. Her lips curled as she grabbed Tee by his hair and pulled his head back. He tried to struggle but it was no use. Tukey reached around the front of his neck and sliced it from one side to the other. Blood squirted everywhere.

Tukey stood and watched him die. Tee choked, squirmed and

rolled around on the floor unable to scream or call for help. He finally died with his eyes wide open. Pulling two trash bags out of her large purse, Tukey sacked up the sheets and comforter. Forensic scientists could detect body fluids very easily. That's why she had Tee shower first. She cleaned up, threw the knife into the bag with sheets and left.

* * *

As soon as Keith hung up with Tukey, he rushed out of the house to go pick up the gun that he had stashed. When he returned, he made sure that he played his music loud. He wanted the neighbors to see him in his car as he pulled up to the house. When the police found Tee's body, he could always say that he was at home when it happened. He would use his nosy-ass white neighbors as alibis because they saw him pulling into his driveway.

Wearing rubber gloves, Keith stashed the gun in a shoe box, deep inside his closet. Selina was giving her son a bath and didn't have a clue what was going on. He fixed himself a sandwich and a beer, then kicked back in front of his big screen TV. He was waiting on the police to show up. If Tee did what Tukey said that he did, they were sure to be on their way, soon.

Keith started dozing off at a little after eleven. All of a sudden he heard someone yelling outside his front door. "Kansas Police Department! Get down!" Then the door came crashing in. "Search warrant," somebody yelled.

He put his hands in the air after he felt the barrel of a gun at his temple. "Don't fuckin' move," an officer said, while the others continued going through the rest of the house. Keith was cuffed and sat on the floor next to the TV.

While the officer read Keith the warrant, Selina and Terry were brought into the room by another cop. They were crying but they weren't cuffed.

"I didn't do nothin'," was all Keith had to say to them.

They searched for about thirty minutes until a tall lean officer came into the living room. He carried the shoe box that contained the gun with a triumphant smile on his face. He looked at Keith.

"You know anything about this gun that we found in this box?"

"Nope."

"I didn't think so." The lean cop examined the gun. He nodded his head after he saw that it was a nine millimeter; the same kind that shot Ben. They bagged it up. "I think we have the murder weapon, sir," he said to his superior officer.

The other officer examined it. "Let's get those guys from LA down here pronto." He looked down at Keith. "Get his ass down to the station."

Selina cried and asked a bunch of questions as they hauled Keith off. Selina wanted to pat herself on the back for playing a good role. She knew exactly what was going on.

Since the bullets that killed Ben were in LA, Keith would have to wait in the county jail for the lab results to come back. Keith knew that they would match the bullets with the gun. But the prints that they found on the gun wouldn't match his. They'll find the prints of a dead man, and dead men couldn't talk. They would have to cut Keith loose, and that would be the end of that. It wasn't his fault that Tee tried to set him up by stashing the murder weapon at his house, then leaving an anonymous tip. It might have worked if he'd remembered to wipe off his prints.

In the county jail they dressed Keith in an orange jumpsuit and issued him two blankets and a pillow, then they took him to his cell. A heavyset young man was sitting on the bottom bunk, combing out his nappy perm.

He looked up at Keith. "What's up?"

Keith nodded. After he made his bunk, he walked out into the day room to use the phone. He called Tukey's mama's house where Tukey was supposed to be. His nose started to drain while he was on the phone.

"Hello," Tukey answered. She waited until the recording was over, then she pressed five to let the call come through. "Hey baby. Are yu OK?"

"I'm cool," Keith said, sounding a little worried. "Look here, I might be here for a few days while they wait on the L.A.P.D. to do their thang. In the meantime, you take care of that other thing I told you to do. What happened with my guy?"

"Him got fucked," Tukey said, referring to Tee. "Yu take care of yaself in dere."

"OK."

"Baby?"

"What?"

"Don't drop the soap," Tukey laughed. They spoke for a little while longer, then she turned the phone over to Mi'kelle. Keith and Mi'kelle exchanged "I love yous" until the phone time was up.

Tukey got off the line with Keith, then made another phone call.

"FBI," a white voice answered the phone.

"Can me speak wit' Agent Jeffery Nowak or Agent Terry Sawyer, please."

"Hold on a minute."

For a brief moment Tukey heard music, then someone picked up the phone. "Agent Nowak."

"Yes, Agent Nowak. This is Tukey Tosh. Do yu remember me?"

"Um hm, but only because of that accent of yours," he said. "What can I do for you, Miss Tosh?"

"Me got a deal for yu."

* * *

Lockdown was at seven o'clock. Keith had spent his day playing cards with his celly and some of the fellas in his unit. Like robots, they all walked quietly to their cells and got into their bunks. For a while, Keith lay on his bunk, thinking to himself.

"So what's yo' name, man?" his celly said to him.

"KB."

"I'm Rico. What you in for?"

"Murder," Keith stared at the ceiling. "What about you?"

"Sheeit, man, I don't even like to talk about it," Rico said sadly.

Keith leaned over the bed and looked down at Rico. "What

you do?"

"I took a case for my girl."

"For yo' girl?" Keith repeated. He couldn't believe what he was hearing. "Tell me the whole story."

Rico sat up in his bed and looked up at Keith. "Me and my girl was selling dope out of this motel, an' shit. I ran out of dope, but she still had some."

"Who, yo' girl?"

"Yeah. She sell dope too. Anyway, the police kicked the door in, talking about somebody sold dope to an undercover, or some ole shit they was saying. She was pregnant at the time. So when they found her dope that she hid under the bathroom sink, I went ahead and took the case."

Keith shook his head. "She would've been having that baby up in here, if that was me. Where she at now? She be coming to see you, an' shit?"

"Sheeit, man that bitch has already been caught fucking around with some nigga." Rico sounded pitiful. "Man, I knew I shouldn't have took that case."

"How much time did you get?"

"Ten years," Rico answered. "But my lawyer said that I have a good chance of giving some of the time back."

Keith lay back in his bunk. He'd had enough of Rico's sad ass for one day. Ten years for some bitch. Dude had to be crazy. Pussy made some people do strange things. Jail was already becoming too much for Keith, and he'd only been locked up for one day. The white man was coming down hard on niggas getting caught with dope. This whole experience made Keith want to get out of the game while he still had a chance. What was going on in his life at the moment was more like TV shit than reality. He had three point two million in his safe and plenty of dope over at the townhouses. Financially he was secure. *Take the money and get out of town* was the first thought that came to Keith's mind. But business was doing too good to just walk away.

* * *

The next day Tukey drove to the apartment complex to pick up some shit for Keith. Keith had called her that morning and gave her the address to Selina's old townhouse where Mann was now staying. Tukey was coming to pick up Keith's money for him.

Mann was standing in the door when Tukey pulled into the parking lot. She hopped out of her car wearing sunglasses, a floral print sundress and sandles. Mann held the door open for her. Rock and Capone were sitting at the table, stuffing money into a bag. Twain and Blue were in front of the TV playing PlayStation.

About a month ago, police started hanging around the parking lot. Sometimes they would park their cars and sit for hours. So Keith changed the business hours to sundown to sun up. In the daytime they would hang over at Mann's townhouse to keep an eye on things.

"You can have a seat," Mann said, closing the door.

Tukey shook her head. "Dat's OK. Me do need to use the bathroom."

Mann pointed toward the stairs. "Up there and to the right," he said. He stood at the bottom of the steps hoping to catch a glimpse of her butt under her short dress.

Tukey shut and locked the bathroom door. She reached up under her dress, dug into her panties and pulled out a wad of fifty-dollar bills. She opened up the cabinet over the sink and put the money on the shelf. She wanted it to look as if someone had stashed it there. She flushed the toilet before she went back downstairs.

Mann picked up the bag that Capone and Rock had filled with money. He handed it to Tukey when she came down the stairs. "Tell Keith that's two hundred grand," he said. "We still got plenty of dope left, so we're cool for now." A curious look appeared on his face. "What he in jail for, anyway?"

"Him had a fight wit' Selina," Tukey lied. "Me gonna go get him."

Keith didn't want them to know the real reason that he was in jail. If they had known that he was in there on a murder case, they would probably run off with his shit, thinking that he would be gone for a while.

Tukey said, "Did yu put the other stuff in here him asked for?"

"Ah yeah," Mann said. He'd forgotten all about it. "Hold on." He ran down into the basement. A minute later he came back up with a zippered plastic bag full of crack. "Here," Mann handed it to her. "That's twenty ounces in there. He wanted it already rocked up, didn't he?"

Tukey nodded her head. "T'ank ya." She hurried out the door and climbed back into her rented Ford Expedition, pulling off fast. She drove for about six blocks to an old abandoned gas station. Parked there were six Crown Victorias and a black van.

Tukey hurriedly took twenty ounces of the crack out of the plastic bag, then put it into the bag that had the money inside it. Then she put the bag on the floor of the backseat. She closed up the bag with the remaining six ounces in it and got out of the car.

The van door slid open as she approached. Eight big white guys were in the back, suiting up in FBI combat gear. Agent Nowak stepped out of it. "Everything go OK?"

Tukey handed him the bag of crack. "They're all around to the townhouse, now. Me bought dis wit' the marked fifties dat ya gave me."

"Good job! What about the girl? Was she there?"

"No, but me suppose to be meeting her later," Tukey said. "Me probation is finished after dis, right?"

Nowak raised his right hand. "Promise. You've been more the generous to us, doing what you just did. I don't understand why you did it. But I guess you have your reasons for it." He patted Tukey on the back. "Now get outta here, before somebody sees you. We're about to go get these guys."

* * *

Keith was awakened early and escorted to the interrogation room. He sat there by himself for what seemed like hours as he waited for the detectives to come in and talk with him. The door opened and two stone-faced black detectives came in and flashed their badges. Both stood about six-foot-four or five inches tall. One was big and yellow with long braided hair; the other one was big and black with half of his hair missing on top. They had to have been LA detectives, because Kansas City cops didn't look like that. They both took seats directly across from Keith.

The yellow one spoke first. "I'm Detective Hawkins," he said, then pointed to his partner, "and this is Detective K-9."

Keith sat back in his chair and returned their hard stares. He refused to let himself be intimidated by them.

"Why they call you K-9?" Keith asked.

K-9 leaned closer to him. "Cause I attack when I'm provoked. And being lied to provokes me. Just so you know."

"Heel, boy," Hawkins said to K-9, then turned his attention back to Keith. "Where did you get the gun that was found in your house?"

"I don't know nothin' about no gun," Keith said.

"You don't know nothin'?" K-9 yelled, rising to his feet. "Don't play that shit wit' me! Where in the hell did you get that gun?"

"All I know is, y'all say y'all found it in my house. Now how it got there, I don't know."

Hawkins said, "You'd better be lucky we ain't in LA, in our jurisdiction. We'd have your tough ass turned upside down." Hawkins calmed down and glanced at his notes. "Do you know who Terrance Jenkins aka Tee is?"

Keith nodded his head. "Yeah, I grew up with him. What about him?"

Hawkins said, "The KCPD found him dead in a motel room this morning. He had been sodomized and his throat had been cut from ear to ear." Hawkins leaned forward and stared at Keith through hard green eyes. "You wouldn't know nothing about that, would you?"

Keith pretended to be shocked. Actually, he was a little hurt that he had to have Tee killed. Tee had been his partner since for-ever. Selina may have brought up the idea to kill Tee to Tukey, but it was Keith who gave the order.

Keith cleared his throat. "No. I didn't even know that he was dead."

Hawkins sat back in his chair. "You know what's funny? The fingerprints that we found on the gun belonged to the deceased. Ain't that strange?"

Keith shrugged. "Maybe he's the one who put that gun in my house. You ever thought about that? Maybe he's the reason that I'm here." Keith voice was rising now. "Maybe whatever he was into is the reason why he ain't alive today." Keith lowered his voice. "Now if y'all ain't got nothin' on me, I'm ready to leave."

Hawkins turned to K-9. "We ain't gonna get nothing out of him," he said in a doubt-filled tone. He stood up and walked to the door. "By the way." He turned back around. "We're still checking on a few things. So you won't be released until tomorrow. Hopefully." Both detectives walked out.

After Keith got back to his unit he called Selina.

She answered the phone sounding upset. "Hello." She waited for the recording to end, then she pushed five to let him through. "Baby, they kicked in the townhouses!"

"What!" Keith yelled.

"They kicked in all the townhouses," Selina informed him. "Mann, Twain, everybody went to jail. I'm scared they're gonna hit us next. I need to get into the safe so I can—"

"Baby, baby, calm down," Keith said. His heart was racing. He hadn't planned on this happening. Selina was right, they might be headed there next. "Baby, I'ma call you right back, I promise."

"No, *papi*," Selina cried. "I need the combination to the safe, so I can move yo' money before they come—"

"Baby, I'ma call you back. Control yourself." Keith hung up on her. Then he called Tukey. Her mama's house number was transferred to her cell phone.

When Tukey answered the phone, Keith said, "I need you to put plan B into effect, now."

"When are yu gettin' out?"

"In the morning. Get everything ready. Tomorrow, I'll meet

up with you at the meeting place."

"What's the combination?"

Keith hesitated for a minute. Once again he asked himself if he could trust her. What choice did he have? He had to get the money out of the house in case the police kicked that house in, too. She'd killed Tee for him, so he figured that he might as well give it a shot. "It's my grandma's death date."

"One fourteen ninety-one?"

"Right. Make sure that slick-ass little bitch gets what she deserves."

"Me love yu." Tukey said, before she hung up. Immediately, she called Agent Nowak again. The last call that she made was to Selina, telling her that Keith would be getting out tomorrow, so they had to move quickly. Tukey also told her that she had a good idea what the combination to his safe was. Selina gave her the address to the safe house so they could meet up there.

Selina's Benz was already sitting in the driveway when Tukey pulled up to the house. Tukey took a screwdriver out of her glove box, then grabbed the bag out of the back seat as she got out of the truck. She stopped behind Selina's Benz and knocked out the tail light with the screwdriver.

Selina opened up the door before Tukey had a chance to knock. "Come on, it's downstairs," Selina said. She had a nervous look on her face. "They already kicked in the townhouses. They might be onto this spot too. We've got to hurry up."

When they got to the basement Selina led Tukey into a small room behind the stairs. Mounted into a concrete wall was a five-foot-tall steel safe. Tukey dropped her bag and hurried over to the safe. The first three combinations that she tried were bogus. Then she screamed out, "Ooh, me t'ink me know it!"

"Hurry, hurry," Selina said anxiously.

This time Tukey turned to the correct numbers and it opened. Selina's face lit up with triumph. $3.2 million dollars stared them in the face, stacked in neat rows. The sight of all that money made both of their faces instantly light up.

"Ya hear dat?" Tukey said faking.

"Hear what?" Selina asked.

"Sounded like a car door. Run upstairs and check t'ings out."

"Pack up the money," Selina said as she rushed out of the basement.

As soon as Selina left, Tukey grabbed her bag and opened it. She pulled out two folded laundry bags. She unfolded and opened them. She reached back into the bag and removed the baggie that had the twenty ounces of crack in it. She stuffed that and the two hundred thousand dollars that she got from Mann into one of the laundry bags. Tukey hauled the laundry bag over to the safe. She scooped out a few hundred thousand dollars into the laundry bag with the two hundred and the crack and pulled the string tight to close it.

Selina came running back down the steps. She winced after she saw that Tukey only had one bag packed up. "Hurry up, girl. What're you waiting on?"

Tukey handed her the bag of money. "Here, take this up to ya car. Hurry."

Selina threw the heavy bag over her shoulders and lugged it up the steps.

When she was out of sight, Tukey raked the majority of the money into the other laundry bag. She locked the safe back up, then headed upstairs. Selina was walking back into the house when Tukey came dragging the bag through the living room.

"Let's go, let's go," Selina hollered, hysterical.

Tukey stopped for a second. "Yu will drive ya own car and me will drive mine. Dat way, when Keith gets out, him won't know us together."

Selina looked at her suspiciously, but then she thought about the bag full of cash that she had stuffed inside of her trunk. If Tukey was trying to shake her, at least she'd have her part of the money. "OK, whatever," Selina said. "Let's just get outta here. We'll meet up at the Holiday Inn off 71."

"OK," Tukey agreed.

Selina took off out the door. Tukey dragged her bag out to her truck and loaded the money into the back. Selina pulled out first, while Tukey followed a short distance behind her. If she would've looked in her rear view mirror, Selina would have seen Tukey lagging farther and farther behind. Selina saw an unmarked police car sitting on the corner as she neared the end of the block. She tried to look normal. She cut on her signal light and made a right turn. Slowly the police car pulled out behind her. He followed her for a few blocks to make her sweat, then he hit the sirens. She pulled over immediately.

Through her rear view mirror Selina saw a police man dressed in regular clothes get out of the driver's side, and a large white man wearing an FBI windbreaker get out on the other side.

"*Shit!*" Selina said to herself. Her hands shook while she went through her purse and looked for her driver's license.

The officer walked up to her window. "You know that you have a busted tail light ma'am?" he asked.

Selina tried not to sound nervous. "No sir, I didn't." She had a big, hopeful smile on her face.

"You need to get it fixed ASAP."

"I will," Selina focused her attention on the FBI guy. "I'm in kind of a hurry."

Before she knew it, the officer had grabbed her door handle and opened her door. "Could you please step out of the vehicle, ma'am? We just want to make sure that you don't have any drugs or weapons in the car."

Selina stared up at the officer in disbelief. "This doesn't make any sense. Just give me a ticket and—"

"Now," the officer said with authority.

The FBI man had already opened the passenger door, reached into the glove box and popped the trunk. Selina's heart pounded heavily as she stepped out of the car. The policeman led her to the sidewalk, out of the way.

"Find anything, Agent Nowak?" The officer hollered out.

Nowak peeped his head around the open trunk door and

whistled. "Looks like possession of a controlled substance and money laundering."

"Controlled substance," Selina repeated, confused. "I ain't got no controlled nothin' in my car! Y'all tryin' to set me up."

Nowak came from around the car and held up the plastic baggie full of crack. He had an evil grin on his face.

"That's not mine," Selina cried. "Honest, I don't know where it came from."

"Cuff her," Nowak ordered.

Tukey drove by just as they were putting Selina into the back of the police car. Selina didn't see it, but Agent Nowak waved at her. He really wished he'd known Tukey's real motive for doing what she did.

Chapter 23

After breakfast, Keith, his celly Rico and a couple of other guys got a game of spades going in the dayroom. Keith and Rico were on the same team.

Suddenly one of the other dudes got pissed off because they lost the first game. "Nigga, that's why yo' bitch left you," he said to Rico.

"What the fuck she got to do with me whupping yo' ass in this game, Nu Nu?" Rico said in his defense. "I bet you if you would've gotten more than two years, yo' girl would have left you too."

The other guy said, "That's why I ain't got a girl. Man, fuck a bitch."

Nu Nu looked across the table at him. "Prince, now you know you're too ugly to get a girl, anyway."

Keith busted out laughing.

Rico said, "Yo' girl might not leave you, but she gon' fuck somebody. Two years is a long time for a woman to put that pussy on hold, Nu Nu."

"What the fuck you know?" Nu Nu said. "Yo' girl don't even come up to see you. And you wouldn't be here if it wasn't for her, nigga. As long as my wife take care of my kids, send me money and come visit, I don't give a fuck what she does out there."

"That's bullshit, Nu Nu," Rico said. "My little brother is probably over there right now, fuckin' the shit out of her little skinny ass." Rico laughed. "And I'm gon' fuck yo' sister when I get out."

"Nigga, yo' fat ass ain't gon' fuck nothin'," Nu Nu said hotly. "She don't want you."

"Nu Nu, she got six kids," Rico reminded him. "She'd better be trying to get anybody that she can get."

Keith and Prince fell out laughing.

Everybody fixed their attention on the guard when he came through the door. "Keith Banks, you've been released."

Keith jumped up from the table without saying a word. He didn't bother to look back as he followed the guard out of there. He didn't want to have any memories about that place. Or the people that he'd met there.

The cab that he called from the pay phone pulled up outside. Keith got in and ordered the driver to take him to the Marriott Hotel downtown. When he got there, they gave him Tukey's message at the front desk. She was in room 207. He could smell perfume trailing outside the door as he stood there. Keith knocked. To his surprise, a light-skinned young tender with freckles on her face answered the door, wearing nothing but a black thong and a bra.

"Hi," she said. "I'm Tukey's friend, Shantí. Come in, she's waiting on you."

Tukey was lying on top of the bed in a two-piece bra and panty set, sipping on a glass of Moët. A soft Jamaican drum solo was playing. Tukey smiled at Keith. "Go wash dat jail smell off of yu so yu can join us."

Keith immediately took off his clothes, then ran into the bathroom. He washed his balls good because tonight he would have two pair of lips on them instead of one. Maybe Shantí would move in with he and Tukey permanently. He stepped out of the shower. Tukey stood in the doorway and watched him dry off.

She smiled. "It's been a long time since me saw yu naked," she said, enjoying the view. "Sexy."

"Who's your friend?" Keith asked while he dried himself off.

"Someone me wanted yu to fuck," Tukey said bluntly. "Trust me. Her like dat in bed."

Keith couldn't believe how much she had changed. "So you want me to fuck both of y'all?"

Tukey walked over to him and kissed him on the lips. "No. Me want to watch yu fuck her." She kissed him again. "While me play wit' meself." She kissed him once more. "Dere will be plenty of time for us."

"Let's do this."

Shantí was laying on the bed, naked, when they walked into the room. The lights had been dimmed and the music turned up. She squirmed on the bed like a deadly snake waiting to strike its prey.

Tukey pulled off her panties, then made herself comfortable in a soft chair next to the bed. For the first time, Keith saw the laundry bag with the money in it, sitting over in the corner. As he approached the bed, he could see that Shantí also had freckles on her bald pelvis. He wasted no time. He slid his face in between her thighs and tasted her sweet pussy juice. Shantí wrapped her short legs around his back and held him down. She lay back and enjoyed what might not ever happen to her again. Keith licked his way up to her small titties. She spread her legs wide so that he could slide his fat dick into her tight pussy.

"Oh, God," Shantí hollered, feeling him go deep into her stomach. She licked and sucked on his ears and neck while Keith stroked in and out of her. Her pussy was so tight that he had already come inside her and was working on his second nut. She pushed him off her, then slid her body down between his legs. Grabbing hold of his hard dick. Shantí put it into her mouth and sucked it slowly. A few times she swallowed so much of his dick that she gagged a little, but she kept on sucking it. Keith grabbed the back of her head while he fucked her mouth like a pussy.

Tukey watched, fascinated that her friend had Keith hollering like a bitch. For some strange reason, she could find no mercy inside her for doing what she was doing to Keith. To her, he deserved everything that she was going to do to him. Even if he was her baby's daddy.

Shantí felt Keith's dick jerking inside her mouth and pulled it out in time for him to shoot his warm nut onto her face. "Ooooh," she said as it ran down her chin. He rolled over on his back and panted until he fell asleep.

* * *

The loud bell on the hotel's room phone woke Keith up. He pulled back the covers and exposed his face to the sunlight that was beaming through the window. He felt around for the phone until he found it. "Hello," he said into the receiver.

"It's checkout time," the voice said.

"OK," Keith hung up. He pulled the covers back over his head. Then he noticed something. He was alone in the bed.

He threw the covers back and glanced around the room. The laundry bag was gone and there was no sign of Shantí or Tukey.

Keith jumped up out the bed and ran naked, to the window. Glancing out into the parking lot, he saw no sign of Tukey. He dashed over to the phone and dialed her cell phone number. It was no longer in service. He slammed the phone down. "Damn it," he cursed. His eyes wandered around the room until they spotted what looked like a note on the dresser. Keith jumped over the bed in a hurry to get to it. There were two pieces of paper. One was a note.

The note read:

Dear Keith,

Me sorry that me had to do such a terrible thing to you. But you did me bad at a time when me really needed you. Me would've jumped off a cliff if you asked me to. That's how deep my love went for you. But you made it evident that the feelings weren't mutual. You had a tiger, and you left me for a snake. Too bad for you.

You lived a good life up until now. But it's over for you. I left you with something that scientists have yet to find a cure for. But there is a solution. Me left it in the drawer next to the bed.

PS: When you fuck someone over, expect to get fucked over.

Revenge is an ugly thing.

Love always,

Tukey T.

The next piece of paper almost made him throw up. It wasn't a letter; it was a copy of Shantí Williams' medical records. For over a year, she had been diagnosed with HIV Two months ago she had been diagnosed with full-blown AIDS In the top right-hand corner was a picture of the freckle faced girl that he had sucked and fucked the night before. Now he knew why Tukey didn't want to join in with them.

The papers fell out of Keith's hands onto the floor. He opened up the drawer beside the bed. A chrome .38 snub nose revolver stared him dead in the face. He picked it up and checked the chamber. There was one bullet in it for him to take his life. That was the solution that Tukey was talking about. And she was right; he was over. You couldn't be a player running around with the AIDS virus. Keith cocked the gun and sat on the bed. His hand trembled as he raised the gun to the side of his head.

Like most young blacks, Keith got into the game because of the fast money, women and the local fame that came with it. That's all he wanted. The big time Tony Montanas and the Nino Browns that he idolized in the movies and on the streets never prepared him for situations like this. Generation after generation, young kids grew up, trying to be like their pimp uncle or their dope-selling older cousin. At the time, the consequences that they saw them deal with, like death and jail, seemed unreal until they were faced with them.

Tears began to flow down Keith's cheeks. The only good thing that would come out of this was that he was going to see his brother. They would be together on the other side. Keith took a deep breath. Then pulled the trigger.

ORDER FORM

Triple Crown Publications
2959 Stelzer Rd.
Columbus, Oh 43219

Name: _____

Address: _____

City/State: _____

Zip: _____

	TITLES	PRICES
	Dime Piece	$15.00
	Gangsta	$15.00
	Let That Be The Reason	$15.00
	A Hustler's Wife	$15.00
	The Game	$15.00
	Black	$15.00
	Dollar Bill	$15.00
	A Project Chick	$15.00
	Road Dawgz	$15.00
	Blinded	$15.00
	Diva	$15.00
	Sheisty	$15.00
	Grimey	$15.00
	Me & My Boyfriend	$15.00
	Larceny	$15.00
	Rage Times Fury	$15.00
	A Hood Legend	$15.00
	Flipside of The Game	$15.00
	Menage's Way	$15.00

SHIPPING/HANDLING (Via U.S. Media Mail)   **$3.95**

TOTAL   **$_____**

FORMS OF ACCEPTED PAYMENTS:

Postage Stamps, Institutional Checks & Money Orders, all mail in orders take 5-7 Business days to be delivered.

ORDER FORM

Triple Crown Publications
2959 Stelzer Rd.
Columbus, Oh 43219

Name: _____

Address: _____

City/State: _____

Zip: _____

	TITLES	PRICES
	Still Sheisty	$15.00
	Chyna Black	$15.00
	Game Over	$15.00
	Cash Money	$15.00
	Crack Head	$15.00
	For the Strength of You	$15.00
	Down Chick	$15.00
	Dirty South	$15.00
	Cream	$15.00
	Hood Winked	$15.00
	Bitch	$15.00
	Stacy	$15.00
	Life Without Hope	$15.00

SHIPPING/HANDLING (Via U.S. Media Mail)   **$3.95**

TOTAL $_____

FORMS OF ACCEPTED PAYMENTS:

Postage Stamps, Institutional Checks & Money Orders, all mail in orders take 5-7 Business days to be delivered.